Gabby Ozems

That Cunning Mask

Gabby Ozems was born in the Gulf of Guinea which is grittily Ghanaian. A journalist, playwright and novelist, he studied at the African University College of Communications in Accra, Ghana and at the University of South Africa.

Fimbo Publishing
Nairobi, Kenya
Virginia, USA

That Cunning Mask
By Gabby Ozems

1.   African Fiction – Novels 2. War 3. African – Social Life and Customs 4. Fantasy

ISBN 978-0-9818626-1-3

Published in the United States by Fimbo Publishing
Visit our website www.fimbo.org

Cover Design by Jeremiah Mitoko

Books by Fimbo Publishing

FICTION

Against the Gods by Crystal Ading' (2008)

An Account of the Deception of David Kyalo by Moses Kilolo (2009)

✳✱❋✺❋✻✦✢✖✳❂✺✱✺◉✦✢✖✢❂✺✱❋✺✻✦

Melodious mild sunk the crimson sun
Over an earth so fated with harm

Above islands primitive as woes

That sally in the union of those

Who hail the curfewed tear of Taila

By which tear the legend of Taila

And the ancient sun got entangled

A ditty they upheld but mingled

Ditty as harmonious as gusto

Telling of a Zowdor Nemoso

Tussling against the Sissi Nanna

Trampling upon the Zomo Nanna

Even though he conspired with the night

The morning our islands went ablight

History shall spare her sworn fiance

As we mourn the son of Kalante

CHAPTER I

They raised me who thieved me from a battlefield, so I know no family and have chanced upon naught in the hunt for my roots. I grew up in the jungles of Isiko, in the land of deadly warriors, but being a son of their enemy they taught me no skill to tend or mend.

Darabi's Dija, that cemetery of woods, where a healer died of fever, where the widow's tear was for her husband's rival, there I met my foremost calling in life. Wood hated me, I knew, and I hated wood, but here I was, the disciple of a lumberjack, so I smiled upon wood.

On the day I was expelled, wood had its muscles tightened against the blades of my trade, blunting them as I hacked into its lanky nape. I conquered, but the kill that fell before the buyer, as I was told, was as hideous as a pauper's purse, so Darabi dragged me to conference and dismissed me with no less than: 'Loafer, loafer without patrimony, go to Maaya; go to the witch, for only such a one can dismember you from doom.'

Hunger then put me in the cult of a charlatan who was a herbalist who traded impotent concoctions. Our market was shingles, boils, barrenness and all manner of diseases that the sons of women grumbled of.

On the morning of our confinement, we had washed a foetus off the inner of its parent till they both became corpses. I swore innocence but my liberty came by Darabi, who was representative of me, for he argued: 'This loafer hasn't a knowledge of herbs, nor has he the eye of a diviner.

His hands are not skilled. His brain hasn't discretion; he wanders into all servitude, profitable or vain.'

Then as I was let out of the courtroom, he crowed, 'O loafer, loafer without patrimony, go to Maaya; go to the sorceress, for only such an one can pull you away from doom.'

Maaya's cult was at the shore of Tilisi and there went I, greeting her in the words: 'Rescue me, O famous witch.'

'Anything for thee,' said Maaya, swinging her wand. 'Whose soul may I murder? Forty cowries a death.'

'Don't murder, good witch,' spoke I, 'fix.'

'Fix what?'

'But … I am a loafer. Fix me. Separate me from doom.'

'That would need … let me see … two, three, five, yes five pots of cowries.'

'But … but, I'm as pauper as I'm loafer.'

'I could accept it in installments on a condition that there's collateral.'

'I have no income, no collateral.'

'Go ask your uncle.'

'I haven't an uncle.'

'Or your mother's sister?'

'I haven't a mother or her sister.'

'Go to your clansmen then.'

'I haven't a clan.'

'Any patrimonial assets?'

'I have no patrimony.'

'That makes you a worm … come on earth to suck. Parasitic ruin.'

'Mmh!'

She walked to the altar that held the candles and their stands. She stood behind the altar, stirring three pots bearing greenish potions, and called to me: 'Come loafer pauper!'

I went and stood before her and her potions.

'Look deeply into the darkest potion,' ordered she.

I deeply looked into all three potions but none was thicker in hue. The lights went out and her voice filled the room, chanting:

> 'Your star is the drabbest in heaven,
> So the yoke chose you from the heathen.
> Your grace is slave in the occult tomb,
> So glory despised you from the womb.
> Fated one, your woe is immortal
> And the cord of your grief, eternal.
> > Drop loafer drop:
> > I doom.
> > Fall loafer fall:
> > I fate.'

The place felt heavy and sinister and gluttonous, thus I fled. As I did, she shouted, 'Just as others are come to lift the mantle, some are come to joy in the victories of the victorious.'

Hope thus lost; I decided to migrate to the islands of the far west. I wept while shuffling through marshes and canes, and with a jar of bubbling spirits entered the abode of my drunk friend called Nomdi. This Nomdi, who drunk with a religious craving, had begun well in life, but was reduced to gin by a whoresome mistress.

'Farewell, my friend,' said I, handing him my jar of alcoholic spirits.

'Whose funeral is this?' he tearfully asked.

'Mine, Nomdi, tomorrow I part ways with Isiko.'

'I'm glad, my friend,' said he. 'Go well; never forget this place, for here life mocked at us. Seed my words in your heart—go with them to the grave. Life is like a thread that hinges on two feeble stands: its mightiest grief is not met in death, but encountered when hope and dignity die as we yet live. Men do not die where they are born, that is proof that tomorrow is dynamic.'

He sipped some of the spirits and placed his hands on my shoulders. They were cold and shaky, and perhaps more ghostly than his dull sickly face had ever gotten.

'Life condemned me to this terrible concoction,' said he, weeping and watching the jar I had given him. 'Behold the pride of Jhene ... dissolved in spirits. Fidani, she is where I fell. She is what undid me. Money, pride and a woman are the captors of the naïve; those are the fiends that robbed me of my life. The world seems beautiful but it is an ocean of snares. Life is a lengthy race haunted by a sinister tactician who snatches all who turn to seek attention. I feared death. I feared his narrow pits, but no more. In that cold messenger of time, I shall find solace.'

We drank to eternal companionship and he said while we parted; 'Farewell, dearest acquaintance. Beware, misfortune gazes attentively on mankind and will race to embrace all who are enticed. Suicide is cowardly. Have sympathy, yet see no justification in this final deed.'

The next morning, on the floor of an ancient fountain that stood at a crossroad, Nomdi lay unconscious, drowned in alcohol, delivered by death, and bathed in the solemn waters of the famed fountain.

My name is Zowdor Nemoso, I don't own the gadgets of these engravings but the writings belong to me.

To the far west went I, to the archipelago called Taila, where dwelled six islands and no monarch. I penetrated there by the west and arrived to a brutal raid which made me yell several shames at them cowardly Tailan men who hid like crabs in rocky gorges behind the Wambian cave Daserwa. They were hiding from death and duty. From death because the raid that was ongoing in their settlements was fatal, and from duty because they had abandoned their obligations as fathers, husbands and sons of the land.

Seeking refuge from that far distance, they listened to the voices of brutally. Fear had permeated the kingdom, causing all who dwelled there to leap many a heartbeat. It was a Numunguan invasion, an unprovoked raid that handicapped the physical and placed the emotional in agony. It was the sort of a confrontation that hacked on the back of a man and peeled off his dignity as though it were fleece that was being sheared from the back of a sheep.

'Muyamba,' an aged man whose name I came to know as Titiadi sharply whispered; his face was green with pain and disappointment, 'do we remain calm when they molest our women and take away our possessions. What would be said of a man who sees fireballs flying over his roof and flees in the name of refuge?'

'He should without doubt be declared insane,' returned the said Muyamba, who was kingmaker of Taila and chief custodian of Wambi.

'All men from Taila are like that man. They merely wear masculine skins. They're gutless, shameful, static ...'

'Patience, old man, patience I say,' grumbled Liyanga, the chief executioner, 'or we'd all get killed.'

'You prefer this pathetic life?' fumed Titiadi. 'Won't you rather die? Arise, people, let's defend the ancestral legacy.'

'With what do we implement that defense?' debated Liyanga.

'With men. Men like you. Men like your tribesmen. Men like your sons.'

Laughing at them pitiful refugees, I crept to kneel beside a fidgety lad.

'What trouble? Were you first to offend them bandits?' inquired I from him.

'A spy! SPY! We're discovered,' shouted he abnormally.

'Where?' asked his countrymen, their heads floating above the rocks.

I sped so hastily that by the time he positioned his finger and pointed at me, I was in front of Daserwa. I hurried to their settlements and hid on a loner of a cashew tree, which resided in some sort of a ceremonial ground and overlooked a garlanded altar.

The warriors of Numungu combed the kingdom from end to end, seizing as much property and women as they could, and made for their kingdom.

Men gushed out of the rocky gorges like hot blood from the stabbed and perishing, and headed for their native islands. The kingdom was in turmoil. From Nuamba to Azumba, there was wailing.

The chief custodians and elders remained in Wambi and camped on the Wambian ceremonial ground, where I was, under the loner tree on which I hid. Here they held an emergency meeting; at which meeting there arose a unanimous point that Taila's continuous defeat was because her warriors never fought as a unit and should one army be formed from the warriors of all six islands, Numungu's aggression could be crushed. A durbar for the formation of an all-Tailan army was scheduled to the dawn of the next day.

My teeth gnashed and my body, which stuck tight to a tree branch, was getting exhausted. My breath was cautious and my movements, calculated. I dreaded the coming of dawn, which was to encircle me with thousands of embittered Tailans, all chanting battle cries. From my hideout, I could hear Nimatua the town crier announcing all around the kingdom.

'Warriors of Taila,' he would yell, while hammering hard on his silver gong, 'I salute you. The elders also send their regards. Men are not the masculine beings that reside on earth: men are the safety of the frontier and the confidence of the union. With a wounded heart and a tearful face, Taila comes to you. "Deliver me from the adversary!" she cries. "Take me back to the days of my ancestors, to the days of peaceful pride." The model of man Taila needs in our time is man with daring heart who shall seek to unite all Taila under one cause. A durbar for the unification of Taila shall be held at dawn tomorrow. Gallant beloved of Taila, come vow to Tailans that you shall take them from this grassy shame to a place of glorious ecstasy. Naamu, people of Taila.'

Throughout the six islands there was jubilation; a celebration of the gallant beloved man about whom Nimatua spoke. But, the people misunderstood Nimatua. They thought the durbar he had informed them about was an enthronement. Some Tailan warriors considered themselves crownworthy, and to them the durbar was going to be the grandest since time memorial. They looked forward to that solemn moment when Muyamba would place a crown on their head and declare, 'I crown you king over all Taila.'

News reached the elders and chief custodians about the happenings on the six islands; especially, news about the Trinity of Taila. In Azumba, a member of the Trinity had summoned his wives and children and was already whistling, 'Sovereign, a-coming, sovereign.' His name was Zomo Nanna and he presently sat on a throne mounted on his tree-house. He wore a model crown and smiled all night long.

On the hills of Agunbe, Tsambo, another member of the Trinity, stood dancing in a palanquin held high by eight men. He held a leopard skull and he gyrated upon his thick, thick ankles. 'Tsambo way!' sang he. 'Tsambo way, way, way!'

Mogoona's was within the Nuamban's. He, the third member of the Trinity, was the best hunter Taila had ever known. He was the pride of Nuamba. On a big stool mounted on Mount Dau, he sat, gazing across the many coasts that wound about. The Nuambans sang to his name and bowed to him anytime they beheld Mount Dau.

News from Wambi, Emorna and Twessi did not talk of things less jubilant, only that these islands did not have warriors who merited singular popularity; hence, the engagement of large numbers of warriors in mass jubilations.

At the first glimpse of dawn, the people of Taila held their durbar. A wave of optimism, sparked perhaps by the previous days misinterpreted announcement, blew across the venue, placing a smile on every face that gathered there.

It was dramatic. The jubilation that followed the arrival of most of the warriors made the early stages of the durbar very lively. I would have enjoyed the joyous air too, if it wasn't my tree branch had taken to dangling irrationally and making crackling sounds. The witch came to mind. I remembered how ill fated she had foretold I would forever be, and this made me sad.

When the venue was fully occupied, Liyanga escorted Muyamba to the ceremonial altar and clashed his swords repeatedly to mark the commencement of the durbar.

'People of Taila, I salute you,' greeted Muyamba. 'We're assembled here today to launch Taila's resurrection. You warriors ought to be united. The rivalry amongst you is what has enabled Numungu to be victorious over the past few years. All of you shall be brought under one leader, who …'

The members of the Trinity curtailed Muyamba's speech with a performance. To show their preparedness towards the position named in the kingmaker's speech, they sped to the altar and performed the Lenli of Kalante: a warrior dance of the Tailan people. They knocked the tips of their weapons against the ground and run about, shouting battle cries.

'Elders and people of Taila,' boasted Mogoona, 'from the lofty coast of Nuamba to the inquisitive jungles of Azumba, there's never been a warrior as fearsome as myself. When I roar, the beasts of the forest flee. In my fury, the eagles high up soar to safety.'

'Mogoona, don't bite more than you can chew,' disputed Tsambo, tapping the Nuamban on the chest. 'Your blabber blossomed from ignorance. Without a tour of the chief farmer's plantations, the okra farmer dwells within his okra shoots, boasting of his weather dependent harvest. I am the Tsambo of the warring jungle, the tornado of the earth, the executioner in your nightmare, the fiercest that has lived. At the mention of my name, warriors sense danger and run to seek refuge in the dark places.'

'Tsambo, be cautious the way you gabble; and, Mogoona, monkeys acquaint by size,' Zomo Nanna cautioned the duo, with a frown as wrinkled as it was ugly. 'I am the Nanna of the renowned Zomo clan of Azumba. I am the reason why their nerves trembled. I am the tension that caused their hearts to skip a heartbeat. It shall be sinful against the ancestors, if the throne eludes Zomo. Elders of Taila, now is the time. Choose righteously. The Nanna of Zomo has spoken.'

Other warriors came to the altar, dancing the Lenli.

'Marvelous!' Titiadi clapped.

'Taila shall have many heroes,' Muyamba said with smiles, 'Liyanga, bring three of the ancestral swords. That gallant, outspoken trio shall lead our men into Numungu. Under their leadership, Taila shall wage war against Anona Sissi.'

'WHAT!' the warriors of Taila fearfully exclaimed.

Fear glowed in their eyes. None found the courage to utter another word. The Lenli shrunk into the dew-laden soil and in its place was a faint echo of Anona's dreaded name.

Liyanga went to a primitive fort and fetched three ancestral swords, which he handed to Zomo Nanna, Tsambo and Mogoona, who reluctantly took them.

'You shall be the face of this part of our history,' he told the trio. 'These swords are the symbol of your authority. With them you shall decree. When you surge, Taila shall pursue. When you withdraw, Taila shall retreat. May our ancestors be with you.'

'NO!' bleated Zomo Nanna, throwing away his sword.

'Have you no respect for the ancestors?' raged Titiadi. 'You shall pick up that sword and behave in a manner similar to that brave man you described yourself.'

'Don't be a hypocrite, Titiadi,' Zomo Nanna quarreled. 'You know better; Anona is not a thing of mockery. Forget about war. Taila shall not confront Numungu. I came aspiring for a crown, not to plot against death.'

Tsambo and Mogoona threw away their swords and supported Zomo Nanna. Many others nodded in favour of Zomo Nanna. This thing made the elders and chief custodians despair.

Then, the high priestess of Ninaya's shrine danced for attention, Zomo Nanna beside her.

'Are we guided by him?' asked her meandering brother, Uono, who was chief custodian of Azumba.

'Truly,' claimed the priestess, 'Ninaya has given his counsel.'

'What was it he advised?' Titiadi happily inquired.

'He recommends that if any should be made king, it should be the Nanna from the Zomo clan.'

'Nay!' wailed Titiadi. 'That selfish, roguish, cowardly, quarrelsome Zomo Nanna? But who shall serve him? Who?'

Wambians shook their heads. Emornans shook their heads. Twessians shook their heads. Nuambans shook their heads. Agunbeans shook their heads. Azumbans nodded.

Announced Liyanga, 'Be reminded, people, that we haven't come here to crown a king. We have come here to plot against our enemy.'

Uono got hold of his sister and meandered away with her.

'Naamu!' Titiadi shouted Taila's battle cry.

'Naamu!' responded the people.

'Listen, every son of Taila, you failed to secure the land of your fathers. All they ever laboured to build, you've rendered useless. In our time, when the great Odu Nyaasa sailed with four hundred into Taila, we did manly wonders. We sang and slew for Taila. Every single attack was crushed and Taila's fame spread far and wide. All that pride has dripped like water from the peforated walls of a basket. Think of posterity; think of what shall be told about you.'

His words were calculated as history, so the elders and chief custodians met aside to work out a resolution.

Meanwhile, the spine of my tree branch was creaking rapidly. The branch itself was tossing emotionally, aided by a careless wind.

'Warriors of Taila,' Muyamba announced after the recess, 'we've decided to crown a king, but we still are not convinced there can be a Tailan resurrection without a Numunguan defeat. All who aspire to be king must battle in Numungu. He shall be king, whoever brings to Taila the head of Anona Sissi.'

That moment, my tree branch betrayed me. It broke and I fell heavily, first landing on one leg and then knocking my side against the trunk of the cashew tree.

'The spy!' shouted one who had earlier called me spy.

'The spy?' queried his compatriots.

'Him,' he who shouted returned.

Half scared, half annoyed, Taila's warriors became an armed circle around me. I thought of a plan: I would pose for a priest.

'Hold on!' spoke I to them, gyrating like some spiritual being. 'You need not be troubled. I am a servant of the gods of your ancestors. I have been sent to rescue you, to take you back to the days of tranquility and pride. I shall lead you into Numungu to murder Anona Sissi.'

'Intruder!' clamoured the warriors, diminishing their circle and frowning more.

'Will you fight the gods of your ancestors?' wept an old woman with a bald battered head. 'O Taila, listen to the voice of divinity.'

'Don't listen to her. Kill the demon!' screamed Tsambo.

'Destroy him!' ordered Zomo Nanna.

'Nonesense, away from him!' intervened Titiadi, shooing the warriors away and bowing before me. 'I trust you, brave servant of the oracle. You've got the voice of Wazeyme. Live long, kindred of my fathers.'

'NAY!' shouted the warriors. 'No false priest of the adversary shall lure us to death.'

'You are faithless,' said the battered old woman. 'Didn't you see how marvelously he somersaulted from the heavens? This is the dawn of Taila's liberty.'

'I saw it,' supported another old woman. 'He landed on one limb and with his side, kissed the bosom of the ancestral tree.'

'We don't care where he landed,' grumbled Zomo Nanna. 'We simply don't want him lorded over us.'

'Yes, he's an imposter,' backed the other warriors.

'I've got a better resolution,' said Tsambo, wearing a hellish grin.

'Kill the bogus god?' his compatriots asked for a hint.

'Nay. Wage war.'

'BAAAD!' his compatriots disagreed.

'We should, or the world would laugh at us. This wretched creature chants the ditties of battle while we howl like frightened dogs. We've got numbers and he stands alone. Let him be single and all of us shall unite under me.'

'Not while I live,' quarreled Zomo Nanna. 'The imposter stands alone and all combine under the Nanna.'

'Under me!' yelled Mogoona. 'Or each island to itself and that priestly ruin stands alone.'

'Sounds better,' consented Tsambo, 'but we shall share Wambi, Twessi and Emorna among ourselves.'

Nearly the all of the warriors nodded in support.

'Do you agree, potent kindred of Taila?' Zomo Nanna taunted.

I said yes.

'So it shall be,' jubilated the warriors.

Their well wishers chanted battle cries and joined in a performance of Kalante's Lenli; the elders and chief custodians applauded to confirm their acceptance of the resolution.

'Naamu, my warriors!' bellowed Muyamba.

'Naamu!' the warriors replied.

'The battle of Taila shall be staged on the moon of Jimra, exactly a month from today.'

'Naamu!' chanted the jubilant warriors.

That's how the durbar ended: all Tailans were eager to war, a war with four goals. The warriors and their well wishers hoped to defeat Anona and return with his head beside mine. The elders and chief custodians hoped that the war would be won, priest or no priest, and that Numungu's defeat would unite Taila for good. The last two goals were mine. I was a refugee of misfortune who had been offered a temporary shelter affixed to the limbs of time. If they aged in favour of Taila, I would retain my space and receive royal treatment. If it ticked against Taila, not only would I have to return to my curse, I also would have affirmed the accusation that I was an imposter; a demonic imposter who had come to lure many to the grave. I desired either a Numunguan defeat in which I should have played a role—or death. Death because beyond Taila I would be a wretched wreckage, lacking lodging, food and purpose.

Three warrior groups were formed towards the war. Zomo Nana assembled the warriors of Azumba in Zumbi and named them Zomo Warriors. Their Battle cry was, 'Osunda! Masanda! Monkeys acquaint by size.'

Tsambo's was the Spear Makambes. Their battle cry was, 'Tukule! None equals the Tsambo.'

Mogoona formed the Jungle Masquerades of Nuamba. That was the largest and most unskilled group. Their battle cry was, 'Mutatar! Tawuder! Mogoona is fiercest.' This slogan annoyed Zomo Nanna and Tsambo so much.

The warriors of Wambi, Emorna and Twessi were numbered and dispersed among the three warrior groups. These three groupings camped where their leaders came from, preparing for the war.

During the dimmest hours of night, when it was six days away from the war, I sat outside my given abode in the comfort of a coy flame, troubled by the noisy crowing of an orphan chick. Nature was at her evil, stealing steam from the sleeping sun and converting it with a harlot breeze to make dew for a virgin day. Eighty yards away, I saw a raffia torch sneaking through the dozing grass. It's end was held prisoner by a human limb, which limb was locked to the shoulder of an aged man whose head loitered about with snakeful curiosity. I was alarmed, so employing a tattered stick I ruffled my fire to death. My sight improved instantly: there was behind the aged man ten youthful shadows, all carrying raffia torches and hissing forth with identical curiosity. When they drew forty yards closer the aged man became Titiadi and his followers became ten lads, each flanked by a gouge and a raffia torch. The gap soon closed and Titiadi stood with his followers before me.

'Your Worship, I'm at your feet!' he saluted.

'Live long, mighty archer,' responded I.

'You are not alone, great one. Here are ten lads from Wambi and Emorna. I bribed them with cowries and gouges of wine, and recruited them into your army.'

'I'm impressed, noble Titiadi,' said I to him.

'Our regards, great oracle,' greeted the young men.

'My sentimental regards,' responded I.

'Great one, you disciples wish to alert you,' Titiadi told.

'I'm very attentive, friends of mine,' was my reply.

'Good god, thy warring foes,' said the eldest of my disciples; 'they seek thee not Numungu. If there's ever a cry beneath the jungle shades, it is the cry of embittered warriors wishing death upon a lonely god. We shall surely be killed if found on your side the day Taila departs for war. I am Monara, son of Kan.'

'Good god, the hidden blades,' said another; 'they swear to crush them through the ribs of divinity. Beware, the archers of Zumbi. Their plot is to brutalize the oracle of war. A quarter the troop shall be assigned to thee. "Death to the oracle," a cry so vengeful is chanted across the land. We sail asunder and escape the snare, but sail with the union and death shall eat us all. I'm Kulonko, friend of my friends.'

'Great oracle, the evil abroad,' said a third. 'Mischief is seeded in the souls of your foes, nursed by envy, guarded by spite, and blossomed of cowardice. Fulfillment dwells in your murder and not in the defeat of Numungu. When the oracle beheads Anona, the war shall be won and he be needed no longer; then shall the evil come to light. Pherfer's advise is return with the union and death we shall have. Return asunder and the snare is escaped.'

'Great god, the ocean encircled,' said a fourth. 'Beyond the waves, where the waters are still, your blood shall stain the duplicate blue. The oracle shall be slain and woe to his disciple. I'm Mena, son of my dad.'

'Immortal one, the talisman of Saundu,' said a fifth. 'It is an evil which weakens the spiritual being. The eye of the evil cult shall spy and hunt you, and even long after your death, shall guard your bones to dust. They call me Dolum, yet my name is Lodum.'

'Eternal kindred of Taila, the request be done,' said the other five. 'Our names are Ader, Dawre, Jetama, Meiro and Siso, sons of the motherland.'

'Live long, sons of Taila,' I said to them. 'We shall set sail a day after them.'

'Foul,' cried Titiadi; 'the battle dwells on you, immortal oracle. I beg that you go ahead of your foes, or they curse the land with their talisman. Humans are nothing to trust. The gods bless the land but we humans oppress it to tears. I kept a canoe for you by the mangroves. It's packed with bread and bows and a basket of venomous arrows. About shelter, you need not worry: Numungu is surrounded by solitary caves.'

'For this reason,' spoke I, 'we shall set sail in the privacy of tonight. You may hurry home and prepare yourselves.'

'We have nothing to fetch,' said my disciples.

'Then go is what we shall do,' said I, smiling, a very dry smile.

My disciples put out their lights and with me trailed Titiadi by a gap of about sixty yards. Titiadi led the way and ensured it was clean of spies. We moved like floating phantoms across fields of rice and millet until we reached a lagoon where was the mangroves.

'Farewell, kindred of Taila. Strength to your men,' whispered Titiadi, who sped off after showing us the canoe he had kept for us.

'We're grateful, great archer,' we whispered back.

The eleven of us dived into the bosom of the brackish lagoon and swam to our canoe. Paddling and humming, we set sail, aided partially by the sympathetic hands of the night waves. Above peculiar waters dark as the night, we surely advanced.

I halt here to relay this baton of our times to another; one in whose bosom dwells the advantage of the legends of the merchants, and whose name is not unknown to the fisher folk by the Nile.

●★★●★

The sky was but an opaque curtain hanged upon the elements of night. It cast a shadow that made a partial silhouette of the earth below: partiality enabled by the bravery of a graceful flame. This flame was co-tenant to a huge pot of local beer and would from time to time as if in wild romance float all around the walls of the pot. Four Numunguan guards, who presently lived up to Numungu's reputation as the most drunken of all kingdoms, owned both tenants.

'Ambition is self-deceptive,' spoke a bearded guard.

'Bujas, you are evidence to your words,' returned his colleagues.

'Ambition will shorten your life.'

'That you should preach to your father's wives,' returned the shortest of the guards.

The bearded guard felt insulted and to counter-provoke said, 'In all of your dwarfed existence have you heard of the dwarfs at Tabilot?'

'Only one as idle as yourself could manage time to learn of dwarfs at Tabilot,' answered the short guard, snobbishly.

'Jauda, is that an inviatation to war?' raged Bujas, drawing his sword.

'I fight not the fallen, Bujas. I am short, but I'm not a fermented bachelor and I do stay afar off my uncle's backhouse.'

'Stop it, two of you,' said the guard in charge of stirring the beer.

'Shut up, Tiyo,' said the fourth guard, 'come what may, I support Bujas in his telling of the Tabilot tales. Tell, Bujas.'

'I shall, great Maako, you who smile in the face of adversity. Have longevity of life and may history remind generations to come that you and I were sworn comrades.'

'I'm flattered, gallant Bujas, you will also live long, comrade.'

'Now shall I tell the tale. The tale which is the true story of the dwarfs of Tabilot. Warring against the realities of gigantic expansions, they decided to build a fortress. The foundation was laid, pillars were erected and the walls were finally ascending. At night they stood afar to admire the work of their hand. "Demonic vanity!" cried their king. "We've been insulted. I'm tallest of us all, but look, that wall is taller than I. History shall make of us a foolery. Attack it. Kill it. Pull down that cemented monster!" That's how the famous fortress at Tabilot got hammered down.'

'Ahaa! Haa! The ill temper of short folk' Maako laughed.

Jauda leaped unto the neck of Maako, squeezing him so tightly that his laughter and words dried up in his throat. A fight broke out between the two. Bujas joined in. He held Jauda's legs and Maako grabbed Jaunda's hands. They carried him shoulder high and sped to the sea. There they immersed him in the seawater, strangling him until he was nearly unconscious. They'd have done worse if the beer maker had not intervened. He pushed Bujas and his comrade aside and rescued Jauda. The duo that baptized the short man run to the pot and fetched two large gouges of beer. They consumed the beer very fast and started a traditional dance. The Southern border of Numungu, which this was, was by now too noisy.

Among the silhouettes of the coast lurked twenty-two alien eyes, two of which belonged to Zowdor Nemoso. The other twenty belonged to Tailan lads from Wambi and

Emorna. They had reached Numungu for about an hour now, having sailed the high seas for a whole day. The flame had drawn their attention while they were still off-shore and they were for that reason docked behind some rocks, ninety yards away from the left end of the flame.

'Those four do deserve a thrashing,' said Zowdor, pointing an arrow at the Numunguan guards.

'Your Kindred have delivered the enemy to us, 'said his Tailan disciples.

'Assuredly. Our arrows are deadly and the enemy at present is like a bat in daylight.'

'We shall dart the venoms into their drunken flesh. Hail the oracle of war!' whispered the Tailans, excitedly.

'Circumstance is the mother of tacticians. Does any of you know how to shoot an arrow?'

'Titiadi served you well, good oracle,' replied Monara.

'How?'

'We are archers from the initiation village. The chief archer bought us into your service with the promise of a shorter apprenticeship, once the battle has been won. These gourds of wine are the seal of his vow.'

'You shall be victorious, lofty lads.'

'No matter what happens,' said Mena, 'I will never regret fighting by your side. May your fame grow like the flames of the dry season and long live the son of Kalante, who bought us into your service.'

'I'm glad to be in your union, brave sons of Taila. Now we devour the prey in the snare. Who are the best four archers among you?'

'Monara, Dawre, Mena and Siso,' answered the lads.

'And among the remaining six of you who are the best four?'

'Jetama, Meiro, Kulonko and Ader,' answered the lads.

'Very well, Monara and Ader shall target the bearded Bujas; his comrade is for Siso and Kulonko; the beer maker shall be hit by Dawre and Meiro; Jauda shall be the responsibility of Mena and Jetama. Pherfer and Lodum, you can shoot at anybody.'

'At your service, wise oracle,' said the lads.

'You shall each pick four arrows and make four swift shots at my signal. Gauge accurately and don't wait to see the effect.'

The lads each picked eight arrows and a bow.

'We will advance forty yards closer,' instructed Zowdor, leading his men onshore. They knelt on some low rocks, about fifty yards to the flame and positioned themselves for an attack. Zowdor stood behind them and watched as they set their arrows to shoot. They nodded at him once they were ready and he signaled in low tone, 'Three! Two! One! Shoot!'

It felt like the quick hour of the sorceress of doom that leaves bare the grave where will be buried the ashes of the doomed; and like an omen from the sea driven onshore by quick tides; and like the destructive race of thunderbolts when nature plots against humanity. So it felt when Zowdor's venomous arrows swam into the environs of the flame and viciously tore through the bodies of the drunken guards. It caused them to echo the fatal name of death; an echo so horrid yet not loud enough to alert Numungu that the enemy incited and barbaric was long onshore.

'We conquered, kindred of Taila,' jubilated the ten lads.

'Not until the angels of death drain every trace of life,' said Zowdor. 'Let us be calm. When they become a carcass I shall race there to perform the final funeral rites.'

The lads hummed a dirge and knelt at Zowdor's feet, as he monitored the dying guards. It lasted six minutes before the final guard gave up the ghost. Zowdor took four bows and went to the corpses. He placed two bows beside Bujas and lifted Jauda onto him. Then he placed Maako facedown beside Tiyo in a way that Maako's left arm seemed to be pressing down the beer marker's throat; beside them, he placed two bows and sped to his men.

'That's a weird funeral rite,' the lads said.

'It's a disguise,' said Zowdor. 'Numungu won't know our business here tonight. Right now, sleep is what we'll do. O lone caves of Numungu.'

'What about the other Numunguans?' asked the lads, zealous.

'We shall await the coming of all Taila. Unity shall come by this war.'

'You deserve the final words, wise oracle,' said the lads, deferring their eager moods.

The eleven took their food and weaponry, and headed triumphantly inland. A solitary cave they did find and in its confines waited eagerly for the arrival of the Tailan warrior groups.

Days withered to hours and hours to minutes so that with the ageing of time came the scheduled day of Taila's departure to Numungu. Nuamba's east coast got engulfed in the violent shouts of impatient pilgrims; pilgrims, not of religion, nor were they of leisure, but of battle. I can behold Zomo Nanna now, as though he were still on the Nuamban coast: that haggard nose of his which sat hideously on a face of undesirable soil, those bile-coloured eyes, his unstable waist and rusty legs. Right by his side I can make out the Zomo Warriors. Happening that same moment was the Lenli of Kalante. Mogoona was at his best, screaming hysterically and hovering over the women. Tsambo's legs were suspended in space, dancing to an irregular angle. His men were around him, exhibiting their own moves. Muyamba's hands were above his head, trying with no luck to command some quite. The Lenli refused to be controlled and dragged on till Nimatua's gong made a metallic cry that softened it and made it look outmoded. The people looked at Nimatua, who beckoned them to look at Muyamba, which they attentively did.

'Naamu, my warriors,' bellowed Muyamba.

'Naamu!' responded the warriors.

'What a dawn! In tender joy shall victory come, clothed in vengeful ecstacy, wishing us eternal peace. Hail this rural coast from whence our battleships set sail. Hail the warriors of battle. May the ancestors grant you strength; may the enemy fall by your mighty spear. Manly is the zeal of your men, Taila. Fearless is the name of your army. Their path is upon the waters and with their song they surge forward. Your beloved's Lenli is their flag. They shall hoist it till the sun goes down and by night the world shall hear our victory song. Once again, Naamu, warriors of Taila.'

'Naamu!' cried the Tailan people.

'Strength to your marrows, sons of Taila,' spoke Titiadi, 'as you journey to do the enemy devour. Death to Numungu, that land of fiends and ruthless scavengers. Peace to your souls. May life smile at you. May you conquer in the unity of war. Naamu, sons of Kalante.'

'Naamu!' cried the Tailan people.

'The waters are ready,' declared Muyamba. 'Climb onto their backs and proclaim the doom of Numungu. Live long, warriors of Taila.'

The Lenli arose and blossomed. The warriors sped to their ships and set sail, all Taila singing and waving after them.

When Taila's battleships had sailed for half a day and the Lenli wasn't as potent nor as sweet as it was before, Mogoona ordered his men to draw close to the spear Makambes: he wanted to have a word with Tsambo. They obeyed. In a short while Magoona's ship caught up with Tsambo's.

'Tsambo,' he called out, 'brother in this struggle. As we set sail, I wondered to myself, "Weren't all great wars won by crafty strategies?" Then I shouted within me, "Eureka! I've found the key to this dreadful task" So I ask you, as I would my mother's son, what tactics do you think would make us victorious?'

'Mogoona,' Tsambo spoke, 'the wise son is sent and not the long-legged. We're only halfway and you've already shown your slight wisdom. Return to your wives, Mogoona.'

'A widowed crab will eat you up,' Mogoona angrily said. 'Greedy demon! You desire the glory to yourself. I will assign men to the head of Anona, so that cowards like you won't have a chance of stealing it in shameful fashion.'

'These are your final moments,' warned Tsambo. 'The enemy you have to watch is me, not Numungu. By your insults you've made yourself an enemy. Death to you, Mogoona.'

'Nonsense!' replied Mogoona, ordering his men to move away.

After a while, he ordered them to the side of Zomo Nanna.

'Greetings son of Zomo,' he greeted the Azumban.

'Just why have you decided to disturb my subdued waters?' returned Zomo Nanna.

'You needn't be like that, compatriot. I consulted with Tsambo a while ago and by talking to him today I've come to realize he is the least of all men. I asked him for a strategy towards the battle and he readily displayed the bankruptcy of his intellect. But let's not waste too much time worrying about the shallow-minded. Tell me, compatriot, what shall our strategy be.'

'Mogoona,' replied Zomo Nanna, 'monkeys acquaint by size and rank. In the ranks of humanity, you're many times behind me, and regarding size, you're a feather before me.'

'The weakest of crows shall poke your eyes. Disgraceful idiot,' Mogoona shouted.

Zomo Nanna felt belittled, an evil instinct was sparked within him. He took a spear and struck Mogoona in the breast. Mogoona fell and his breath ceased, that was the onset of a bitter bloodshed. The Jungle Masquerades and the Zomo Warriors attacked each other. The uprising pleased Tsambo. He had wanted vengeance on Mogoona for insulting him. The Zomo Warriors having initiated it for him, he gave them his support by declaring war on Mogoona's men. The jungle Masquerades had to battle on two fronts; this made them vulnerable. They killed so many of their opponents, yet failure was inevitable. They were defeated and not a single one of them was spared. Now, the Zomo Warriors and the Spear Makambes wanted to do away with each other, but each feared the might of the other. Until they reached Numungu, they sailed coldly apart, each observing at regular intervals the behaviour of the other.

'Tsambo,' called Zomo Nanna when they were almost onshore, 'as goes these ships, so Anona shall be attacked. You keep to your northward direction and I would to my south. Attacking Numungu from those extremes, we shall battle until the palace.'

'Well said,' Tsambo devilishly accepted.

It was the early hours of morning. Dew still resided on the low flora of the Numunguan coast, chilled by the sea breeze, which blew around three Numunguan guards as they tooted their horns to alert their kingdom of forthcoming danger. They were massacred by the Tailan warriors, who, racing onshore, attacked them with spears. Tsambo headed north with his men and Zomo Nanna went south with his, both groups trumpeting loudly and singing battle songs. They monitored each other and once they were out of sight, deserted the journey north and south. They both converged central instead, in search of Anona Sissi.

Zowdor and his lads in their south-eastern cave heard loud trumpets declaring war. They took their weapons and sped towards the direction of the trumpet sounds. The Zomo Warriors, favoured by proximity, first reached the palace. They tore down its bronze gate, but discovered to their amazement that it was empty. The loneliness of the place rid them of all human fears.

'Numungu surrendered at the sound of the trumpet,' they said, laughing.

'People of Numungu, today is a day mourning,' declared Zomo Nanna. 'The god of chaos has visited your land. I will tear you into chunks and feed your flesh to the bird of the sky. I am the Nanna of the Zomo clan of Greater Taila. My wrath is unpleasant and today you'll know. I promise you pain, tears—'

'Tire not your lips, dear compatriot,' Tsambo shouted as soon as he entered the palace. 'Anona Sissi, the beast of the jungle is at your throat. The end has come, people of Numungu. Today the spears of destruction have risen against your kingdom.'

The Lenli begun and gathered momentum. Soon the floors of the palace were vibrating. Taila's warriors in their duel against the alien floor looked up to one structure: a tall tower whose summit was a lookout. Since it was to them the only remaining symbol of Numungu's past glory, they looked at it with a triumphant air of mockery. The structure sometimes seemed to frown in rebellion and when it did the Tailans showed it their soles to remind it that it was part of the conquered kingdom.

'The adversary is on the run,' Zomo Nanna said to his countrymen. 'I pronounce us victorious. What remains is a hunt for the ruler's head. Before that hunt, I say we search all the chambers of this palace to make sure he's not in hiding here.'

His suggestion found total backing, for it came at a time when the rays of the sun had illuminated the Lenli, making the Tailans an eager uncontrollable force. The two leaders remained in the large compound while their followers split into several groups and searched the palace chambers. The chambers were filled with heaps of valuables, beer forming the most part of them. There were also underground chambers storing dusty skeletons vandalized by mice. In the seventh minute of the search, the two leaders encountered something that made them think a divine being had visited them.

'I had a premonition,' Tsambo said to Zomo Nanna.

'Even I had one,' responded Zomo Nanna, religiously. 'I saw something like a flash of lightning. It flew fast to that lookout, then I didn't see it anymore.'

'Maybe the ancestors want to communicate.'

'Perhaps.'

As their expectant eyes roamed above the palace, waiting upon divinity, a shooting star, which they were certain didn't fall from the heavens, shot into the side of the thatched roof near the lookout. It had a tip like a burning cloth, a hand like an arrow's shaft, and a smoke akin to that of earthly fires. Tsambo rubbed his eyes in an attempt to rid them of defects unknown, and when he was confident they were functioning without flaw, said, 'Comrade, that is the flame that might undo the victory song.'

Two more fires shot into other areas of the palace roof. That moment, the Tailan leaders knew that all the desolation and quite were a snare, and like naive infants they had marched their troops into it.

'It's a trap,' they alerted their men. A chaotic race to the damaged exit followed, but it didn't rescue the Tailans. Numungu's archers shot at any Tailan who entered the passage that led to the exit. Taila's warriors therefore returned to the palace compound.

The source of the mysterious fires revealed himself. He was an executioner with a basket of arrows, and to the tips of the arrows balls of burning cloth were tied. His Plan was to hide behind the lookout and prudently set the entire roof ablaze; now that the Tailans knew of him, he cared little for prudence. He hastily moved about the lookout, attacking the roof on all ends. The desperate Tailans shot spears at him. Few times did they come close to hitting him, because most of the time he worked from behind the lookout. This frustrated the Tailans. He jumped off the roof when he was out of supply.

'Welcome, gods and beast of Taila,' a dogmatic voice announced from inside the lookout. 'Here, warriors, gifted and mighty, have fallen. These walls have eaten blood. They have witnessed the destruction of renowned armies. Flames are not at all dear to me; in fact, I dread the nudity of fire, but today I shall use it as a weapon, for your demolition. Your feet are in the belly of hungry flames. Your end is now, friends of my foes. Death is all I wish you; die.'

A march similar to the parade of sojourning ants through hostile territory followed the announcement. Many executioners bearing large bronze shields ascended the palace roof and lined up before the lookout. The owner of the dogmatic voice leaped out of the lookout and stood behind them, so that their shields shielded him completely. It was Anona Sissi and the Tailans shrank when they saw him. They drifted back, fearing he might jump into the compound and devour them.

'Sons of Mungu,' called Anona, 'give no peace to the alien warrior. Long live the union.'

His bloodthirsty men responded with a song that said:

> 'Anona the son of Kubiise,
> Earth admired you at birth;
> Anona the gem of humanity,
> Thy milk is the blood of war;
> Anona the King of warriors,
> Wild birds shall chant thy fame.
> The ghostly sign once pursued thee,
> A dagger of ice the tool of death,
> Yet she sought thee in vain:
> Where lives our Nanna
> Death failed to invade;
> What shall thus subdue the King?'

Anona's wild appetite for praise thus kindled, he danced backwards until the eaves of the roof and somersaulted to the ground. He went around the palace, dancing to the tune of a drum and commending his men for their heroic roles in the ensnaring of Taila.

Although the flames grew destructive and ripped off the palace roofs, it did no more than cause the Tailans to cough; Anona's men weren't immune, they coughed along. This made the king furious. He distributed spears to his men and sent them up every tree that stood anywhere close to the palace. From the tops of those trees, Numungu attacked Taila. The target misty and pacing about, Numungu shot her spears with the mindset of a rainfall; shooting into every unit of space, be it vacant or occupied, and this way the opponent had not a tactical chance to escape.

A cry so melancholy broke through the smoke of the fire. It diffused swiftly into the whole of Numungu. It came from wounded Tailans and it was this cry that brought Zowdor and his lads to the battle. For hours, they had been searching for the Talian warriors in vain. Once they heard the woeful cry, they managed to locate the Numunguan palace.

They joined the battle from the south, making a buffer of a fetish hut, and piercing Anona's men with toxic arrows. They firstly shot down the Numunguans on the trees, and then forced those on land to desert the south. Anona tried to re-establish his southern front. He assigned his best swordsmen there, but again, the new entrants, by their venomous arrows, gained control.

Anona felt vulnerable. He took a shield and raced behind it towards Zowdor and his lads. He hoped to get the customary response: the customary cowardice of Tailans; their customary fleeing from battles, and the customary triumph Numungu always enjoyed over them. That he nearly got, for the ten Tailan lads, alarmed by his furious race, moved a hundred and seventy cautious yards away from the buffer. Their leader was courageous, he remained behind the hut and once the Numunguan king reached it, showed himself. Anona went at him with the shield. Zowdor flung himself around the shield, tussling with the Numunguan king for possession. Anona pulled the shield away, and Zowdor pushed against it. It hit Anona's jaw, so badly that he let go off it and knelt down, moaning.

'To his rescue!' signaled the guards keeping the exit, when they saw their king go down. They left two men at the gate and sped towards the hut. Zowdor took the shield, and hurling it hard against the king's head, fled westward. Fifteen guards went after him, while their colleagues attended to the king. The Tailans realized the exit lacked able security, they raced to it, and, with a stampede which flattened the two guards keeping it, escaped. The east coast was where they went, and though pursued by executioners, they escaped Numungu unharmed, sailing in a single ship. Zowdor's lads abandoned the war, at the point when they saw their countrymen running towards the east, and made for Taila.

The chase was on. Spears the threat of his life, Zowdor maneuvered through the thick woods of Numungu. The low grass grabbed his feet with their tiny blades, trying to capture him for their warm-blooded neighbours. He squashed them with his feet and kept the race alive. The Numunguans had fifteen spears, and in wasteful fashion they parted with their limited weaponry. The race led all sixteen participants to a fenced garden, Zowdor within the fence and the natives at the exit—a really wide exit by design. Their arms wide open, the Numunguans advanced toward Zowdor. He run to the fence and climbed to its apex. He quickly observed behind it. There were pairs of large logs surrounding it whose barks looked very old. Many yards away, he saw eight guards around a pot of wine. He hid his face from them.

'Finally, demon,' said the leader of the guards to Zowdor, 'your games come to a close. Come with us to the Sissi Nanna or drown yourself into the underworld. Death is calling, demon, he's come for you.'

The Numunguans moved briskly to the fence and begun to climb. Zowdor jumped and landed on a log behind the fence. It shattered like a thin crispy shell and he fell into a hole which the crash left uncovered. It was a long violent fall into a dim, dim dungeon.

There was grief on the seas that led to Taila. Two pompous leaders with waxed hearts were weeping. A fraction of the men that they controlled stood with bare chests in a corner, trapping seaweed.

'What with yarns and sticks?' the haughty leaders asked the weed-pickers.

'We shall go with weeds above our crowns, so Taila will know that there's no victory song,' the weed-pickers told.

'Tsambo,' whispered the one haughty leader to the other, 'red oil hangs above our white attires. We can either pluck it aside or allow it to burst and soil our speckless white.'

'Alert your men,' returned the other leader in a low, satanic tone, 'and I would mine. When the trumpet cries, all the hybrid should perish.'

The leaders alerted their men and the trumpet did cry. The warriors from Twessi, Wambi and Emorna, against whom the plot had been, were put to death.

The Zomo Warriors and the Spear Makambes arrived at Nuamba's coast performing the Lenli and singing a victory song. The rest of Taila were already there, gathered around ten lads carrying seaweed, and didn't join in the Lenli, nor did they sing a victory song. They looked rather astounded.

'Victorious is your motherland!' yelled the warriors when they got onshore.

'And the ruler's head?' queried Titiadi, suspiciously.

'We damaged Anona with a horrible fire,' said Zomo Nanna.

'He roasted beyond recognition,' added Tsambo.

'These ten were in Numungu,' said Titiadi, pointing to ten lads, same which carried seaweed, same which were with Zowdor. 'They saw you in your cowardly flight to safety. You should be thankful to the kindred of your ancestors. He overpowered Anona and gave you room to escape.'

'We escaped by our might!' fumed Zomo Nanna. 'Be cautious, Titiadi, no one ...'

'Shut up,' Muyamba angrily spoke. 'Every one of you should be ashamed of himself. You made light of our project. The love of a vain crown you held so dear, and it you set before Taila's cause. The ancestral dream is a bore to your ears, and what tomorrow holds you'd rather a throne.'

'Tsambo, do you know of the creepy Weterian tale?' asked Zomo Nanna.

'In picturesque format,' sniggered Tsambo. 'Before peeping into a narrow, crooked, dark tunnel, you should, as a precaution, consider the sort of a reptile that resides there.'

'Tsambo the star above Agunbe,' flattered Zomo Nanna, 'you were born to partner me, but society made me your enemy. The enmity ends here. Together, we shall walk through this barbaric land, your enemy my enemy, my foe your foe. Shake me, loyal ally.'

The two shook hands and departed with their men, Azumba their destination.

The Tailans stood on the Nuamban coast, looking searchingly across the seas. They dreaded the future, near and afar, for with it could come the vengeance of Numungu.

CHAPTER 3

❋❋❋+❋❋❋❋❋❋❋❋❋❋❋❋❋❋❋❋❋❋❋❋❋❋❋❋❋❋❋❋❋❋❋❋❋❋❋+

The dismal chamber of doom, the cemetery of decay, and the still gust of death: but what arsenal has the devil more satanic? So what if the chamber of doom housed savage mice; and the cemetery of decay was crammed with ghastly skeletons; and the gust of death was a hauntful wind, alive in every passage of time? Won't a dweller of this hellish place be doomed immortally?

Zowdor knelt dizzily in this place. He saw the face of the witch of Tilisi. It still had the lips that cursed him, and the lower lip motioned as though to visit its downhill neighbour, a chin, but instead initiated a malicious campaign that filled the upper lip with evil intent. United, they recited the very words that had cursed him:

> *'Your star is the drabbest in heaven,*
> *So the yoke chose you from the heathen.*
> *Your grace is slave in the occult tomb,*
> *So glory despised you from the womb.*
> *Fated one, your woe is immortal*
> *And the cord of your grief, eternal.*
> > *Drop loafer drop:*
> > *I doom.*
> > *Fall loafer fall:*
> > *I fate.'*

This campaign incited the gust of death against Zowdor. The gust became a whirlwind and on its whirling shoulders carried the words of the campaign. Terrified, Zowdor run anarchically about the chamber. The savage mice were awoken from their slumber and they immediately made a sport of the situation, their sport being a game of hurdles whose hurdler was Zowdor. He would run like a pursued dear, leaping over the mice until he bolted into the cemetery of decay and run into one of its residents, and this resident crushed against its neighbour, who also crushed into its neighbour, leading to a chain of crushes that left twelve skeletons disintegrated.

The last in the chain, hardest hit, grew vengeful. Wrestling the dungeon floor, it tumbled head-only towards Zowdor. Zowdor fled and fortunately the bodiless skeleton made a detour into a dark passage, no more to be seen.

The place returned to its creepy quite. Zowdor feared an underworld evil might conspire with it to decimate him. He shut his eyes.

Not long after, a soft, pathetic cry arose.

'Uuuu! Help!' it sweetly called.

It came from the dark passage into whose bosom the bodiless skeleton had disappeared. This made Zowdor afraid, yet he felt a strong compassion towards the sweet voice. He opened his eyes.

'Help … somebody … please!' the voice like untainted honey arose again.

It forced tears out of Zowdor. His heart yearned to venture the dark passage, to give deliverance to the bearer of the angelic, feminine voice, but his conscience discouraged him. 'What if the evil that seeks thee to kill dwells there?' cautioned his conscience, and owing to this he swore not to venture the dark passage.

Then, again the cry arose.

Zowdor weakly ignored it.

And again, but fragile this time.

He gazed at the entrance to the passage.

It came sweeter.

He moved five steps close to the entrance.

And sweeter than before.

He ventured his head into the passage.

Observing around and noticing the place still kept its calm, he went to the entrance.

And sweetest of all.

He ventured his head into the passage.

Now seductively, for it so melodiously said, 'Generous one, quickly come or I perish.'

'She's a living,' Zowdor said to the gust of death, as if to get its approval. 'That voice is too sweet and fragile to belong to your kind. It comes from an angel.'

At the time that the voice walked into the dungeon again, Zowdor had already succumbed to his human desires and was in the parameters of the passage, moving meticulously in search of the voice.

The journey down the passage was an awkward ritual burdened with constant appeasements, in that at every further yard a limb or some other make of a bone would be dislocated from its skeleton, and when this happened, Zowdor had to repair the whole union and appease it with a better lodging. As he plunged into the depths of bona fide darkness – void of contour, beauty, and still of ugliness – he watched out for the bodiless skeleton. The melodious seduction of the feminine call led him on, and when he had traversed the passage for four full minutes, he reached the vicinity where moaned the soft female voice.

It but ceased. He panicked.

'Who are you?' he faintly inquired.

'I am one mishandled by life,' responded the voice. 'The royal who shall die the slave's death. The dead whose soul cannot find the ancestral place.'

'Are you human?' asked he, bewildered.

'I was, and not at a time far gone. Then, the day was dissimilar to the night, and I could tell an aroma from a stench. In my Lembe, life, like drizzling nectar, smiles down on men. The alien pursued and entrapped me. In his coffin he buried me alive: a coffin of stone, grim as a trampled mamba. In the array of the good times that have divorced me, I can tell you of so much. I was a coastal lass, the daughter of a sailor. I controlled a stately marina, which served many ships and from that trade, I made a handsome fortune. Fortune brought fame and fame established my name at the lips of men—lay and honourable.'

'Which name was?'

'Damoya.'

'Damoya?'

'Like that. I don't boast it was beloved, but a hundred times before noon it got mentioning. Now the world neither knows nor hears of me. I sit behind this wooden mountain, weeping till long after the workman retires.'

'Hush, Damoya,' consoled Zowdor, settling before the door behind which she sat. He felt it with his hands: it was made of logs, several of them held together by ropes.

'Do you belong here?' she asked him.

'I don't.'

'You were abducted, right?'

'No.'

'No? What then?'

'What shall I tell?' Zowdor spoke in a depressed tone.

'How you got here?'

'I have nothing honourable to tell. I've been nothing before. Who cares for my name? Few I suspect believed that I deserved one. I am the weed that knows not from what it came, wandering the earth with needless liberty. Death. The curse dwelled in his city, hibernating sluggishly. He called me not. I went onto him and invited him to this deadly gamble. I'm here in the service of strange men, warring in their favour.'

'Ooo, that was why!'

'Why ... what?'

'The whole of this month, it's been violent up there and I suspected a war was on. In fact, I thought my people were come to rescue me.'

'The whole month?'

'Yes. It begun and halted and begun anew.'

'That wasn't you all along?'

'No. I've been here with my men only a week now.'

'A week? That's strange! And where are your men?'

'They fled. Say no more. Talk will lengthen your misery. I'll work at the seal right away.'

He sprung up and exerted all his human strength on the bound logs.

'It's too hefty,' he complained to her.

'He made them interlace the ropes when he locked me in. Try to undo the knots.'

'You mean somebody entered here?' inquired Zowdor, searching for the interlaced ropes.

'Yes, the ruler. He brought me by the gate on the notherly end, where the stairs begin.'

'I've found three knots on the left.'

'Chew them loose! Show no mercy!'

'Be calm: this wooden monster falls today.'

He undid the first knot. So the second and the third, and while he shifted right in search of new knots, a log removed from the structure and heavily fell into the chamber.

'UWU!' an aged masculine voice briefly screamed.

'What was that?' asked Zowdor, drawing back in fear.

'He's harmless,' assured the female voice.

'Who's he?' asked Zowdor, still afraid.

'My father. The log got his foot.'

No one said nor did anything. It was the aged masculine voice that tore apart the suspicious quite.

'Greetings, good lad,' it said.

'Greetings, old man,' responded Zowdor.

'I'm grateful.'

'Life, old man, such is life. Today's tear is yours, so Tomorrow's could be mine. Anyway, lets tear down this seal right away.'

The trio pounced on the bound logs, Zowdor undoing the knots, and Damoya and her father forcing out the logs. Their effort left a hole in the wooden seal, huge enough to admit a buffalo, and through this hole Damoya and her father escaped. Employing Zowdor's culture of appeasement, the trio ascended the dark passage into the dungeon of doom.

When Damoya and her father first stepped into the passage, Zowdor saw them as two humanlike silhouettes with dangling spirals above their crowns, but now that Doom's dungeon had replaced the silhouettes with semi-detail, he could make out two authentic human forms. They looked peculiar to him, for their features were quite similar to those of the villain of a marine tale he knew. Wide-eyed, he stared from father to daughter, then from daughter to father, and again and again and again.

Damoya was astounded. 'Everything all right?' she uneasily asked.

'Almost,' Zowdor laughed. 'Sidola is the prettiest, fiercest of all marine devils. She's got wild tufts, just like your father's, held in a headband again similar to his, only hers sit at the foot of the tufts. Her face is a duplicate of yours and if I wasn't shy, I should say you borrowed them curly nails from her. Ahaa! Hoou!'

He shut up. He had to. Because his company, they were not amused. His comments had made them dull. He tried to right his wrong, and so smiled technically at them. They looked away, uninterested in him and his foolery.

'Do you want some food?' he vainly asked.

'FOOD!' they went wild.

'I'm sorry … thought I brought some with me,' he absently told them.

They looked at him with spite.

'And just where did you say the gate was, Damoya?' asked he.

'I'm hungry!' howled she, settling onto a skeleton.

'You really haven't got any food? Even peas?' begged the old man, settling beside his daughter.

'Nay, old friend,' replied Zowdor. 'So tell me: did you war against Numungu?'

'I'm a peaceful sailor, not a bandit of any sort,' growled the old man, rubbing his belly.

'May the ruler die on a cold, pagan night,' said Zowdor, without a trace of foolery. 'He sinned against a peacemonger?'

'My days are lengthened by your decree, venerable lad,' said the old man. 'That ruler has wronged me enormously. Yet, what was my crime? Sailing beside his domain.'

'May disaster burrow through his fields!' spoke Zowdor, his hands akimbo.

'Listen, good lad,' spoke the old man. 'Every year, before the harvest, I buy valuables from the merchants who pass through Lembe; then, at such a time like this when the harvest is at its peak I sail with my family around the kingdoms, trading with foreign tribes. This year, as any other, I took my valuables and started around the kingdoms. The first month was tranquil and trade was good, but the second was a curse: it brought me to this ruthless place. I lost my wife, son, seamen, and so much wealth.'

'Pity.'

'They showed no sign of an evil intent when we first noticed them heading our way. We thought they were come to trade, so my son and his mother went to make the exchange. The Numunguans told them they were come to confiscate our ship; my son protested and they tried to bind him. His mother got in the way. She wouldn't let them take her son. They threw her off the ship. My son jumped after her. I went with my men in rebellion, but got smashed by a club and when I next saw the world, I was in Anona's palace. At first, we were entertained, for the king wanted my daughter to wife. She refused. That's why we're here. He used to offer us food until one afternoon when Damoya vowed to eternally hate him.'

'My condolences, old man.'

'What do you call yourself?'

'Zowdor. Zowdor Nemoso.'

'My name is Yiddi.'

'UNION!' they shook hands and said. 'May liberty come to this union.'

'The exit is that side,' said Damoya, pointing to the base of a steep, blur staircase. She noticed Zowdor watching her fingers and she timidly hid them.

'Sorry about what I said about you and Sidola. Will you forgive me?' Zowdor begged.

She nodded and took to playing with a leg bone.

'I would have ripped apart that huge gate … to search for food,' said Zowdor, 'if it wasn't that the exit is secured by guards.'

'Eight guards bearing the mischief of eight lanky spears,' warned Damoya.

'That freezes my blood,' said Yiddi.

'With a hefty bone like Damoya's, what is there to fear?' teased Zowdor.

She giggled.

'That is the way, the method, the key, the stratagem!' cried Yiddi. 'We shall go with bones, bones of the innocent but dead who want vengeance but are trapped.'

'What do you mean?' asked Zowdor and Damoya.

'We would hide in the dark corners beside the gate, drumming on the gate; once the Numunguans hear of our drumming, they will come to patrol the dungeon. That would be our escape. When they open the gate, we shall go at them with hefty bones.'

'Adventurous ... but ...' started Zowdor.

'But risky,' completed Damoya. 'Very risky!'

'Risky?' cried Yiddi. 'Confined or speared, we shall eventually die. Spearing is better anyway—it won't leave us as hungry as confinement would.'

'I say we face the spear,' seconded Zowdor.

'I didn't say we shouldn't,' said Damoya, defensive.

'I've got a new problem,' said Yiddi.

'Say it with courage?' his daughter told him.

'Lembe is too far away. The canoes on the Numunguan shores cannot make it there. I need a ship.'

'Where's the one you brought here?' asked Zowdor.

'The Numunguan destroyed its sails.'

'I could get you one from Taila.'

'Where?'

'Taila. Them for whom I war.'

'They would give me a ship? What about seamen?'

'Anything, as long as you've got the head of Anona Sissi.'

'They may keep their ship and their crew. That is a disproportionate trade.'

'Kill the talk and get a bone like mine,' ordered Damoya.

The men obeyed. They got a hefty bone each.

'My soul is taken by vague things,' said Damoya. 'Fear, pessimism, cowardice, hunger. I say we strike tomorrow.'

'Silly girl,' quarreled Yiddi, pinching her nose. 'I am commander of here and I say ... behind me now.'

To the stairs went the trio, tiptoeing, one after the other. Cautiously, they ascended it, encouraged by starving bowels. Tiresome as it was, they reached the apex, where lived the gate.

'Now let us rest for some minutes,' whispered Yiddi, panting.

'Nay. I say we drum right away,' murmured Damoya.

'Young woman, were you entered by some ghost while there in the chamber?' the old man asked his daughter.

She didn't answer him.

'This is called mutiny,' he told her.

Yiddi's decree prevailed, so there was about five minutes of rest, after which the trio gathered at the huge wooden gate. They hammered it till they heard the Numunguan guards inquiring among themselves: 'Just what was that.'

They split, Yiddi to the left corner, Zowdor and Damoya to the right corner.

'Be always invisible and never strike until I strike,' whispered Yiddi to the youngsters.

'Noted,' they whispered back.

Veins worked faster, pushing blood through arms that fretted with revenge.

'Okanta,' the trio heard a Numunguan say, 'go with these three. Go see what nuisance defies my decreed peace. No spoilsport of condemnation shall discourage me from my nap.'

Earth was the immediate victim of those words. Indecent feet trampled her and caused her to mime tears. She painfully endured the gruesome maltreatment of the feet, allowing them to traverse her onto their destination.

The time was come for the trio. Repentance was too late now, because the gruesome captor was already at the gate, undoing its fasteners. The Numunguans loosened the fasteners. They opened the gate and were about to enter when their instructor loudly ordered: 'Okanta, send two men downstairs and remain with one at the exit.'

Obeisance was done to the order. Two guards stepped into the dungeon. Yiddi spared them; his allies emulated his act, enabling two Numunguans to descend the stairs unharmed.

The next passersby were migrant mice—a snobbish couple. They scurried to the exit, stopped as if to return, then wagged their tails and spat into the dungeon, before walking out into the cheap liberty won by others. The trio envied this couple, and were pained as they watched them motion into the fresh breeze that knew no limit.

The two Numunguans behind the gate showed no interest in venturing the dungeon. Yiddi sought to lure them into range, so he dragged his feet. The two Numunguans rushed in to patrol; Yiddi launched an attack on them, which received immediate backing from Zowdor and Damoya. Viciously, but briefly, the alien trio did away with the native duo. The alien trio stole the spears of the native duo and returned to their hideouts before the guards on the exterior came to the scene. They came, three running and one walking behind, issuing orders. The running men approached the gate while their instructor stood thirty yards away.

Zowdor noticed the tips of three spears moving by the side of the gate closest to Yiddi's corner. He feared for the old man, so he removed his sandal and when the owners of those spears entered the dungeon, threw it across the stairs. This distracted the Numunguans, making them turn their attention from Yiddi's corner to the stairs. Yiddi and Zowdor, who had the spears stolen from the native duo, jabbed the Numunguan trio in the ribs, doing this so speedily that they conquered in a brief time. They stole the spears of their new victims and were returning to the extreme ends of their hideouts, when the busts of the two Numunguans who had descended the stairs popped up. They speared one in the throat and the other in the chest, leaving the population of the guards to just one.

'COWARDS!' yelled he that remained: a dumbfounded instructor. 'Come out and face me if you trust in your strength. Depart from the shielded places; show me your face.'

He looked expectantly into the dungeon, ready to shoot at anything that would show itself.

'Face me now!' he yelled on.

Yiddi jumped into the frame of the gate and withdrew immediately. The instructor was tricked: he shot his spear. It flew through the vacancy of the gate's frame and landed on the dungeon floor. The instructor was without weapon and he fled towards his camp. The trio dashed out and went after him. He was a chubby, lackadaisical fellow and they no trouble capturing him. He was pounded with hefty bones until his blood froze.

'Liberty!' married Damoya, shedding a tear and hugging Zowdor.

'How graceful she appears in stature!' Zowdor mumbled.

'You think I am?' she happily mumbled back.

'I meant Liberty. She is gracefully statured.'

'Food,' shrieked Yiddi, 'or I'll make a meal of this carcass.'

The youngsters laughed. The old man went to the camp of the fermenting instructor in search of food. He found the roasted thigh of a she-goat, and this he shared with his allies.

Zowdor went to the dungeon and returned with five spears, wiping them impatiently.

'We'll need those to sail successfully,' Yiddi told him.

'They're meant for the ruler,' responded Zowdor, wiping more seriously.

'We're done here, Zowdor,' spoke Yiddi. 'That ruler will lead us back to the dungeon. Moreover, we're three and he owns a kingdom.'

'Escape won't be articulate if that ruler remains alive. He will learn of our escape and send his men after us.'

'We can hurry to Taila. We might get help from there.'

'Taila cannot shield us from Numungu. We have to complete this thing. That's the meticulous escape there is.'

'I have no business with war, good lad. Go is what I shall do. Time is the enemy in this escape. I shall go immediately.'

Yiddi took two spears and grabbed his daughter by the hand. She kissed Zowdor and with her dad parted ways with him. There was not a smile upon her countenance as she was dragged away. She had the face of a bona fide widow.

'This is suicide,' said Zowdor to himself, a while after he last saw the Lembeans. 'I should follow them and go wherever they go. The sailor might remember my generosity and teach me the art of riding tides. Suicide is a vanity, and it finds justification in pathetic folk.'

He took three spears and trotted forth.

'HELP!' bawled Yiddi.

'HELP!' bawled Damoya.

Yiddi's bawl was static; Damoya's bawl was dynamic, in that Yiddi's bawl remained within the distant woods but Damoya's drifted nearer to him. He trotted along the trail by which they had parted from him. It led him into the woods. Damoya was under pursuit. Her pursuers were two Numunguans with clubs. He speared one Numunguan in the heel. He speared the other beside the armpit: both knelt down in agony. Zowdor grabbed Damoya and went with her as if to the dungeons but they sneaked into a thick part of the woods. They stood on a potato bed, a-spying everywhere.

Yiddi was carried in the grips of three men to the place where Zowdor speared the two Numunguans, who still cried painfully. Four swordsmen came from the south wearing suspicious faces.

'Did you encounter any invaders?' asked a swordsman, eyeing Yiddi.

'Not exactly,' answered one of Yiddi's captors. 'The Tailans are gone but ...'

'They are not!' swore one of the men that Zowdor speared. 'Go tell the king his attacker lurks somewhere within the woods.'

'Did you see him?' asked the swordsmen.

'He did this to us and stole the king's bride. He took her that way.'

'Go with the sailor,' ordered the swordsmen. 'Deliver him to the king. We shall go after the girl. But do tell the king's decree to every man you come across: Taila shall be invaded in two days.'

Yiddi's captors made with him towards the palace and the swordsmen went towards the dungeons in search of Damoya.

'They're taking him to that horrible king,' wept Damoya. 'What shall we do, Zowdor?'

'Hush, Moya, I have a plan,' consoled Zowdor.

'What plan?' asked she, anxious.

'That king wanted to make you his wife, right?'

'Yes ... and then?'

'We could use you to set him up.'

'He'll kill me if he sees me.'

'False. The longings in the hearts of men are perfectly parallel to the activities of their minds. The heart is the weakness of the mind. The mind is slave to the heart.

Invincibility belongs to that hermit who hasn't a lust. One that had, yet did not have is most vulnerable.'

'Zowdor!'

'What?'

'You make me feel like some harlot.'

'I'd rather a ransom.'

'Mmm, ransom. But even if I pretend to accept Anona, he won't let us out of Numungu.'

'Our aim is not to ask for his favour, but to trick and assassinate him.'

'How? His palace is chocked with warriors.'

'You shall cause them to disappear. All you need to do is to go to Anona with a harlot tear that can melt his metallic heart. Once it is melted, use it against his wisdom. Daze his intellect. Tell him in seductive ways that a thousand men have invaded his western border and are drifting silently towards his palace, that they are two miles away. I am sure he will send his men west.'

'What if some remain?'

'You needn't worry. I'll battle that. When you do see me, or when you're sure I am very close, assassinate the king.'

'How?'

'Take this,' he plucked the blade of his spear and gave it to her. 'Hide it in your attire. He must not see it. It would be better if you put it behind you, where your spine meets your waist. There, it would be easier to reach when the moment comes.'

She drew up her gown and hid the blade in her girdle, at the place where her spine knew her waist.

Instructed Zowdor, 'Now go quick after them that seek you. Let them transport you to Anona and prove yourself a worthy ransom.'

'I'm scared, Zowdor.'

'Think of Yiddi. Imagine that the sword is at his throat. Does that incite you? Does that call out to you? Good. Go now. Time is no kinsman of ours.'

'See you, Zowdor.'

'See you, Damoya.'

'Be cautious.'

'Be smart.'

Waving, they parted, Zowdor via the route by which Yiddi was taken, and Damoya via the route by which her pursuers had gone in search of her. She wailed loudly, pretending to be calling out to her father. Her pursuers heard her and came to capture her.

'Where to, young lady?' mocked one swordsman. 'Anona will be delighted to see you. If you're fortunate, he will just dismember you with a sword of mine. Otherwise, in a dungeon creepier than where you were, you'll rot to death.'

The swordsmen dragged Damoya to Anona's palace. It was a hurried journey and sooner than she had expected, she was walked through the long passage of the palace, into the palace compound, and to a crowded shed where sat Anona and his throne.

'Haaa!' Anona sarcastically grinned.

Damoya only sobbed innocently.

'Gorgeous flower from the Nile,' so Anona addressed her, 'look what you're left with. I gave you the world, yet you preferred a cage. I gave you a castle, but you wanted a barn. I gave you my friendship, but you called me your enemy. It breaks my heart, yet I cannot be at peace with an enemy.'

'Forgive me, my lord,' pled Damoya, looking genuinely repentant.

'What did you just call me?' Anona specially grinned.

She answered him with tears, crying from a pair of eyes that were blameless, pitiable and seductive.

'Quit suffering them arms of hers!' Anona ordered Damoya's captors, who until now had her hands firmly gripped. 'Do you have no sympathy in your hearts?'

'Forgive me, my lord,' Damoya wept on, looking around for Yiddi and not finding him. 'I'll serve you. I swear to be yours. Please do not hate me any further.'

Anona was delighted. He walked to her as if he would do something relevant, but he only smiled and returned to his seat.

'Take her to the shrine of Tori,' Anona ordered an executioner. 'Tell the royal maids to bath her and change her attire. I'll return to you flower of the Nile. At present, my mind is filled with vengeance.'

'No!' she wildly wept. 'Please don't send me away. There was a man in the dungeon. His cohorts came to murder the guards. They freed him and captured my dad and I. They had an argument so we got a chance to run. They kept pursuing us till your men took us; then, they went west. They're still in the land. Please don't send me away, lest they capture and slay me. There's too many of them, my lord.'

'Where? How many of them?' fretted Anona.

'A thousand or more, my lord. They have swords and spears. They are in the west, two miles away, and silently they advance towards your throne.'

'You heard the flower!' Anona yelled at his men. 'There's no time for a detailed plan. All you've got to do is massacre them. Take none of them for granted: fattest, thinnest, weakest. Move, my warriors. Return victorious. Kill them. Be merciless. Death to the alien warriors. Ayiso, halt, halt. Ayiso, remain with two executioners.'

Incited, barbaric, chanting brutal songs, the warriors of Numungu charged towards the west. All, but three of Anona's men, were engaged in that comedic marathon. Their departure from the palace made the place spacious, which spaciousness enabled Damoya to see her father. That sorry old man dangled about a dangling pole, his hands jailed in a noose that hung from the pole, a leg of his skipping sorrily about, and his face the unhappy showcase of his sorrowful self.

'O, Pa-Yiddi!' his daughter wailed, making her palms the grave of her tearsome face, and travelling to the pole that held her father.

'Pardon me, Flower,' spoke Anona after her. 'Ayiso, free the sailor.'

Damoya, assisted by the three of Anona's men who stayed, freed Yiddi from the dangling pole. The old man heaved and requested for water immediately. Water he was given and taken to Anona.

'You no longer are my enemy,' Anona smiled at him. 'The day has reconciled with the night, so peace you shall have for as long as it remains so.'

Yiddi merely nodded. His daughter's fingers crept into Anona's palms and she kept a whorish smile that made him want to die. He stared at the wench that stood before him: she was a shameless seducer, who employed all manner of speechless evil to entice the very evil that had caused him his wife, son and fortune. He was ashamed to have her for a daughter. He didn't feel liberated—he felt manipulated.

Meanwhile, outside Anona's palace prowled the very daredevil that had knocked him to the ground: Zowdor was there behind the buffer-hut. Numungu's deployment west was not unknown to him. He was in the nearby bushes by then. Now, he monitored the palace. At intervals of two to three minutes, a Numunguan would pop out of its doorless exit, patrol thirty yards to the left, same to the right, then return.

Well acquainted with the environs of his prey, Zowdor diverted his gaze to the inanimate society around him. His aim: to recruit its working class, specifically those that fell under the trade of warmonging. A basket of toxic arrows, which was not unfamiliar to him, was his first recruit. Not far from where he had found the basket lay a maimed bow. He cured it and made it his second recruit. The shield that dazed Anona was his final recruit.

Zowdor now programmed his gaze to the exit. He allowed the Numunguans to patrol it twice more. Tiptoeing speedily but noiselessly, he converged at the exit and stood five yards away. Crime was the virtue of his present mind, crime against criminals, the politics of cursing the sorcerer with his own destructive sorcery.

Patrol-time came again. A Numunguan was sent to do the usual manning of the exit. Spear in one hand and club in the other, he walked through the long passage. Zowdor heard him come. His gait was accompanied by a tasteless sound whose source was mysterious. Zowdor positioned a bow and arrow in shooting posture. The Numunguan's head came foremost to the outside, followed by a quarter of a yard of his spear. Just as his neck tried to regulate his head to make a left turn so he could examine a figure that was spotted by the side of his eye, the figure shot at him—Zowdor being that figure. Zowdor's shot caught him in the cheek, and caused him unbearable pain.

The Numunguan stepped out of the exit and threw his spear. Zowdor blocked it with the shield and went on the offensive. He shot the Numunguan in the waist. At this point, Anona's man fell, wailing and wobbling in pain. Another Numunguan run to the scene. He was an easier prey. Zowdor shot just once, near his navel and down he went, a downward motion that was the last move of his mortal self.

The palace stood in fright by now, its owner, the king, being the most frightened. He wasn't seated in his chair nor was he out of it. His eyes glanced into the long passage whose crookedness allowed him limited patronage.

Damoya walked about him. Something about her behaviour got him concerned. She moved briskly, her hands almost epileptic. She would touch her gown in ways that made it seem it tormented her. She was tensed. She was afraid. She was breathless. Anona's heart pitied her. He took her and hid her behind his throne, for at that moment, he only saw might in that one wooden giant, which neither shook nor panted.

Yiddi frowned. He shut his eyes. He yearned to die. He insulted them both, not to their hearing.

Without words, Anona ordered his last man to go face the exterior mystery. This he craftily did with his forefinger, poking it toward the long passage, while grimacing to discourage the last executioner from any act of inertia.

Sorrowful last executioner, he did the passage enter, and slower walked he than a tortoise.

Damoya moved her head to the side of Anona's chair, observing him, wondering if the time was best for her mission. 'He lacks security and harmony of mind,' concluded she. She tucked her hands into her gown, into the place where her spine wooed her waist, and reached carefully for the hidden blade. She buried it in her palms and observed the king some more. His eyes were devoted to the crooked passage—to its monitoring.

Zowdor had heard the executioner's slow movement through the passage and had been waiting with an arrow against his bow to strike. It was nearly two minutes, but the Numunguan had not appeared. Zowdor went to exit. He spied into the passage that owned it. The Numunguan was within, crawling on his hands and knees, his one hand holding a spear. Zowdor tensed his arrow against the string of his bow and hopped into the passage. The Numunguan stood up and threw his spear. Zowdor bent, escaping narrowly. He shot Anona's man in the leg. The Numunguan didn't fall; he only screamed and fled, hopping on one leg.

His scream inspired Damoya. She knew by it that Zowdor had conquered the ruler's man. She leaped onto Anona's chest and pierced him with her blade. She was about to pierce him afresh when he held her two hands and squeezed them mightily. She bawled.

It was now that Yiddi liberated his eyes. A beast was bullying his little girl, whose modus was no longer whorish, so he felt a fatherly pain and went to grab Anona's throat, suffocating it dearly.

The last executioner hopped to the scene and joined the struggle. He fisted Damoya's head. She fell to the ground. This gave Anona a break, for the threat of Damoya's weapon had been eliminated. He focused fully on Yiddi, firmly fisting the old man in the tummy. Yiddi freed Anona's throat; the punches of the Numunguan king were mighty. Anona got to his feet and knocked the sailor to the ground. He wrestled the sailor, and his man tackled the sailor's daughter.

These four fighters were joined by a shield bearer: Zowdor, who being more concerned about a skilled male fisting a frail unskilled lass, rescued her urgently. He crushed the male's head with his shield and smashed him off the female. He and the female then joined in the fight of the wrestlers. The domineering one, also owner of the palace, was whom they attacked. The shield bearer squashed him with his shield and the wench punctured his head with her blade, helping the wrestler below to gain superiority. He overturned the wrestler who owned the venue and, with the assistance of his allies, sent him to the nameless chasm that marks the end of all mortals born by women.

'The Tailans need only his head, you said?' Yiddi breathlessly inquired.

'No more than that,' Zowdor assured him.

Yiddi galloped to a chamber that had served as a kitchen in the heydays of the palace and returned with an axe and a trumpet. He stood beside Anona's corpse, jerked the axe and said, 'This triumphal decapitation is not only to obtain a favour from Taila. It is also meant to console the souls of many who died without justice. May their souls guide us to safety.'

Yiddi hacked off Anona's head and gave it to Zowdor.

'Union!' bellowed Zowdor.

'Union!' Yiddi bellowed in response.

'Let's go away,' Damoya wept. 'It's getting creepy.'

The men laughed, not at her, but at Numungu, at Anona Sissi, at his gullibility.

Anona's head in their possession, the trio headed east. The journey was long. The sun scorched with no humour, but when your heart slaps your chest bone and your blood cooks inside of you, as the trio's did, you're not bothered by climate. They went to a rocky shore that looked like it seldom had fisher folk. Several canoes were there, some aged, some new, some mysterious, some under-construction. The one they stole was mysterious and they pushed it to sea. ROCK! ROCK! ROCK! Lo, upon the waters, sailing speedily as though they were in a race, the trio that conquered Numungu.

Above the deep sea, at twilight, when Numungu was well behind, Yiddi kissed Anona's head and gifted himself to sleep in the front corner of the canoe.

Damoya was seated at the center of the vessel. She had a paddle and she rowed consistently, her every paddle displaying the fear she had of Numungu. She didn't desert her fears until the canoe reached the point where Taila was visible—Nuamba's coast the closest of all.

'So graceful in stature,' Zowdor rubbed her arms and said.

'Tell that to Liberty,' she giggled.

He came behind her; and he whispered into her ears:

> 'Sweet lass, my fine ocean lass,
> And how longs my soul for thee
> Who in charm exceed the mass.
> Tears dewy my vow to thee,
> That by my life, companion,
> A dirge shan't know thy spirit.
> Bless the tune of communion
> Whose strain our merging merit.
>> The foe is gone;
>> The king shall die;
>> The sun will tone;
>> The sea may dry;
> But ours shall be named endless,
> For our merger is deathless.'

Damoya detached herself. A critical frown wore she, while uttering:

> 'Love! but what bandit are you,
> Who shamelessly thieve with mirth
> While you do the victim woo?
> Calm to the abyss of death;
> Then jolly, the spell is thrown:
> Same that would be the razing
> Of hearts into which are sown
> The addiction to baiting.
> Mangled the sufferer whines
> By voice eerie as an incense,

Yet at the graveyard still pines
For that fiendish sweet nonsense.'

Zowdor knelt before her and implored:

'For thy love, tenacious score bandit I,
Tameless lass, for whom I fear no scandal.
Axed is my throat, yet I'll pursue the tie;
Though threatened by thy suitor, the vandal,
My heart does continue this hurdled plight.
I wonder, but why do men maidens woo?
What if the potter intended our sight
To serve us direction and entice us too?
So let no woman from now despise man
For good sin which the maker might have sown.
Clemency! O graceful statured woman,
Sinless I came, carrying no vice my own.'

Damoya glanced coldly at Zowdor, slapped his fingers
when they tried to touch her and scolded:

'Now an innocence for men he claims;
Sanctimonious vipers whose fang maims
The very fair species that bore them,
Piercing womankind with deadly firm
Blades of infidelity and woe:
Unlike the soft verse with which they woo;
Let my sorry heart never fall prey
To that sick sport accursed by foul play.'

'Damoya,' Zowdor muttered in a fragile tone, 'I thought
you ... why do you not smile at me anymore?'
  'Why should I if I don't want to?'
  'Damoya?'

'I say this to you and your kind: womankind is not the object of man's dogmatic whims.'

'I didn't mean to ...'

'As if I were asleep when you tried to manipulate my will.'

'Let's not fight. The problem is mine. My thoughts are infested with scenes and scenes of you and ...'

'Cleanse your thoughts then. Sorrowful vanity. They will only cause you pain.'

'You excelled, sweet lass; my art is dead.'

He quit the verbal exchange and lay on his back, staring dejectedly into the sky.

'Mankind cheated me also, Zowdor,' she softly said.

He looked at her. She wasn't furious anymore. He asked her to forgive him.

'So quickly you gave up,' she told him, 'and just as her I'm left with tears.'

'That's a strange, unfaithful statement,' he told her.

'We went, when I was little and foolish, to a bay. Diamo and I. A lass wooed his lad, a prince, for he wore a crown. He was stubborn and made her cry. I was pained and swore to avenge when my prince comes to woo.'

'I am no prince.'

'You're better than one.'

'I'm nothing.'

'Don't say so, beloved,' she went to lie by his side. 'I'll be your wife, Zowdor.'

They engaged in a hug, a lengthy one. Zowdor's lips had embarked on a journey to the sailor's daughter's lips, when the sailor flexed his limbs and cleared his throat. The journey halted, but resumed when the sailor was thought to be deeply asleep. He sat up, his eyes wide open, at a time that the journey was close to completion. The duo engaged in the journey leaped apart: the lass to the center and the lad to the back corner. They were intimidated by the occurrence; hence, the girl's restriction of her sight to the floor of the canoe.

'That first island is Nuamba,' said the lad to the sailor. 'We can dock there.'

'Mmh!' the sailor simply exclaimed.

Glorious triumphant trio! In majestic waters ornamented by silvery-brown corals and shrimps and flora and fish and tides and blue, they sailed to Nuamba's coast.

CHAPTER 4

'Twas awhile after twilight when they docked at Nuamba, making their journey two twilights old. The island was a plain that showed a vast picture of itself, yet they saw no sign of human life.

'Nobody lives here,' said Yiddi. 'See how desolate the land is.'

'It's a funny ghost town,' said Damoya.

'Strange ...' Zowdor wondered aloud.

'I won't paddle anymore,' moaned Damoya.

'Why don't we alert them with this trumpet?' Yiddi gave the trumpet he took from Anona's kitchen to Zowdor. 'I intended to use it near Lembe.'

Bearing the trumpet, Zowdor went to a pear tree and climbed onto its branches.

'So amoral!' Damoya giggled. 'Look, Pa-Yiddi, is not he a mess. The world has no pity: even over him a woman would be lorded; then, corrupt his heart would become.'

'Daughters of women, warriors at lies; with a heavenly smile they harm. There's no flaw in your claim that your kind would corrupt him.'

'But father?'

'Pharaoh is not greater than the Nile; not in might, not in years.'

'I was going to tell you ... before I ...'

'You naughty lass! Come here. Men chaunt praise songs to patriots, commending the virtue that is an obligation. That lad fights the fight of strange men; god is he, not a patriot. He can keep you.'

Zowdor sounded the trumpet while scanning the island from end to end, and as the minutes decayed he sounded it louder.

On the paramount island that stood in the center of the archipelago, stood Muyamba and Titiadi. They weren't alone though. No. Thousands of Tailans stood around them, all fretful—the assembly did not include Azumbans, who, apart from their chief custodian, were all in Azumba.

'Titiadi,' Muyamba spoke to the chief archer, 'if that trumpet sound is Numungu's declaration of war, then plagued is the motherland.'

'Crucial, my friend,' spoke Titiadi. 'I've fought in battles where the commander was a gutless lunatic; in battles where the bravest warriors had cartilages for chest bones; in battles where only a quarter of the warriors bore weapons; but ... an army of women and infants? I've never fought beside one. Woman is the disputed frontier that ignites the battle; Infant, the ally whose massacre marks the climax; when mingled, they are the defective front that will eliminate the triumphant end.'

'Incompetent lords,' mocked Nier Nsora, chief custodian of Nuamba. 'The nature of woman is now shield to the chicken-hearted overseers.'

'Nsora,' Muyamba shook his head, 'these are difficult times.'

'Exactly as I was saying;' Nsora drummed mockingly on his belly, 'you don't match the demands. Step down, old men, it would benefit this kingdom.'

'Such disrespect!' cried Titiadi. 'And the outrageous segment of it is that it comes from none but Nsora. Who composed the tribal song that led to the crucifixion of fourteen Nuambans?'

'Nsora!' Muyamba shouted with fulfillment.

'Who traded four hundred sacks of state grain for a defence force that never showed up?'

'Nsora I think.'

'Who else? And who was it that made the women of Nuamba boycott communal service because he had been suspended from a council meeting?'

'Nsora it must be.'

'But who else? So who if we must count his misdeeds could last until tomorrow?'

'Nsora again, I suppose?'

'False!' bellowed a chubby woman. She also was Nuamban.

Titiadi and Muyamba gave her a mean look that did not silence her.

She cast a circular look upon the gathering and spoke: 'I know you are sick as I am of this wreckage labeled authority. Till when shall we wait? Till when shall we leave our destinies in the care of witless leaders? When shall I stand with a cheerful face beside yours, against no background of intimidation? Do we wait while the blood of our sons and husbands are drenched into the bellies of unprofitable wars? People of Taila, this sickly leadership shall not deliver us. Here ...' She lifted Nsora's hand. 'I bring you the new Taila. Behold the Somma rain before which a bare flame is fog. Nier Nsora, our people are all ears, address them.'

'Dikomo,' Titiadi called her: that being her name, 'I will have none of—'

'Reserve that,' Nier Nsora intervened. 'You'll need it against Anona, especially at that minute that brings a sword to your throat. Now is the time for statesmen, the time to do the duty of the state.'

'Are you following, Muyamba?' asked Titiadi.

'I am, great archer. But, is not statesmanship another name for selfish, political ambition? Perhaps, not always so, but on this day it is so.'

A trumpet sound came thundering across the kingdom. The Tailans formed a tight belt round Titiadi and Muyamba.

'Nier Muyamba, they're coming!' some cried.

'They'll kill us all, Nier Titiadi!' others cried.

'My son's leg is fractured,' a mother cried. 'How will he escape Anona.'

'Patience, people,' Muyamba spoke to the people, after consulting with Titiadi, 'we'll hide at Daserwa. But before that, we shall go quickly to the nearest settlements, pack those of our belongings which are easy to carry and dump the load on the west coast. That would make the Numunguans think that we fled.'

'They won't do it,' objected Nsora. 'What a stupid idea! We may as well dig graves and burry ourselves, so Anona would think we disappeared.'

'Move, people, ignore him. Numungu will soon charge through the land,' Titiadi told the Tailans.

'Don't,' Dikomo instructed.

'What should we do then?' asked the mother whose son's leg was fractured.

'We'll go where there's a safe hideout,' answered Nsora.

'Where?' the Tailans desperately inquired.

'Where warriors roam the coastal lines.'

'Where's that?'

'In the land of true warriors.'

'How far from here?' asked the Tailans, somewhat excited.

'An island away.'

The Tailans smiled at him.

'Azumba!' told Nsora.

'Foul!' most of the Tailans debated.

'Where else?' debated Dikomo. 'Look around you. What do you see? Children, women, old men. Don't be fooled. There's no escape in this place. I'm off to Azumba; what about you?'

She moved away from the gathering and waved at them.

'I'm off too,' said Nier Nsora. 'The next time the trumpet cries, I would be far apart; safe but mournful, worrying about my beloved Taila. What if Anona's crocodile-jaw swords are thrusting through your bodies? What if your children's heads are on the rocks at Daserwa, tossing under club? What if the warriors who do this have hearts made of steel? How my tears will flow for thee. How my heart will pain and bleed. Farewell, good people of Taila.'

He left the gathering and joined Dikomo. Their hands behind them, the Nuambans hummed a dirge and marched eastward. The woman with a fractured-leg son carried her son and run after them. In groups of divers sizes, other Tailans broke away from the gathering and went after Nsora and Dikomo. The gathering eventually reduced to two old men – Muyamba and Titiadi – and thirteen members of their nuclear families.

'They could be right,' Muyamba said to Titiadi.

'Their strategy is crude politics. It's nothing but a showoff,' replied Titiadi.

'We serve this land, Titiadi. Will the workman dictate to his mistress? Our allegiance is to the voices of our people, in whose midst our two voices become a murmur. Deserting duty in rebellion against Nsora is treason.'

'Well, let's hope this goes well,' Titiadi succumbed.

'Let's go,' Muyamba said to the fourteen with him, who obeyed and went with him to join the other Tailans.

The Tailans went to the east coast, overloaded themselves into the canoes there and set sail for Azumba, under the leadership of Nsora and Dikomo. Hasteful was the journey to Azumba. No canoe wanted to be left behind. Some even felt the canoes were slow, so several yards to shore, they dived into the sea and swam to Azumba. The Tailans all converged at Zumbi.

Zomo Nanna's village was desolate and hadn't Zomo Warriors, nor Spear Makambes. No other Tailan lingered about it. A bird on a swinging barrel suspended among trees and a partridge were the current dwellers of the place, but their language was exotic.

'Azumba fled,' the Tailans despairingly complained.

'Tarry in your conclusions,' Nsora told them. He walked beneath Zomo Nanna's tree house, whistling the Azumban's name.

'You see what I told you, Muyamba,' Titiadi loudly complained. 'It's only a showoff. They will endanger us.'

'Who invited you?' fumed Dikomo, going beneath the tree house and partaking in the whistling.

'Let's return, people,' urged Muyamba. 'Our shield is not in this place.'

'Tarry, people of Taila,' Nsora spoke. 'The chief of Azumba is in his slumbers. There's nothing to fear. The only cobra anywhere in Taila is whom we seek; with whistles enchanting I shall lure him into this assembly.'

'Let's depart, Taila, there's no one in the land,' warned Titiadi.

'Don't heed the chief archer. He foretells as though he were an oracle. The door of the tree house will swing open soon, just persevere,' Dikomo told the people.

Titiadi went to the ladder of the tree house and climed to its balcony. He gave its main door a knock. Many times he knocked, but dead silence was the response. Titiadi therefore stamped the door continuously with his leg and it detached from its fasteners. He peered inside and shouted to the people: 'Your cobra and shield has fled as I said. I could topple this structure if you still have doubts.'

A raffia bag appeared on the right end of the barrel and scared off the bird. The bag had eyes, human eyes peeping through two oval holes.

'Topple it!' roared the bag to Titiadi, though it had no lips.

Titiadi showed the bag his palms and shook his head, trying to convince it that he didn't mean what he had said.

'Topple it!' the bag roared again. 'Go on.'

Titiadi hurriedly descended the ladder, to prove to the bag that he really didn't mean his words. The bag disappeared. Seconds after, two human legs appeared on the opposite end of the barrel. They flew downward, adjoined to a waist, a belly, a chest, two hands, a neck, and the raffia bag. These segments, excluding the raffia bag, settled into a human form that the Tailans were familiar with, the form of the owner of the village, the form of Zomo Nanna. The two hands grabbed the raffia bag and tore it asunder, revealing the content of the bag. A human head it was, the head of Zomo Nanna. Zomo Nanna eyed the crowd and called: 'Tsambo, it was a plot. Surface.'

Another raffia bag appeared, this time from the soil behind the tree house, at a place where many heaps of lifeless wood had been dumped. It also had two eyes, which the Tailans immediately identified as Tsambo's. A human form emerged beneath the bag, which also they identified as belonging to Tsambo. Tsambo destroyed his raffia bag and walked up to Zomo Nanna.

'From thence came the blaring,' Zomo Nanna reported to Tsambo, pointing the Tailans with his tongue.

'Ooooh!' Tsambo nodded thrice.

'Not we,' Nsora explained.

'Not you?' Zomo Nanna and Tsambo queried him.

'Yes, not we,' Dikomo spoke and walked to Tsambo.

'Then who?' Tsambo asked her.

'Numungu. Anona has come to kill us, so we came to you. Be king if you want but hide us. Hide us right away. Where are the Zomo Warriors? Where are the Spear Makambes? Secure the island. Do it right away!'

New raffia bags emerged from the heaps of wood. They spied the crowd. Dikomo spotted them.

'Come, brave warriors,' she called, Zomo Nanna and Tsambo looking on furiously. 'Come secure the island. Numungu is not far apart.'

The new bags came to Tsambo and Zomo Nanna and inquired from them the reason why 'snobs from neighbouring Taila' had come to crowd the village.

'Anona's wrath whistles through a trumpet sound,' Dikomo beat Tsambo and Zomo Nanna to the provision of an answer

'Nobody vested a power to your lip. Shut up!' Tsambo slapped her head.

'Don't take her seriously,' pled Nsora. 'She stands on heroic soil. She can do nothing but be glad. This place is safe; let's leave the women here and go secure the coast.'

Tsambo smiled.

'Are you conspiring against me?' Zomo Nanna demanded with a shake of Tsambo's arm.

'I smile because I am glad,' replied Tsambo. 'Life has respected herself. I asked for a chance as this and I thought I would have to set it up, but see; I played no role. I only have to chase them away, to the enemy meaner than I.'

Zomo Nanna laughed.

'Have mercy,' begged Muyamba.

'Leave now!' ordered Zomo Nanna, frowning at the Tailans from Wambi.

'Us men can return. Keep the women,' pled Titiadi.

'Did you hear the snake,' Zomo Nanna mocked Titiadi.

'Because he spoke, they're going now,' said Tsambo.

'Osunda! Masanda!' bellowed Zomo Nanna.

'Monkeys acquaint by size!' cried his warriors.

'Get whips,' Zomo Nanna told his men.

'Tukule!' Tsambo bellowed.

'None is greater than the Tsambo!' cried the Spear Makambes.

'Fetch whips,' Tsambo said to them.

'Taila,' announced Zomo Nanna, 'my whips are coming at your backs. When they spank your skin, remember the snobbish thing you did to me at our last encounter.'

The two warrior groups fetched whips. They spanked and kicked, racing after their unarmed compatriots, their whips slashing everywhere fleshy. Yelping and galloping, the Tailans that came from Wambi headed for the west coast, their pursuers' whips still smashing all aspects of their bodies. Sorrowful was it. The woman with a fractured-leg son, carrying her boy, run behind her countrymen, her body struggling to keep up the pace. She trotted amid heavy trashing and reached the coast few yards behind her countrymen. To their canoes and quick to sea, paddling boisterously, Tailans who from Wambi came. The waters bubbled, the paddles scrambled, the canoes competed while the crew aboard shivered and moaned.

The hauntful trumpet sounds filled the air once again. This happened when the Tailans had just arrived on Wambi's east coast. The blaring was fiercer than before, for its source seemed to be drifting inward. Alarmed, the Tailans did another race, this time to Daserwa and its surrounding rocks.

The trumpet sounds were moving inward because Anona's murderers were on the seas, headed for Wambi, desperate and blowing a trumpet: it was growing dark and they were exhausted and starving.

'Those pathetic morons have directed Anona here. They have stirred Numungu against us. Which cruelty will undoubtedly be the brainchild of Titiadi and Muyamba,' so spoke the Zomo Warriors and Spear Makambes of the oncoming trumpet sounds. Wherefore, they sent word to Cerithi, the forested village in which their families and the rest of Azumba, save the chief custodian aforementioned, had taken refuge. The word was, 'Haste yourselves! By a lie Taila has swapped places with us that Numungu's noose should throttle us in their stead. But off we go, to swamp village Yadoma, so when Anona finds Azumba unoccupied, he shall divert his wrath to Taila and this very thing shall rid the land of tyranny. The joy that awaits us can only be envisaged.'

Away! Away! Sprinting, quickening horsefully into unaware canoes. Shoving them to sea and parting with the land of their fathers. They both parted: the group that sent the message of departure and that for whom the message was meant.

Refuge seeking in and around Daserwa carried on for a wearisome three hours. Fear was the name of the wind that blew about. An old fellow stood at the entrance of the cave, his forefinger, the right, thrusting frequently into the void before him, giving the impression that he may be close to finding a remedy for the horrendous circumstances of the time.

His behaviour irritated another old fellow. This other one hid behind a stone within the cave and when he could tolerate the finger thrusting no more, he honked, 'Look, people ... the same recklessness that cost us an able shield. Titiadi, quit the foolishness and return to your hideout.'

The finger-thrusting fellow did 'quit the foolishness' but returned not to his hideout. He hurtled, hovered, spread his wings and claws, and thudded on the irate fellow. The irate fellow squealed and slapped his palms on the floor. The finger-thrusting fellow then got hold of the irate one's legs, pulling him round about a stone. The irate fellow developed a whooping cough, which he coughed like a ditty, and the ditty-like cough was, 'A-whoot! A-whoot! Whoa! Whoa!'

The irate fellow was nearly fortunate, this was when a rotund, anchor-bellied compatriot of his charged into the duel, the anchor-belly of hers defying all natural dictates of fair play. She mowed down the two men, gluing them to the floor, and lay breathing heavily, unable to lift herself.

Another backup came to the duel, for the finger-thrusting fellow this time; it was an elderly fellow and he caught the anchor-bellied's hand and hauled it to a perpendicular, and hauled it level, thereby leaving her entire mass to glue down the irate fellow alone. He hugged the armpits of the finger-thrusting fellow and helped him up.

'What nuisance!' honked the finger-thrusting fellow, breathing hard; he trampled his glued adversary's knuckles with his heels. 'Next time I'll drag you in a zigzag, then bang your head and crush your back.'

'Your prowess at wrestling is magnificent,' said the finger-thrusting fellow's saviour, thrusting forward his hands, as if to endorse his claim.

'There's a maggot on my head,' said the finger-thrusting fellow.

'Maggot? Show me,' requested his saviour.

'Not a material maggot, Muyamba. The maggot of instinctive doubt.'

'What begat him?'

'Not so great a factor.'

'Well, make it known?'

'Numungu has been in Taila since nightfall, yet all we hear is that inconsistent blaring of a trumpet. No battle cry.

No verbal declaration of war. No sound of charging warriors. The mood of this raid is too serene.'

'Indeed, but perhaps Anona plans to strike in the dark hours of night.'

'Unlikely. No stranger attacks you wearing a blindfold. Muyamba ... I'm going down there.'

'Anona will poke your heart!'

'He'll see no segment of me. Did you ever see the day hand over the duty veil to the night? So perfect is the process that mortal humans are incapable of knowing: in such manner, I'll spy on Numungu. Let's hope there's no immortal in their midst.'

'Titiadi the lurking leopard,' Muyamba the saviour praised. 'The bona fide porcupine who for ever possessed his spines. You are the metal that slices a metal. The whale that fought Orlorra; before the river drowned you, you swallowed half of it. You are the wind that whistles in the ears of warriors; they can either listen or pretend they didn't hear. Titiadi the heartbeat of Taila, the evidence of her heroic past, Taila shall always remember you.'

'Off I go,' said Titiadi, fingering his saviour's hair.

'May the immortal among Numungu blaze to death ahead of your arrival,' Muyamba prayed and danced once with Titiadi, a rectangular dance, whereupon Titiadi exited the cave.

The settlements were unlighted. Trees were scary creatures, scarier a smaller tree, the bigger the better, reason being that the smaller trees posed as humans. So pure was the darkness that it took one familiar with the island while day yet perched its coast to know it now that the darkness had cursed it.

Titiadi advanced, sly as a chameleon, watchful as a fetish mouse, spying and smuggling himself deep into the settlements. He halted awhile, unsure of where to tread next.

A trumpet sound hinted him. It was akin to that which had brought him questing. From the north it came, from far enough to be the coast. Titiadi put his path in that direction. He employed haste in his gait and strode to the foundation of a coastal hill. Beyond it was the seashore, the shoreline, the seascape and possibly the trumpet and its lord.

Quivering, Titiadi started up the hill, his gaze loitering all around him. Almost uphill fear gripped his heart, so he lay on his chest and steered his body onto the crest of the hill. His gaze detected three and quarter human forms made of stone, or clay perhaps. He slid forward till a time when his upper body was resting on the slopes overlooking the space right above the shore. What he felt has several names, terrified being one of them. He tilted his head left, to enable him have a left-sided view of the human forms; he tilted it right to enable a right-sided view, then shook his head so his eyes would dance in their sockets and be cured of all imperfection.

The dancing accomplished, he positioned his gaze where it was before, but an uncanny occurrence connived with his own fears and caused him to tumble sideways downhill. The blaring of a trumpet was the uncanny occurrence: one of the human forms took a trumpet and blew it.

'Awu! Ummh! Wohhh! Ouch!' growled he downhill.

Tumbling left him in an upside down posture, and a new spectacle was detected by his gaze. The three human forms had become three oceanic demons, two of them with an unearthly fashion of hair. The fourth, the quarter form, had become a bodiless oracle with Anona's make of head.

'Cohorts of the Sissi Nanna!' squealed Titiadi, leaping to his feet and speeding uphill. 'Cohorts of my Nuamban foes! You shall not conquer. I am the Tiadi the lord of the Lenli. I was born onto the laps of the Lenli. Named before birth;

born after the soothsayer's predicted time. Orlorra could not swallow me.'

Zowdor applauded. He handed the trumpet and quarter human to Yiddi, and walked to the foot of the hill, Titiadi thrusting a finger at him from uphill.

'Live long, brave archer of Taila,' said he. 'You are the strength that strengthens a warrior. My gratitude, brave archer.'

'He doesn't flatter me to doom, I hope?' spoke Titiadi, less terrified. 'Tell me, flatterer, I hear in your utterance a voice that belongs to a kindred of my ancestors, a priest of their shrine, whose countenance is quite like your present countenance. Are you he or are you merely the demon that dwells in his skin?'

'I am he.'

'Which of them? Take sides?'

'I am him for whom you hired ten archers. Him for whom you kept a canoe. I am he who promised Numungu's head, and see behind me, the head of Anona Sissi.'

'Lifeless head of the bandit!' Titiadi raced downhill, bypassed Zowdor and went to the head; Zowdor followed him. 'Haa! Hee! Hee! Did you smite his cranium? His eyes … shut are they, dead, haughty no more. This head, which tormented many, now will go to the ancestors, bodiless, without limbs to fight. How much flogging they will give him! Give it me. And what's your name?'

'Yiddi, I sail the seas of afar,' the sailor responded, handing Titiadi Anona's head.

'And you, fair Wakiti?'

'Damoya, good archer,' answered the sailor's daughter.

'Together with them, I axed Anona's head,' Zowdor told Titiadi.

'I'm grateful, friends of the Oracle,' Titiadi shook hands with the Lembeans.

'But where are the people?' asked Zowdor.

'Poor folk. They grieve at Daserwa, my king. I shall fetch them quickly. I have a request, which I do not mean to impose on you.'

'Anything,' Zowdor encouraged.

'Well, I know godly folk despise evil, but my evil, if you consider how mischievous its victims are, ceases to be an evil. My request is simple. You simply have to hide in those coconut trees over there. At the peak of the event, I'll simply ask you to attack, whereupon you'll simply dash out and show Anona's head to whoever pursues me.'

'Why a plot so eerie?' Damoya giggled.

'Very simple, Wakiti Moya, Titiadi has got devout foes, who deep into the night plot his destruction. Up the hill, fair Damoya, Titiadi shall be the moron, then the enemy's appetite will be whet. Please don't refuse?'

'We shall do it,' the trio assured Titiadi.

'And do blow your trumpet if I take too long.'

'We shall,' they again assured.

Titiadi went uphill and the trio went to the coconut trees at the far right, if judged by one facing the seascape.

He raced like the frigid wind of the Kalahari, heedless as a tornado, stumbling a dozen times, singing sometimes, yelling at other times and finally produced himself before the cave.

'Son of Wazeyme!' he called for Muyamba. 'Produce yourself.'

'You survived the immortal eye,' Muyamba said, running to him. 'Titiadi the feral archer. The stone that crushes a stone. The bad weed of the earth; they may weed you but not until their legs are badly injured.'

Titiadi sent his lips to Muyamba's ear and narrated to him the story of the trumpet's owners, exactly as had transpired. The two held hands and jubilantly danced about a rectangle.

Wearing inquisitive faces, the other Tailans surrounded the dancing duo. Nsora, the irate fellow, having escaped the anchor-bellied's glue was present within the surrounding Tailans, Dikomo, the anchor-bellied, by his side. Nsora grew tired and spiteful of the rectangular dance.

'Enough!' he told the dancers. 'Childish vanity.'

They ignored him.

'What has been the outcome of your quest?' he put to the finger-thrusting dancer.

'PEBBLES!' yelled he who knew how to thrust a finger.

'How dirty he looks!' sniggered Dikomo. 'Hope he didn't go hiding in some tunnel.'

Titiadi dived and caught her by the neck. He ruthlessly pressed the bone of her throat. She held her belly and yowled, acting as if she was nauseous. The people feared she would die. They implored Titiadi to free her. He refused. She yowled louder and acted the more nauseous. The people held Titiadi's hand and she managed to slip out his grips. She punched his jawbone and sped off. He went after her. The sympathetic hands of the people blockaded him. He failed to get her. He stood fuming.

'Leave that vagabond, Titiadi,' Muyamba spoke to him. 'The people are eager; speak to them.'

'Naamu!' Titiadi cried, eyeing Dikomo.

'Naamu!' the people returned.

'It has been said by the sages of the past that there's not a smoke without a blazing nuisance. And, long before it rains the clouds mobilize moisture. The trumpet sounds that drove you out of your homes emanate from a moisturized nuisance, which could kill you, or make you glad if tackled on time. My quest was horrific and life-shortening, tiresome and health-threatening, I shall charge a fee before disclosing—'

'Yes! I knew it!' yelled Dikomo.

'Tell her to shut up,' Titiadi told the people, who said nothing.

'I wonder how some get to be so greedy,' resumed Dikomo. 'Out of a mere hike to some dusty tunnel, he wants to make a fortune. We shan't pay a pebble.'

'You,' fumed Titiadi, trying to dive, but to no avail, tens of muscular muscles clung to his torso.

'Nier Titiadi, just name the amount?' the people spoke to him.

'I was going to need a cowry each, but due to the arrogance of that Nuamban, I've decided to pacify my anger with an additional cowry, making two of them.'

'Are the children included?' the woman with a fractured-leg son angrily asked.

'Do they belong to clans of the colonies of Raneb?' quarreled Titiadi. 'Since you've said it, every protruding foetus will have to pay.'

The people grumbled and swore not to pay any amount, even if it was a broken pebble. Some hooted at Titiadi and called him a tyrant.

Feeling insulted, the chief archer mumbled a dirge and went to sit on a stone inside the cave. 'Cohorts of my Nuamban foes,' he grumbled, 'I toiled in vain.'

'Needless talk!' snickered the people, pleased with themselves. They felt victorious and were happy they did not contribute too many a cowry as two times the whole of Taila into the pocket of a lone man. They remained victorious for close to seven minutes; then mightily the trumpet cried anew.

'We'll pay!' they knelt before Titiadi and pled. 'We promise to pay.'

'Cowards,' sneered Titiadi. 'I'm charging an extra cowry. Dikomo will have to pay six, three for her, three for whatever evil is stored in her belly, be it mortal or immortal. Till I see the cowries at my feet, my lips will remain shut.'

Obediently, the people brought their cowries to Titiadi's feet. He kept his gaze on Dikomo. She did not pay, so at the end of the payments, he announced that the cowries he needed most had not been paid. The people asked among themselves, trying to identify the deviant and when they failed to do so, they enquired from Titiadi.

'It's she whose eyes glare most at my feet, casting spells on the cowries of Titiadi,' the chief archer dropped a clue.

The people tried to find a pair of eyes that related to the description: they found too many and couldn't single out one.

'These eyes originate from the island of Mogoona,' the chief archer dropped another clue.

The people searched in one, and only one, place this time. An anchor-bellied woman occupied this place, and indeed her eyes were seriously glaring at the cowries, not in a holy manner.

'Stubborn woman!' they pounced on the anchor-bellied, looting every cowry that dwelled in any part of her attire, and handed them over to Titiadi, nine of them.

'Sixteen sturdy Tailans?' requested Titiadi.

That instant, forty athletic Tailans assembled before him.

'Cleave,' he ordered the forty.

They cleaved.

'This score must remain here and guard the cowries of Titiadi,' said he to one half, which half formed a triangle round the cowries.

'The rest of you should fetch two long poles capable of doing the work of a palanquin. Hurry, I'm an impatient ruler.'

This second twenty also were obedient. They dismantled a bench in the cave and took two long poles from the wreckage.

'We've got them,' they showed the poles to Titiadi.

'Good,' said he, 'now I'll group you properly. You two, place the rear of this pole on you right shoulders. Precisely. You two, place the front of the pole on your right shoulders. Good. Two of you, pick the rear of this second pole onto your left shoulders. And, you two, pick the front. Onto your left. Yes. The remaining twelve of you should stand behind them. You're their replacements. Muyamba, I want you to lead the procession. Proclaim my name as we move, so my enemies shall know that I forever remain the son of the Lenli. Peopled-palanquin, squat for your lord. Come closer. I will sit now; one leg here and the other there. Chim! Now, Taila, behold your soothsayer and lord.'

Muyamba leading the way and chanting praise songs, Titiadi's palanquin moved out of Daserwa. The people followed with his approval and he steered the procession northwards.

Dikomo felt manipulated. The cheers that went for Titiadi hurt her conquered soul. she prayed loudly, asking a foreign oracle to topple Titiadi. That didn't happen. She took a stick and scurried ahead of the procession. Whenever the chief archer demanded something she marked a stroke in the soil, somewhere unlikely for mortal feet to tread.

Titiadi noticed her troubles and decided to worsen them.

'My toes hurt,' he would intentionally complain. 'Peopled-palanquin, move slower.'

At other times he yelled, 'Women of Taila, is this how you treat your husbands? Allowing them to go hungry all day? I won't tolerate such cruelty. If I have to lead you to your fate, my belly has to protrude like my enemy's. Be quick. Get me something to eat.'

Whenever some other body walked pass him, he would quarrel, 'What arrogance! What do you think you are? A kingmaker? A chief custodian? Or the chief archer of all Taila?'

Muyamba chanted on. Dikomo marked till her pamls became sore. And Titiadi, the farther he went, the noisier he got. Eventually, the procession reached the hills of the north coast.

'Go up the hills,' Titiadi instructed the people.

'Up the hills?' asked they, fearful.

'Yes, what is to be feared is down here, not up there.'

Quarter curious, quarter optimistic, quarter scared, quarter pessimistic, the people started up the hills.

'Go to the total summit and glance at the shore,' Titiadi instructed.

The people went to the total summit and glanced at the shore.

'It's empty,' they said of the shore.

'Steal another glance,' he instructed.

They stole a glance.

'Empty,' was their report.

'Steal again. This time watch for long.'

They watched attentively, adjusting their eyes to all possible angles.

'Empty,' they reported.

'That is impossible? The three and quarter humans were there,' insisted Titiadi.

'What three and quarter humans?'

'Look again.'

The people looked. Their report remained negative.

Titiadi jumped off his peopled-palanquin and run uphill. He caught a dozen glances of the shore. 'Where are they?' he asked the people.

Dead silence. The people angrily stared at Titiadi, some tapping their feet, some grinding their teeth.

Dikomo burrowed her way through the crowd, closely followed by Nsora. They burrowed up to Titiadi.

'Bandit,' Dikomo hooted.

'Quite,' Muyamba shouted at her.

'Let her be,' the people sternly told Muyamba.

'I wish to go down there,' Titiadi told the people.

'To do what?' demanded the people.

'To search the three and quarter beings,' replied he.

'He'll flee!' alerted Dikomo.

'Allow him,' Muyamba told the people.

'We will on two conditions,' said Nsora.

'State them?' Muyamba said.

'Your position,' stated Nsora, 'and his freedom. If he tries to flee, we shall confine him for ever and you shall be demoted.'

Muyamba pondered awhile and said he had accepted the condition. Titiadi also accepted.

'Very well,' spoke Nsora. 'Liyanga, give me two executioners. They will accompany Titiadi to the shore. Don't worry, people, everything will happen under my nose. I'm following them down there.'

'That tactic is sick,' argued Dikomo, wrapping a cloth shabbily around her anchor-belly. 'Why travel to the valleys of Kooa when Henegi has brooks that burble with life? What if the executioners turn out to be his henchmen? Take me instead of the executioners. I'll tie one end of my cloth to his waist, which will check his speed as we descend: there's no way his skinny body can drag along my able self. I'll tread so close to him that it would seem to him he was back in the womb of a woman. That sabotages all his chances of survival and rounds up our coastal duel.'

'It's good,' the people told Nsora.

'That bandit has to be held tight, so I can tie him,' spoke Dikomo. 'Any two volunteers?'

Ten people stepped forward. Like a wrestler's coach, she moved about, examining them.

'Nice muscles. Yours are too girlish. Neat fists, they'll make no good punches. Firm grips,' with these comments Dikomo selected her two volunteers.

Titiadi was firmly held as she tied her cloth to his waist, telling him, 'Titiadi, start trotting. As soon as Nier Nsora signals MOOVE you GOOO!'

'Clap, people, clap,' Nsora ordered. 'Dikomo, ready yourself. Don't let him move an inch without you. Clap, people, we'll soon be moving. I'm gathering momentum. Now dance, dance. You can jump if you want. Get ready, Titiadi, and … MOOOVE!'

His waist firmly held in the anchor-bellied's cloth, Titiadi led the way downhill, Dikomo jumping into every little gap that opened under his feet. Cheering from the people was grand. Nsora followed with an eagle's eyes. He coached the anchor-bellied and made sure her belly was forever pressing tight against the chief archer's back. The people just loved it.

Near the foot of the hill, Titiadi swiftly turned and snatched the end of the cloth from Dikomo. He bolted downhill and headed for the coconut trees.

Many Tailans charged downhill and went, with Dikomo and Nsora, after Titiadi, who halted when he was five yards away from the coconut trees.

'Attack!' roared he.

Out came the three and quarter humans he had told the Tailans about, one of them hoisting a trumpet. The oncoming Tailans halted and screamed and turned and fled. They and their compatriots uphill merged and run to a place where the shoreline was unseen.

'Titiadi the ally of death,' yelled Muyamba, who alone stood uphill, to Titiadi. 'The monster in their sour dreams. The crafty spirit that makes a coast feel eerie. The fish that swallows a fish. The snake that contaminates a snake. You are the gritty soil that prevents a river from reaching the sea. Naamu, son of the Lenli.'

CHAPTER 5

Ah balmy bonfire! A jollification at Taila was its guest. At the center of the kingdom it glowed, at the place of durbars. Its eyes were a pair of victory chalks; its nose was the warm breeze of immunity; its lips were the ditties of a songbird; its arms were the sultry embraces of ecstasy.

It was conceived on the north coast, at a place where the shoreline was invisible. It was conceived when three and a quarter humans led by a kingmaker and a chief archer met the fleeing multitude of Taila and gave them the message of victory.

'Anona's head is this quarter human,' the kingmaker had said of the quarter human.

'Sovereign is the morrow of Taila,' the chief archer had declared.

'Bow, people, to the kindred of your ancestors,' an elderly woman with a bald head was the speaker of these words.

Taila bowed to the Zowdor whose other name was Nemoso. They bowed to his allies, the sailor and his daughter. The sailor told of how he had been robbed and confined by the quarter human and asked for a ship so he could sail back to his Lembe. The Tailans promised to give him a ship and two score men to be his crew.

The chief archer proposed a bonfire and the proposal met unanimous approval. So, inward strode the entire assembly – the chief archer and the three and quarter humans leading the procession on palanquins – to the ceremonial soils of Wambi.

The trio from Numungu was treated to huge chunks of mutton as women sang praises to them. The sailor noticed his daughter's eyes. The Tailans also did. Her eyes, dreamy as they were, stole. They stole glances, at a lad, the Zowdor.

'Go sit yonder,' the sailor said to her.

'Shhh!' she said and ate some meat.

'Swap seats with me. Come sit by your damsel,' said the sailor to Zowdor.

'Did you tell him?' murmured Zowdor to the sailor's daughter.

'He was a-spying,' the sailor's daughter murmured back.

The sailor got up, saying to Zowdor, 'Let's swap.'

Zowdor swapped and he wasn't made unhappy by the swap.

Meanwhile, four Tailans stood a few yards away. They continuously thieved glances at the trio from Numungu and thrust fingers into the direction of space that if one followed would lead to the trio. Their lips were busy and their faces were serious. Two half-hours was the age of their conference, after which they came to surround the trio from Numungu. Their identities, by clockwise manipulation, were Titiadi, chief archer of Taila and chief custodian of Emorna; Muyamba, kingmaker of Taila and chief custodian of Wambi; Nier Gorua, chief custodian of Agunbe; and Nier Jerda, chief custodian of Twessi.

'Lembe is far, far away,' said Gorua to the sailor.

'I'm quite skilled at my calling,' returned the sailor.

'The spear is a murderous invention. It has killed many a skilled man,' spoke Jerda.

'The spear, though murderous, is not craftier than a vigilant sailor with good skill,' argued Yiddi.

'I counted seven score sailors on the seas around,' Jerda told Yiddi. 'Only one of them escaped the pirates, and as he went, I saw blood dripping from his chest; then his face became a wraith and he could captain his ship no further. His ship fell off the waves to the ocean's foundation. And you know what?'

'What?' asked the sailor, becoming disturbed.

'There were four score seamen with him, all armed, and he perished. But you could escape the pirates.'

'How?'

'Stay here for three months. Once the harvest season is over, the pirates shall move north, then you can sail peacefully.'

'Uuh, that's a long time.'

'Lightning bolt us if you ever get bored,' swore Titiadi.

'You can rule Taila while you await your departure,' offered Muyamba. 'All three of you can rule. The lass will be queen and you'll rule east, while the oracle rules west.'

Damoya touched her head. She formed a crown with her hands and tried it on. The men stared at her. Their stare intimidated her and she hid her face behind Zowdor.

'I'll give you a gold crown, Wakiti Moya,' Titiadi promised her, 'just say you'll be queen.'

'Give me two crowns,' she said, her face still hidden. 'I'll wear one for Zowdor and the other for Taila.'

The men laughed. Zowdor didn't. He felt awkward and looked below the assembly.

'Will you wear our crown, great oracle?' Muyamba asked Zowdor.

'He will, if it looks like mine,' Damoya showed her face and said.

The older men laughed.

'And, you, great sailor?' Jerda asked Yiddi.

'Let the young woman answer,' Yiddi laughed.

'Give him a crown. A golden one,' whispered Damoya, thrusting her finger at Zowdor's cheek.

The older men laughed another round.

'Nimatua! Nimatua!' called Titiadi. 'Come here urgently.'

The town crier went to Titiadi. He had been singing when the chief archer called him.

Says Titiadi to him, 'We're off to Wazeyme's stone palace. While we're away, host these lofty ones.'

'I'm honoured,' said Nimatua, taking over from the four chief custodians, who went speedily to the stone palace. I'll tell you of Cheops, no Raneb.'

'Who's greater of the two?' asked Damoya.

'Cheops,' answered Nimatua.

'Tell of Cheops,' she told him.

'When another story of Geesa is told, a new life is breathed into the lung of the Nile,' Nimatua commenced. 'In the years Cheops ruled Egypt, there lived a famed sculptor whose name was Petaki. This Petaki was the most notorious of any breed of he-whore imaginable; and it so happened that in his middle ages he kept a foreign mistress, whom he would meet every full moon. An inn along the Nile, the only one in Egypt at the time, was where they would meet, until one planting season when a tornado swept away the inn and its keeper. Now, Petaki had a quarrelsome wife, and he dared not drop a hint of his infidelity. Troubled, he sat behind a map of Egypt, thinking hard of a place he could entertain his mistress on her visits. Even on the map, Geesa looked secure, but it was a cold place at night, and Petaki was no friend of the cold. He decided to have Cheops build him an inn at Geesa. Come the morn, to Cheops went he. "Great Pharaoh! O mighty Pharaoh!" cried he. "Your fellow gods have shown themselves to me. They were with tears at Geesa. Unsafe they said they were, and this they ask of you that you build a fort about which guards would be stationed to guard their tombs. On the full moons, their spirits come out to dine, so the guards should give them privacy." Petaki was an honourable son of the land and Cheops believed him, instructing, "You, Petaki shall see to the building of the fort. I'll provide the material but the fort should look like the foundation of a pyramid and bigger it should be than the foundations of all pyramids at Geesa." Petaki smiled. "I shall set to work tomorrow," he told Cheops. With abundance of material and over a thousand men at his disposal, Petaki completed the fort in four months; a fort with the shape of a pyramid's base, bigger than the base of every pyramid that stood at Geesa. But Cheops, as Petaki, had ulterior motives. He had forever envied the pyramids of the other Pharaohs and would scowl anytime he came across them. Petaki's inn was to Cheops the foundation of his own pyramid, which he intended to be biggest of all the pyramids. Full moon after full moon passed and Petaki would go to entertain his mistress at Geesa. One full moon, Cheops was bored and not even Shoret, the exotic dancer, could entertain him. "The Pharaohs dine tonight," said his queen to him. "Go to Geesa. Go entertain yourself. What is done there, you also can do. Are you not Pharaoh?" Cheops was driven in a chariot to Geesa, but a mile away from the pyramids he made the charioteer stop and he journeyed on foot to the pyramids, talking to himself. "Very soon," he pointed to the fort Petaki had built and told a sphinx, "I shall rest my bones here and my eyes shall see above your head. I shall be lord of Geesa, greater than all." He walked to the fort and entered by a side exit. He heard voices, so thinking they belonged to the spirits of the past pharaohs, he crept silently to the chamber in which they dwelled. A veil was the seal of the chamber's exit and he drew it aside with his hand. He spied on the pharaohs, but they were no pharaohs. Petaki lay laughing, a woman against his chest. "Emissary of the pharaohs," so Cheops addressed him, "what godly ritual I've witnessed." Petaki and his mistress leapt asunder, alarmed. "Spare my life, venerable pharaoh," wept Petaki. "If you shall build me a mountain?" negotiated Cheops. "If you shall mount a pyramid for me upon this fort and place before it a solid image of myself, with eyes that can see above every pyramid and sphinx?" Petaki bowed at the pharaohs feet, "I shall," he swore. "Your eyes shall not only view above Egypt, but also above the world." The pharaoh shook Petaki's hand and promised, "I give permission to every pyramid in Geesa; you may entertain yourself as you please but never smile at a woman in the pyramid of Cheops." Petaki vowed to limit his deeds to the other pyramids. Cheops smiled and went home a happy man. Petaki spent the rest of his life at Geesa, building and entertaining his concubines. Cheops smiled till his death, for everywhere in Egypt, his pyramid was visible.'

All laughed merrily.

'If I were Petaki's wife,' said Damoya, eyeing Zowdor, 'and perchance I got to know of such infidelity, I would bind him and sacrifice his mistress to the sovereignty of Cheops.'

All laughed the more, save Zowdor.

'And ... and,' she talked on, eyeing Zowdor aggressively, 'if I were Petaki I better be without mistress, not an alien, not a local.'

All laughed some more. Zowdor yawned.

The four chief custodians returned to the ceremonial ground performing a rectangular dance. They had four gold crowns, which lacked polish, yet were lined with elegant fabric. The youth of Taila were engaged in a circular dance round the bonfire and the four chiefs stood at one point of the dance, refusing to move, so that the dance died.

'Naamu!' bellowed Gorua.

'Naamu!' all Taila responded.

'Before the battle,' spoke Muyamba, 'we promised a throne to they who behead the Sissi Nanna.'

'You're not going to offer those crowns to outsiders,' Nsora quarreled.

'O we will,' the woman with a fractured-leg son picked a flaming plank and firmly said.

'This is abominable,' spoke Dikomo.

'Silence will benefit you,' the fractured-leg's mother told the Nuamban.

'We stand for the well-being of Tailans,' Nsora and Dikomo campaigned.

More Tailans drew planks from the bonfire.

'We shall grill you if you object any further,' the fractured-leg's mother said to the Nuambans.

The Nuambans did not heed. They walked to the four custodians and the anchor-bellied Nuamban snatched one of the diadems. Planks hammered her head, her back, her legs, and several aspects of her. She freed the crown and fled. She was gone but the planks remained thirsty. Her henchman's body became victim. A good spanking he was given before he too fled.

'Sin is in the air,' proclaimed Titiadi, 'a godly sin. Nothing shall hamper us. This moment we crown a fearless trio. Muyamba, do it quickly, lest our enemies spoil the ceremony.'

'Shame on us,' said Nier Jerda. 'We didn't bring them any majestic chairs.'

'The stone palace is faraway,' complained Titiadi. 'We shall hesitate no further. Is a crown and a people with allegiance not all it takes to be a ruler? Crown them, Muyamba, go on.'

Muyamba went to trio that beheaded Anona, Gorua accompanying him with a flat board on which rested the four crowns. Muyamba stood before Damoya, picking a crown and suspending it above her head. He gradually lowered it and as it sat upon her head, declared: 'Over the six islands of Taila, I crown you queen. Be bold. To the adversary who lets you no peace, give him war. Taila is your offspring: chasten her if she deviates from the norm. Taila is your servant: dismiss her if she disobeys your dictates. Taila is your master: her wish should often outshine yours. Taila is yours: give death to them that threaten her peace. Rule, my queen. The spirits of our ancestors are with you; they shall bring fame and might to your throne. Live long, queen of Taila.'

'Naamu!' roared the Tailans. Lenli. They danced that anarchic dance, the Lenli. Vaulting, breaking, shaking and singing of a foreign bird and its sister. That the bird was a-scavenging and its sister was at a burial.

'Silence. Not done yet,' shrieked Muyamba.

His words were a boneless punch slapped against the groin of a rock. Anarchy lived on and only left the ceremony when his disciples were panting and could not vault nor break nor shake.

'This other crown,' Muyamba put a second crown on Damoya's head, 'is to be worn for a godly duty, particulars of which I should not be telling. But I am confident the kindred of your ancestors is aware of the duty.'

The assembly laughed, not including Zowdor. Everywhere he turned, there were eyes, peering, demanding answers. He squatted beside his seat and inserted his head under it as if he was repairing some fault. A face appeared in front of his. It had gold above it. 'Damoya!' he squeaked and withdrew his head. The assembly went hysterical with laughter.

Muyamba took a third crown. He rested it on Yiddi's head, declaring: 'Over Azumba, Nuamba and Agunbe, I crown you king. Yours is the islands of past glory. You shall be the peace of the east. The immoral east is history from tonight. Rule, my king, do with the land as you wish. Many hands shall try your strength. Wear the paws of a leopard and look through the eyes of a homeless cat, then trounce the foe of Taila. A smile of yours shan't be enjoyed by our enemies. Live long, my king.'

Anarchy was reborn, with song again. The song still spoke of foreign birds: it told of the sister of the first bird. That it was at the burial of its lover, a chameleon. And this chameleon, it was very dead, yet its eyes won't die; and they flew out of their socket. They saw the bird but bypassed her and wooed an insect. The bird cried. It as well rolled on its little chest. The insect was a hunter, a starved hunter, wandering with a stolen dagger. The insect jabbed the chameleon's eyes and ate them. The bird stopped crying and sold her lover's body to her scavenger brother. The disciples of Anarchy were the tellers of this tale. And as they told it, they danced.

'Uuu! Terrible! Terrible! Terrible!' shrieked Muyamba. 'Halt for the last! Halt for the finale!'

Anarchy left at his own discretion. When he was gone, Muyamba suspended the fourth crown above Zowdor, all Taila applauding and humming a victory song. Muyamba placed the crown on Zowdor's head, with the declaration: 'Kindred of Taila, I crown you king over Wambi, Emorna and Twessi. Dauntless deity, who from a tree occurred, this is a jot of our gratuity. Roam the west like a beast and feast on every poacher. The east is twin to your west, borrow her your mortal eyes and keep the immortal ones where you reign. Be a testy oracle, always at the heels of the foe. Rule by your bias. Live long, my king.'

Anarchy. Back he came. He: Anarchy. His disciples were with dance and song this time too. The song was for the bird that bought a carcass. They sang about how he swallowed a blind carcass that happened to be a glutton. And the only time the carcass was not hungry was when it was eating. That it ate the bird's bile, which caressed its appetite, so prior to its decay it ate every other organ therein. A famine visited the scavenger bird and it wanted to discharge and make festival of its decayed carcass but it had no intestine.

Anarchy's sport was replaced by a spy sport. Zowdor's eyes inaugurated the sport: they did by spying for two score seconds and not blinking. This thing amazed the Tailans. They followed Zowdor's eyes to the spectacle of his interest. Gorua and Damoya were the spectacle. Damoya was giggling and slotting words into the chief custodian's ear. When that meeting elapsed, Gorua stood on a tree stump and told the Tailans: 'A power of the land has aired a crucial word. Simply, no bachelor, be he king or deity, qualifies to reside in Wazeyme's stone palace.'

'False,' argued Titiadi. 'Muyamba, where on the tablets is that inscribed?'

'Nowhere,' replied Muyamba.

'Nowhere,' other voices announced.

'The queen is the maker of this rule,' clarified Gorua.

'Forgive me,' begged Titiadi, bowing. 'In fact, it's on the tablets. I'm at fault if I say it was never inscribed. Will you regard the norm of your kindred, good oracle?'

Zowdor nodded.

'Marry us, Nier Gorua,' Damoya sat beside Zowdor and said.

The Tailans sang a matrimonial song. Gorua went to the queen and her groom.

'Do it like a robbery, quick,' Damoya instructed in a low tone.

'Queen Damoya,' Gorua said it loud enough for all to hear, 'will you marry this oracle seated here by your side?'

'I shall,' she vowed.

Taila applauded.

'King ... King ...' Gorua slapped his head while stammering. 'But what is the name of the oracle? O I forgot.'

'Yes, what is the name of the oracle?' asked Titiadi.

'What is it?' all Taila asked Zowdor.

'Zowdor Nemoso,' answered the king of the west.

'That's an awful name for an oracle,' said the old woman with a bald head.

'I am not a priest,' confessed Zowdor.

'Not!' the Tailans exclaimed, searching at their neighbour's faces.

'Where I was born I know not, but I was raised in Isiko. Life was drab where I was, so I decided to wander in search of that which lay beyond. My quest led me here, into the heart of a battle, onto the shoulder of a tree, down to the jaws of mean warriors, who wanted me dead, so I became a priest. Pardon me.'

The Tailans searched at Muyamba's face.

'The better he is,' announced Muyamba. 'If an oracle got us this peace we'd all be made to serve the shrine, but look, he did it for the love of Taila.'

The assembly applauded, some wept.

'But he still is oracle,' announced Titiadi. 'The world would fear us less if it was heard our oracle was human. It shall never come from any lip that humans rule Taila. Show me your hands, all who shall violate this decree?'

No hands went up.

Damoya beckoned Gorua to proceed with the marriage ceremony.

'King Zowdor,' Gorua resumed, 'will you marry the queen?'

Damoya nudged Zowdor. He returned the nudge, saying to Gorua: 'I shall.'

Yiddi blessed them and they danced for the assembly. Anarchy's disciples joined the dance. Damoya sought to entertain them. She took her second crown and put it on Zowdor's head. The people laughed at Zowdor. He pinched the skin upon her spine. She squealed like a duck and climbed a tree stump, from where she decreed: 'Any king, oracle, son or daughter of the land who fights a peaceful Tailan shall pay two pots of cowries, even if that king or oracle was husbanded to the victim.'

The Tailans laughed at her. She quit the ceremony altogether.

Same trumpet that had earlier caused Taila to tremble blared again. It was blown by the chief archer, who announced: 'This is to inform all who are unaware, that the throne has been reinstalled.'

'That trumpet is misleading. And the sound it emits is awful,' complained Jerda.

'We shall sail to all five islands and announce the reinstatement of the throne,' decreed Gorua.

'Why suffer our bodies?' spoke Titiadi. 'All whom are unaware of the enthronement are in Azumba. There alone we shall announce.'

The Tailans went musical. Their instruments comprised of gongs, metal pieces, sticks and a trumpet. At the eastern coast fear gripped most of them, so Titiadi went with a stubborn few to Azumba. Titiadi led them to Zomo Nanna's village; it wasn't peopled, therefore they went to other parts of Azumba, searching north, south, east and west, and finding no Azumban.

They returned to Wambi, announcing: 'Azumba is gone. Azumba fled from the trumpeting of only three and quarter humans. Tsambo fled too and as he fled his knees soared high as the hills. His eyes were a chicken's tears. His hands were a rabbit's ears. Zomo Nanna's heart is pounding on a foreign sea, his tongue hanging beneath his chin. A turkey's heart is braver than Azumba.'

CHAPTER 6

They were an army. And they sneaked pass the shoreline. Red bands ringed their heads and wrists, and there was villainous vengeance in their eyes. Compact were their lines, as they started up the hills.

'SHOOT!' Commanded the chief archer of the kingdom they had come to attack.

It rained arrows from the top of the hills. The arrows had a fatal sting: they were impregnated with venoms, so that when they tore through flesh, they separated soul from body.

The invaders were overpowered. Their population declined to a trivial fraction of its original size, forcing their commander to order a retreat.

As the archers their arrows shot, the invaders, their ships their current station, their rudders steered, sorrowful and weeping home.

The fleeing army was Numungu and the victory was Taila's; the attack came a week after the reinstatement of the throne.

Fearing a possible invasion by Numungu, the triple-monarchy, the day after their enthronement, decreed that a defence-force be formed. The chief archer was tasked with training the entire kingdom in the art of archery since the males that were counted were either too aged or too young, and this task he masterfully accomplished, for in three days there was a kingdom of archers, shooting at trees and birds throughout the day. A full day was set aside for the making of toxic arrows, thick bundles of which every Tailan kept in wait for Numungu.

Spies were placed all around the kingdom to monitor the coming of Numungu. Theirs was also a job properly done, for on the evening Numungu, after invading Nuamba and finding it empty, crossed the shoreline at Wambi, Taila lay on her hills, arrows tensed, ready to defend her land. And O, yes, she did defend it.

Time fermented, eating two ripe moons, and another that symbolized the sailing season recommended to the sailor prior to his enthronement. Happily, he summoned his subjects and told them he would return to his Lembe the coming week.

'Have we been a dreary company, my king?' Nier Gorua asked him.

'Your company isn't dreary, but I owe the dead a ritual: I go to bid farewell to the family lost,' he answered.

'The pirate swords have not vacated,' said Nier Gorua, in a compassionate tone.

'Danger yet lurks?' inquired the eastern king; his voice was dry.

'Worse danger than before,' answered Nier Gorua. 'How dear rebellion is to deviant hearts! The amateur pirates have taken over the trade. The lords have been murdered and swords have been ground ahead of the mariners' arrival.'

'Uuuh!' groaned the king.

'But, you can survive the swords,' Nier Jerda comforted him.

'How?'

'Count three more moons.'

'Uuuh, very long.'

'Lightning smash us level if you ever get bored!' swore Titiadi.

For fear of getting slashed by a pirate's sword, a thing he deemed worse than nostalgia, the sailor remained on the throne, going daily to a shore and imagining himself behind a rudder, sailing to his Lembe.

Close to counting the first of his three moons, his daughter, the queen, conceived. Glad was the heart of his, so he summoned his subjects.

'I'm honoured among my kindred,' he told them. 'A generation is added to my name.'

'The heir is here!' celebrated the people.

'So … let's see?' Nier Jerda said to the king, counting his fingers. 'That adds six more moons.'

'Uuuh, why?' groaned the king.

'The god of the seas circling Taila is a barren man. Countless wives he's been with, yet he's got no child. An oracle once revealed that all stillborns around here are murdered by him and dumped into a cage.'

'Uuuh, wicked, wicked!'

'Worse if the foetus floats on his seas: he cremates them alive.'

'That will not happen to mine. What did he do wrong? Can't he just be peacefully born like all humans?'

'Then rule six more.'

'I shall, for the child unborn.'

Five moons came and parted. Most of the time, the eastern king thought of his Lembe, mourning his wife and son, boiling Anona's skull so it would forever remain scorched.

Zowdor. If not for his abused pair of ears, it would have been flawless to say that the western king was a spoiled king. Female voices in particular were the abusers, two groups of them. First, the tender tellings of his talkative wife; and then, the ever-complaining voices of Tailan women.

'Zowdor,' the wife of his would usually call, 'look at the tinniest toes of mine, these two. Yesterday, after supper, they grew bigger than my thumbs. But see now how little they've become.'

He would laugh and rub the toes.

'Nemoso,' she would sometimes call him, 'this is an inquisitive baby. When I think of you, it runs to the left where beats my heart, and when I think of things imperial it tugs the threads that hung from my brain.'

At this, he would laugh and ruffle her hair.

She would never let him wander a half-mile away. When he in a corner strode, she would quest with her maids until he was found. She loved him and her love was difficult, very difficult in that it was too religious and demanding. Her love gave him no space, yet he loved her deeply; and, better than any hunger-stricken vulture ever loved a corpse. Together with the eastern king, the couple decreed from the Wambian stone palace built by Wazeyme, the first king of Taila.

The women of Taila, ever-complaining they were. There was always a case in the kings' court, the majority of them for the western king. There were cases of verbal assault; cases of marital interference; cases of utensil thieving; cases of man-snatching; cases of gang rivalry; cases of unfair terms of polygamy; cases of foodstuff thieving; cases of inappropriate gazing; cases of suspected gossiping; cases of amateur harlotry against another woman's suitor; and other worldly cases that men work their minds hard at, but are left less competent in the comprehension of that one phenomenon called woman.

Zowdor's ears were told into by Tailan women, and grumbled into, and sobbed into; and there came a time that their notorious tellings got him bothered. This compelled him to summon them and ask those who were not Wambians to return to their native islands.

'Our king,' replied the non-Wambians, 'we call him king of the east yet he dwells in the west. We call you king of the west but you dwell in the center. We may go where we were born if the kings of those places will go with us; otherwise, we will dwell here in this place.'

Queen Damoya was by Zowdor's side and he said to her, 'Pa-Yiddi is the cause. He must go east. I will roam Emorna and Twessi.'

'Shame, Zowdor,' she groused. 'My pa loves you so dearly, yet you treat him with no love at all. You want to send him east, where an enemy prowls.'

She left the palace, wearing a frown.

Zowdor called aside the non-Wambians. He scanned their lips. Many showed signs of tellings. This made him furious and he wanted to send them and the eastern king away, but he feared his Damoya would frown forever; he needed more for her to smile, than for them to leave.

'You may stay,' he eventually decreed.

Later that day, as Zowdor knelt before his Damoya begging her to smile, a Nuamban woman and her daughter brought tellings. They were the wife and daughter of Nier Nsora. A notorious scarf bound the wife's head, the type worn in polygamous fights. The duo carried four pots and an effigy.

'There's a big, big battle about to quake Taila,' the wife loudly told.

'Who? Who?' Titiadi, who had come to visit the triple-monarchy, dashed out of a chamber, Yiddi behind him. 'Who is to battle Taila?'

'Come, good men,' the wife said to the chief archer and the eastern king, 'you also shall judge.'

'Who is to battle Taila?' repeated Titiadi.

'My queen,' the wife directed a finger at Damoya, 'didn't you decree that any king, oracle, son or daughter of the land who fights a peaceful Tailan shall pay two pots of cowries, even if that king or oracle was husbanded to the victim? Didn't you?'

'I did,' replied Damoya.

'These are two times the fine,' the wife handed four pots of cowries to the queen.

'Which peaceful Tailan did you fight?' asked Titiadi.

'She hasn't fought yet,' answered the daughter.

'You haven't?' Titiadi put to the wife.

The wife shook her head. 'My queen, look at this effigy,' she said, handing the effigy she and her daughter had brought to Damoya.

Damoya was confused. She looked carefully at the effigy. 'What is this?' she asked the wife.

'It's the effigy of the god at Moru shine. It used to guard Nuamba, but the rains swept it into a valley. There's still some power in it. I've added it as supplement, in case there's a shortage.'

'I still don't understand,' the queen told the wife.

'I'll tell you,' said the wife. 'This day, I'm about to battle against them that provoke me in painful ways that are not physical. You, my queen, shall condemn me and ask a fine. I've paid two times the amount, because the enemies I fight are made of thick skin. There shall be a first battle to soften their outer skins; which after, I shall attack their sore inner bodies. If after these two battles they go unharmed, I will have to battle their souls. The effigy is my payment for the battle against their souls.'

The triple-monarchy and the chief archer were bewildered. They met briefly aside and on their return offered the wife a chair, telling her; 'Explain how your adversaries provoked you in painful ways that were not physical.'

'This effigy from Moru shrine will punish my husband' started the wife. 'He is a disgusting, unprincipled man. In the last six months we've been spending the nights asunder. Whenever I confront him, he gives the excuse that the ghost of his late wife, my senior, is haunting him and would kill him if we spent a night together. But, Nora was lying. We caught him today, after the meeting. We caught him with Dikomo.

'You left out the trips,' the daughter reminded the wife.

'And aha, many times, my husband would ask leave to a foreign shrine to seek charms against his dead wife's ghost. Once he was gone, Dikomo would be missing from Taila. My husband never returned a cured man; and now I know why.'

'Your case is good ,' Titiadi gave her a handshake. 'I will pay additional pots for you. Keep the effigy to strengthen your muscles. Go with strength, daughter of the land.'

Right about the time the chief archer encouraged the wife, a young woman joined the assembly. She was skipping. She was noisy. Her temper was bad, and she spoke, 'Ma, they're bound for Azumba. They're in our new canoe. They've got a big box with them and the woman is smiling and eating.'

The wife grabbed her effigy and saying nothing trotted out of the palace. The daughter, the young woman and Titiadi trotted after her. The four went to the east coast. They saw Nier Nsora and Dikomo cruising on the Azumban seas. A great distance it was that lay between them and the cruising duo; the wife's eyes discharged.

'I'll harm them,' she told Titiadi.

'You should,' he returned.

She took a paddle and sat in a canoe. 'Push me!' she ordered the daughter and the young woman.

'Don't follow them,' Titiadi advised. 'Rest your muscles. On the waters you'll be vulnerable. We'll get them when they return.'

'The chief archer is right,' said the daughter and the young woman.

The wife got off the canoe. 'I'll bide here,' she said. 'Blood shall be the remnant of them the minute they return.'

'We shall stay with our mother,' said the daughter and the young woman to Titiadi.

'Good,' spoke Titiadi, 'I'll go home quickly and get you some food and water. Do you need any weapons?'

'Bring me a club,' said the daughter.

'I'll need a metal,' said the wife.

'I will as well need a metal,' said the young woman.

'Don't yell too much and don't be too active. Reserve the power in your muscles. I'll be back soon,' Titiadi instructed and trotted off.

The three women stayed on the coast. Club and metals they got. Food and water they got. Seconds graduated to minutes. Minutes graduated to hours .Hours graduated to days. But Nier Nsora and Dikomo did not return to Wambi. Nine was the number of the days that managed to convince the three women and Titiadi that Nier Nsora and Dikomo were not returning in any brevity of time. All four concluded the duo might have eloped and on this basis called off the coastal wait.

Those nine days that convinced the four Tailans gained weight, or rather they aged, by a score and a single day; six months was the length of time King Zowdor had endured at the mercies of the pregnant queen who had dynamic toes. Then came the troops. They came by the south, moving in two rows as they bypassed the smelly cave Tarada; one row at the right of the cave and the other at the left. They had a muddy complexion, were a skinny folk with deflated jaws, wore unwashed clothing, and it could have been argued without resorting to prejudice that their heads had never felt a comb in their whole lives.

Judging by the direction in which their malnourished limbs steered their canoes, it was a certainty they would dock on the south coast of Wambi. There their eyes looked. There their shoulders faced. There their sails directed the wind.

Arrows of theirs rubbed tight against the strings of bows: arrows of archers who had come to do the manning of the coast after learning from spies about the skinny troops on the seas. The sun above was high, splashing its rays on the muddy troops, giving the archers an excellent view of their unkempt assailants.

The archers had a commander. His legs were impatient, his hands also. He had a sure forefinger and would once in a while thrust it toward the assailants. He coached with signs and at the behind of a tuft of grass he hid. The south coast was not a highlander; the south coast was a lowlander on whose back grew coarse weeds. So behind tufts of these weeds, the archers, spirited as their commander, lay.

His eyes, the commanders, had the hue of a carrot. Those organs, his eyes, closely observed the assailants, the particulars of their population. It was a weird composition. Just as Taila, women dominated their force, and it seemed the women were braver than the men, because they sailed ahead of the men. The assailants' canoes and the commander's gaze moved as a pair. They were like mating larks. Harmoniously, they proceeded, slashing the length that resided between Tarada and the shoreline into two. They proceeded again, biased now; they offered Tarada the better of the distance. Again they proceeded, offering Tarada over two-thirds of the distance.

Archers, their commander, their bows, their arrows, all knew too well; the drums of battle were playing, calling the warrior to duty, releasing from dormancy every slice of frozen blood.

Assailants, muddy-complexioned troops, skinny folk, across the shoreline they marched, women in front, weapons unseen. He drew air, the commander commanding archers, through his mouth, down his throat, contemplated it in his voice box and let it out via a nasal opening. He then accumulated air in his throat, molded it in his brain that if it should come out it should mention the word 'shoot' and motioned the tip of his arrow about, thrusting it toward the assailants, worrying about which of them to shoot first.

A flag was hoisted above the assailants. Its bearer, a female, was aged and pitiable. It was a white flag; white as the breast of a gull; luminous as the tresses of a cataract displayed against the eastern sun. The assailants had surrendered.

'Crime is when a vulgar swain marries with the modest fair. Injustice is that time of the year when a virgin rain is given to be stored in filthy, muddy soils. Sin is sarcastic; it happens when nature, our mother, lights the way of the murderer, assisting him in his flight,' so thought the commander commanding archers, as he contrasted between the muddy hue of the assailants and the brilliant white of their hoisted flag. He saw no fairness in the juxtaposition of the two. This brought him sadness.

He pushed his bow and arrow upwards, high enough for the assailants to see. They saw and suspended their hands above their heads. He monitored them through dents created at the waist of the grass, where its blades did not tangle. They saw his eyes peering at them. They peered back. He peered in return. They returned the peer. He peered; they peered; all peered and the peering turned competitive. The commander thrust his head into the space above the grass and peered at the assailants with might.

'It's us, Nier Titiadi,' they peered and yelled.

'You … who?' asked the commander, peering.

'Us,' they answered, but did not peer.

The commander's archers jerked their heads to the tops and sides of the weeds behind which they hid. They joined their commander in peering at the assailants.

'Who are you?' the commander, still peering, put to the assailants.

'Azumba,' they, as though they were embarrassed, said.

The commander lay down his weapon. He knelt behind his tuft of grass, thrusting his forefinger. His archers, because they saw their commander drop his weapon, disengaged their arrows from the strings of their bows. Their commander showed his face meanly to the assailants, now Azumba. 'SHOOT!' he commanded.

His archers repositioned their arrows against the strings of their bows.

'Don't!' an old fellow stopped them. 'Don't shoot.'

The archers disengaged their asrrows.

'Who's commander of you?' the commander put to his archers.

'You,' they answered.

'Then shoot.'

They returned to shooting position.

'Don't, I say,' the old fellow stopped them again.

The commander marched to the old fellow and protested, 'Muyamaba, just why won't you let them shoot those devils.'

'Titiadi, forgive me,' pled old Muyamba. 'Forgive them also.'

Suddenly, women wailed and men sang a dirge; Azumban women and men. A woman was carried on a bamboo stretcher by two men, to the commander. Her hair was partly burnt; her skin was bathed in ashes and she was shaking and slapping herself as if a fire in her body burnt. She had a suffering voice. It cried out for help. It bore witness to her misery.

'She seeks Nier Uono,' her carriers said to the commander.

'Who's she?' the commander asked, peering at her.

'The sister of Nier Uono,' answered her carriers.

'O priestess of the shrine!' sympathized Muyamba. 'Lay her down.'

She was laid down.

'Muyamba, you've done wrong,' said Titiadi.

'She's dying,' pled Muyamba.

'She should. The Grey Oracle should strengthen our warriors, but she used it to curse them. You vowed to me, Muyamba. You vowed never to pray to that oracle.'

'I never will.'

'Then leave her to die.'

An old man with hardly any courage in his joints meandered to the woman on the stretcher. His unsteady eyes patronized her painful body. Deep compassion stood in his eyes. He had no tears but his countenance showed more melancholy than widowed dirge.

'Uono, forgive me,' spoke the woman to him; smoke accompanied her words; it leaked from her mouth.

He touched her face. She eyed his eyes. He tried to smile. She took his hand in hers.

'What happened?' he tenderly inquired.

She answered, 'The Grey Oracle. He came with Ninaya.'

'You saw Ninaya?' Muyamba interrupted her.

'I did. His teeth were maroon.'

The archers drew close. Curiosity dwelled on their faces and they asked the priestess: 'Did Ninaya have a message for Taila? What height was he? Was his gait rickety? What did he say?'

'He came on wings: on the wings of the wind. His hair was pure as salt. The Grey Oracle stood at his breast; his breast was a cluster of shields. Precious stones hung from his ankles, and as he came they lighted the earth.'

'What did he say?' demanded the people.

'Furious things!'

'Furious?'

'Not against you … you, he blessed.'

'Bless him too.'

'Ninaya sobbed into his palms. He kissed his tears and sprinkled many drops on your faces. He kissed your faces and smiling called you his beloved. He said your islands shall flourish and war shall not haunt you. Your kings shall rule from an eternal throne.'

'Live long, my kings,' jubilated Titiadi, waving at Zowdor and Yiddi. 'Ninaya himself has bestowed eternity on your thrones. Ninaya the gallant king from Azumba. He who seized the adversary's Grey Oracle and made it vow allegiance to Taila. The great sends his regards. Priestess of the shrine, what more did he say?'

'What remains was said in fury.'

'Say it!' demanded the people.

'Ninaya cursed Azumba.'

'Bless Ninaya!' bellowed Titiadi. 'He should have murdered all Azumba and left you, as he has, to give us his message; then, as you conclude, he would crush you also with a rock.'

The archers laughed; the priestess moaned.

'But, before the crush of you, complete the curse,' honked Titiadi, elated.

'Ninaya cursed us. Us, he accused of sin. Sin against the land of his ancestors. Ancestors who with blood and sweat built him a home. Home which he now will plough down with flames. Flames from an oracle. Oracle which Azumba and her priestess abandoned. Abandonement whose rocky heart shall reduce us to ashes. Ashes … even the infant Azumban.'

'Ninaya! When shall I see your face?' Titiadi knelt down and religiously said; his hand beckoning heaven to: nobody knew what it beckoned.

'Cannot the oracle be appeased?' inquired Nier Uono.

'What now?' quarelled Titiadi; thrusting a finger at Uono, 'Shall you bribe the spirits of your ancestors? Ninaya has decreed flames. Let his flames be honoured. O, Ninaya, when shall we meet?'

'Cannot he?' Uono inquired again.

'Only by a king who shall perform for Azumba a ritual. Ninaya's other fury was that the rest of Taila walks with an ethereal countenance. Countenance upon the necks of the brave. Brave ones who lead with holy decrees. Decrees whose absence has made Azumba headless. Headless, and see how we err?'

'Hear her, my kings, Ninaya admires your throne. Yours is the ethereal countenance of Taila. Live long,' spoke Titiadi, thrusting three fingers.

'What ritual?' inquired Uono from the priestess.

'It has to be done beneath the light of this coming moon. The oracle has to be taken to Ninaya's tomb. All Azumba shall kneel before the tomb, and the king will alone enter with a concotion of salt and octopus-blood. He'll place the oracle at Ninaya's skull and sprinkle the concotion on the walls of the tomb. Ninaya shall pardon Azumba and foretell the future of Taila.'

'We're grateful, Ninaya,' said Titiadi. 'People of Taila, their ancestor is the one who has crushed them with rocky flames. We now know how to appease Ninaya; there's no need for the priestess. Our king shall go to the tomb, but only after Azumba is ashes. Uono, we'll build an altar for Ninaya, so he spares you; and, when Azumba is gone, we shall give you men and women to be your tribesmen, to live with you on your island.'

'This priestess is my mother's daughter and her people are the offspring of my tribesmen,' Uono told Titiadi.

Titiadi thrust a finger at the skinny folk beside the shoreline. 'The Zomo Warriors are also the offspring of your tribesmen, yet they did not spare you when they scourged Taila away from Azumba,' he told Uono.

'All Azumba have wronged Taila, and even I am very angered. But shall we kill them to obtain revenge?'

'Ninaya will!'

'Mercy, Titiadi.'

She abruptly had a fit, the priestess. Her fingers curled; her toes quivered; her eyes and body shook, and she rolled off her stretcher.

Nier Uono helped her back onto the stretcher. He held her hands. 'What did you see?'

She laid her hand on his chest. 'The oracle has brought Ninaya's message. If we find a foreign king who's willing to perform the ritual, Ninaya will not refuse.'

They felt threatened: the archers and their commander. And this threat made them see the muddy folk, once again, as assailants. On her stretcher, the priestess, who shook and quivered and curled, annoyed them.

At Muyamba's face one could discern fear. He led the commander away from the crowd and beckoned the kings and two chief custodians to part with the crowd. A conference resulted away from the crowd, a conference of six men worried about that which the priestess last told to her brother. Their eyes converged at a pivot which floated at their center: a pivot visible to them alone; on it their eyes tensely remained, occasionally spying the priestess, occasionally spying her skinny tribesmen, always with suspicion.

Muyamba heaved and uttered, 'Should Ninaya's final words reach the canoes yonder our present freedom would be compromised.'

The five with him nodded, their eyes cleaving to the pivot. Their lips were tightly sealed, devoid of words, devoid of remedy.

Muyamba twirled the pivot with his hand, taking their focus of it to his hand. He swiped this hand above his head, leading the eyes of the five men in a curvy maze. They kept to the hand, as they had to the pivot, hoping some mystical solution from it would come. Muyamba with a frosty question terminated their vain attentiveness. 'And just what do you say we do?' that's what frosty question he hurled at them.

'A-zum-ba ... A-zum-ba ...' stammered the chief custodian of Twessi; peering below the place where the pivot had been.

'Speak up!' Muyamba shook the jaw of the Twessian, as if that should make him fluent; but, it rather muted him.

Titiadi's forefinger thrust against the place of the pivot, reinventing it, directing all eyes to it, an expectation visible in every eye that converged there: expectant of words, witty or barbaric, from the chief archer.

'With able weaponry ... not powerless,' faltered the chief archer, thrusting his fingers into his hair, 'and the priestly oracle, which I have no fear of, shall we banish Azumba or murder all foreign rulers?' He looked at the bemused faces of the five with him and thrust five fingers about, making a face that revealed to his company that he was not sure himself of what he meant.

'Why don't we bait?' suggested the chief custodian of Agunbe.

'Bait what?' asked his company.

'We quench their flame and they build us a battle-force?'

'How?'

'There, yonder, after the wailing women, muscular and pompous some months back—Zomo Warriors and Spear Makambes. If they'll sober and be used to construct a defence belt, why not quench for them a flame?'

'Haa! Those gutless, gutless, gutless cowards with feeble hearts!' Titiadi thrust his fingers at the assembly of men sitting behind the Azumban women.

The members of that assembly had their eyes glued to the coastal floor; and most of them faced the archers with their backs, murmuring dirges that seemed to be coming from toads, unfed ones.

'Nier Titiadi, I like the idea of baiting; however, should you propose a better remedy I will give you my support. Until then don't be a complication,' warned the chief custodian of Twessi.

'O, I've got a better remedy. We have more arrows than the number of Azumbans you can count. I say we shoot them all,' muttered Titiadi, absent-mindedly.

'The occasion calls for seriousness, Titiadi,' begged the chief custodian of Agunbe.

'I could accept baiting, but on a condition,' said Titiadi.

'What condition?' his company asked.

'From here, the Spear Makambes and Zomo Warriors shall all match to the initiation village. I, Titiadi, the son of Kalante, shall instruct them for three full months before I graduate them into a battle-force.'

All five with him nodded. Their faces lit and each shook his hand.

'On deeper consideration,' added Titiadi, 'I don't think it would be safe to take the Zomo Warriors today: their fire could affect the rest of Taila.'

His company nodded.

'Now debate the ritual itself,' said Muyamba.

'Which of my lords will go to the ritual,' inquired Nier Gorua from the kings.

Yiddi glanced at Zowdor. Zowdor replied with a glance. Then, they both looked away.

'I think it's me,' said Yiddi. 'The east is my domain.'

'Worry not, my king, I'll be with you,' swore Titiadi, thrusting two fingers at his archers. 'A quarter of these archers, the best among them shall come with us. Zomo Nanna is fond of whips, but his whips shan't subdue our arrows.'

Upon this the conference ended, the six leaders returned to the crowd. Once there, Titiadi peered at the priestess and thrust his head at Uono, instructing; 'Go, Uono, to your people. We've suspended the grudge. Tell them our king shall deliver them, if their men and their men's allies shall train at the initiation village, and accept induction into a battle-force. Their men's allies shall match this day to the initiation village and their men shall join after the ritual.'

'They will do it,' assured the priestess, grinning and rolling slightly.

'It should come from their lips,' Titiadi thrust Azumba a finger.

To his feet, Uono jumped, meandering, skidding down a docile slope, onto the shoreline. He rotated anticlockwise, eyeing his muddy tribesman and their Agunbean allies. In that slow whirlwind of his a shrill command was heard: 'Go this day Azumba; go to your homes and look forward to the moon of deliverance. All Agunbean men, to their wives, mothers, sisters and smallish little children may go; but before such going, must follow the good and bad Titiadi to his initiation village. Azumba, men I mean, you should join Agunbe, once the fire of your doom is terminated.'

He stopped to whirl and fastened his lips. He shuffled; nay, he meandered away from his people.

The Spear Makambes matched after him, wearing starved artificial smiles, controlling their eyes with great skill so their eyes wouldn't wander into the gazing zones of the archers.

Stampede. Titiadi caused it. He bundled four bundles of arrows under his armpit, grabbed a huge bow by its throat; then roaring, he galloped into the matching Agunbeans. They fled. Titiadi galloped further, prancing over the shoreline. Azumba cleft; and through the gap that resulted, he advanced, fiercely and noisily, until he got to the backs of two men whose faces faced the sea.

'Face me!' roared he.

They hesitantly obeyed.

He saw their faces. He knew their faces, which once were coarsely, yet cleanly, bearded and rotund. The faces were now muddy and skinny and defeated. Titiadi dumped the bundles of arrows and the bow on them. 'Take these, Tsambo,' he told the skinnier of the two, 'and follow me. Are you better or braver than those Agunbeans behind Uono? I shall teach you not to be haughty.' Here he shifted his gaze to the less skinny one. 'Zomo Nanna, it shan't be long before you join me at the initiation village. After me, Tsambo, move.'

All dispersed: some quietly, some briskly, some lazily, some noisily, some teasingly, some shamefully, but all dispersed. Titiadi danced as he went, calling to the kings, calling to his archers, calling to the Spear Makambes, and calling to their leader: one who carried a bow and bundles of arrows.

At their court, the kings found the queen in a bedridden state. She lay on a feather-bed with her head outdoors, looking out for them. They sat themselves beside her. She spoke to them; her voice was gone, because she had been wondering aloud their fate on the battleground, while they lingered there.

'I will never leave you to yourselves again,' she uttered with what was left of her voice.

'It wasn't a dangerous front,' they told her.

'It wasn't?'

'In fact, it wasn't a battle,' responded Yiddi.

'What then was it?'

'In your state you need rest so I'll be brief with you. Azumba has returned and it happens that an oracle in their land has cast a spell on them. This coming moon, I am to go there to perform a ritual.'

'O Zowdor, it is your making,' wept the queen. 'My father has loved you more than everything, yet you're bent on sending him east where an enemy prowls.'

'By our love, my hands are clean,' vowed Zowdor.

'Then, don't send him there.'

'It's not my desire, fair Damoya, but that of them whom we rule. Pa-Yiddi can stay; I'll go in his stead.'

'You won't, Zowdor,' sobbed the queen, 'promise me?'

'I have to; it is necessary,' maintained Zowdor.

'Go with me then,' she begged him.

'I think it would be better if I went with him,' said Yiddi. 'You should stay behind.'

'No. We will all go. United we conquered in Numungu,' said Damoya, insistently.

With the queen dwelled the final say. The triple-monarchy was attending the ritual; that was a decree, not to be debated.

CHAPTER 7

Titiadi was at it, instructing the Spear Makambes. In the first week they cuddled in bed till the morn was without dew. Titiadi got jealous, for he the commander would be long awake by the time they arose. He reacted with water, watering them through the thatched roofs of their lodgings, every morn.

It pained them and they went to him with a complaint, complaining, 'Nier Titiadi, you're an unkind man with a solid, cruel heart.'

Titiadi thrust a catapult and a pebble at them and rejoined, 'Kindness pursues his foe because a hiding place is nigh; Unkindness chases, because the sounds of battle are thundering and his foe is without a hideout.'

He tensed the pebble in the catapult and pointed the weapon at them; off fled the spear Makambes.

Titiadi was at it the second week, instructing the Spear Makambes. Come the twilights, to sleep went the Spear Makambes. Titiadi got jealous, for he the commander stayed awake till long into the dark. He reacted with a timetable, fixing supper so late into the night that the Spear Makambes could not sleep by the twilight.

It pained them and they went to him with a protest, protesting, 'Nier Titiadi, you are a men of unreasonable dictates, whose heart is solid and cruel.'

Titiadi thrust a club, a catapult, and a pebble at them, then rejoined, 'The reasonable assists his dying neighbour, though his neighbour is guilty of evil; the unreasonable picks a whip and goes at the heels of the innocent.'

He hoisted the club; tensed the pebble in the catapult, and pointed the weapons at them; off fled the Spear Makambes.

Titiadi was at it the third week, instructing the Spear Makambes. Come the noons, to the village's cluster of sheds went the Spear Makambes, resting and dining with the senior apprentices. Titiadi got jealous, for the joy with which the Spear Makambes rested and dined surpassed that of the senior apprentices. He reacted with a ban, banning all junior apprentices from resting and dining at the sheds.

It pained the Spear Makambes and they went to Titiadi with a grumble, grumbling, 'Nier Titiadi; but you are such a cruel hearted man full of partiality.'

Titiadi thrust a machete, a club, a catapult, and a pebble at them, then rejoined, 'Impartiality says all men deserve to be treated with dignity; Partiality says we alone, or nobody.'

He brandished the machete; hoisted the club; tensed the pebble in the catapult, and pointed the weapons at them; off fled the Spear Makambes.

Titiadi was at it the fourth week, instructing the Spear Makambes. Come the daily chores, there would be a wife, a mother, or 'smallish little children' at the village's reception, wanting to see a husband, son, or parent. Titiadi got jealous, for the senior apprentices never dodged their chores. He reacted with a ban, banning all wives, mothers, and 'smallish little children' from visiting the village.

It pained the Spear Makambes and they went to Titiadi with a criticism, criticizing, 'Nier Titiadi, you are an unfair human with a solid, cruel heart.'

Titiadi thrust a bow and arrow, a machete, a club, a catapult, and a pebble at them, then rejoined, 'Fairness sees a woman's tears, then brokenhearted, extends her a hand in assistance; Unfairness beholds a weepy woman and her tearful son, then haughtily, he flogs them with cruel whips.'

He tensed the arrow against the bow's string; brandished the machete; hoisted the club; tensed the pebble in the catapult, and pointed the weapons at them; off fled the Spear Makambes.

Here was the day, which owned the moon, moon of the month of Jovva. They said Azumba was sick; they said Azumba was weak; they said Azumba was cursed; they said Azumba would burn; they said Azumba would die.

Here was the royalty, which held the sovereignty about; which was charged with healing Azumba; and charged with strengthening Azumba; and charged with quenching Azumba; and charged with reviving Azumba.

Here was the command, which commanded the archers' weapon. He swore he would go to Azumba. He swore he would bear a catapult; swore he would bear a pebble; swore he would bear a club; swore he would bear a machete; swore he would bear a bow; and swore he would bear some arrows.

Here was the union of his archers, which warred in the service of the sovereign. They claimed the throne was eternal; they claimed their venoms were potent; they claimed their commander was insuperable.

Evening was the season. Dim glittered nature's lamps. Birds were asleep. Fowls had retired from society and the bats that lived in Taila were there upon the sky.

The going was in the hands of a sea who had spilled over her banks and was whining like a defrauded demon. Cuddling was not her present sport. At present, they who put their path on her back were tossed and bumped.

The triple-monarchy, the chief archer, the chief executioner, and a quarter of Taila's archers were in the going.

'Go with the peace of our ancestors,' the rest of Taila had said to them before they climbed the eastern seas of Wambi.

'May their peace remain with you also,' had been their response to the rest of Taila.

The sea arched her hands like a mattock and angled her soles like a mallet, her liquid-belly spurting perilously, banging and zooming, dancing and calling for attention, rendering the going shaky; so, struggling for stability, the travelers thumped her with paddles.

She killed her celestial hue. If she was rude at first, now she was brutal. She elevated her belly, allowing her mighty waters to slant onto her flanks. She lifted her mattock-like hands in rage, and erected her mallet-like soles in anger; then, she postponed the attack, fearing her soft belly might cushion the travelers if she struck them on it. She pulled them to the firm sands of the eastern shoreline, which was the shoreline of Azumba, and sent her hands and soles to the point from whence the travelers had commenced their journey.

'From here I can charge and accumulate enough force to smash them,' she said, speeding their way.

They saw her speeding to them and they panicked enormously. Upon their heads is where they put their belongings, and, bless the ancestors: her mattock-like hands and mallet-like soles demolished none of them.

Behind the shoreline, tom-toms sat on the flanks of drummers in white: white, their scarves, their smocks, their sandals, their sticks, their drums. Among them was Azumba's chief custodian and he welcomed the travelers on Azumbas behalf, stating, 'Azumba welcomes you, good kings, queen and people of Taila. The priestess' word is that victory decrees Ninaya. White he instructed should be the attire of Azumba. She has with her the oracle and the concoction. A prayer was said at her shrine, hours ago, for your safe arrival. Come this way, good people.'

Their toms-toms bleating, the drummers embarked on an inward journey. Cheering, the travelers trailed the tune of the tom-toms. It gladdened their hearts and led them through the abodes of drunken crabs, beneath the nests of dozing birds, beside the tunnels of prominent rats, sweeter each time it advanced and led them into an arena which was Azumba's ceremonial ground.

Here, they found a conference and nothing more. A conference of bouncy, attentive men bearing square drums, of no smoked priestess with an oracle and a concoction, of fewer than a dozen women carrying beer and eatables, of no 'smallish little children', of men with observant countenances, ever talking undertone; and this conference was aborted the instant the travelers were in close range of it.

Uono was wordless. Uono was bemused. Uono was ashamed. Uono developed a pair of wagging eyes, for his eyes, shamed by the disorderly appearance of the arena, dreaded collision with the eyes of the travelers.

Gyrating, nay meandering peculiarly, he inquired from the members of the just-ended conference: 'But where are the women who gracefully sway their waists? But where are the smallish little children with garlands for the kings and queen? But where is that tuneful troupe whom I left yonder? But where are the dramatic masquerades? And where did the oracle, the priestess and the concoction go? Tell this venerable lot. Relate the details to them. Uono did not create this jumble!'

A member of the just ended conference led two women carrying beer and eatables to the rulers. He sat on a square drum, an ecstatic air about him. 'Here, I bring you nourishment and the friendship of Azumba?' said he, pointing to his chest and to the women carrying beer and eatables.

'The pretentious politics of fallen men!' snickered Titiadi, plus a thrust of his finger. 'Give nourishment to the bird: it is she who has enriched your soil with manure and entertained your spirit with songs. Give friendship to the south wind. It is he who tears down the home of peaceful men: he will pass by your portion of the earth if you gave him your friendship. But know this, Zomo Nanna, you are not far from my village.'

Belittled, the conference member shifted his square drum to Uono. 'Nier Uono!' he called; Uono offered him attention. 'I will tell you the priestess' decree.'

'What else do I await from you people?' scolded Uono, meandering his ears closer to the conference member.

'A wind descended from the sky,' narrated the conference member, 'and took the priestess and her oracle. It booted off the concoction, revealing, "An evil eye has watched this potion." And …'

'I swear it meant your eye,' honked Titiadi, paying the conference member an attention that was quarrelsome.

'An order was given to the priestess to take all the women to her shrine,' continued the conference member, after eyeing Titiadi. 'Ninaya shall appear there and choose one of them, whose hands shall prepare a new concoction. The priestess promised to briskly return.'

'The best version of the truth is that of the eye, not the ear, not the mouth,' Uono told the kings and queen. 'Says the Nanna, a wind ruined this place. A wind spoiled its elegance. However, the thrones we mounted for you still sit in majesty. Come, my kings and queen, come reign; Azumba is the eastern gate of your kingdom. Azumba shall sing for you and give you nourishment.'

'Not now,' said Titiadi. 'Song is good, but nourishment should wait. Azumba has to be cleansed before men touch the produce of her soil.'

'True,' Uono nodded. 'The big chairs are for the rulers and the benches are for you, people.'

King Zowdor, King Yiddi, Queen Damoya, and the other travelers strolled elegantly to their seats, saying in a festive tone to the conference members: 'Greetings, Azumba. Peace upon you, Azumba. Taila wishes you well. Be blessed, sons of Ninaya. Be blessed, daughters of Ninaya. Ninaya shall grace your gathering, Azumba. Soon, Ninaya shall dissolve his wrath.'

Time that was ample, if measured by adequacy of rest, passed

'Address your subjects, good oracle,' Uono said to King Zowdor, directing him to a podium.

King Zowdor strolled majestically to the podium. He waved at the conference members, who waved back. Zomo Nanna waved with his square drum, violently. Titiadi's eyes were on the Azumban and he showed him a bow.

'I salute you, people of Azumba,' spoke King Zowdor. 'Sovereignty is coexistence. I'll prove to you by a story of Teeth and tongue. A war they once waged. Teeth got terribly shaken. Tongue was left with a sore body. "Rift!" swore Teeth. "Rift!" swore Tongue. "I'll leave you unkempt!" swore Teeth. "I'll leave you unclean!" swore Tongue. Unkempt was Tongue for many morns. Unclean was Teeth for many morns. Unkempt and unclean, they became weak; and weaker after more rifting; and sickly after a long time of rifting. Their enemies, the hot ground maize, the fish, and the henchmen of their enemies, combined against them. The fish put a plaque in the dents of Teeth, and helpless was Teeth in his efforts to be rid of the fish. The hot ground maize and his host of liquid-veggies put a plaque on the skin of Tongue, leaving on him every unfortunate scent that ever caused an uprising anywhere in the world. They were an eyesore, Teeth and Tongue. A nose would seal its entrance whenever they met one. They were hated and met unceremonious treatments every distance they trod. That should not happen to Taila. Solidarity is a fortification for fallible mortals. Peace unto you, Azumba.'

Applaud from the gathering. Zomo Nanna did not applaud; Titiadi showed him a bow.

'Address your subjects, good king of the east. 'Uono said to King Yiddi, directing him to the podium.

King Yiddi replaced King Zowdor on the podium. He smiled at the conference members, who smiled back. Zomo Nanna smiled unceremoniously behind his square drum. Titiadi's eyes were on the Azumban and he showed him an arrow.

'My best wishes Azumba,' spoke King Yiddi. 'An equitable union is the spine of a lasting autonomy. Ilier the goat: he once said, "Soil, you are dirty. Soil, you are slimy. Soil, you are ungrateful. Soil, you are an opportunist. Look how fair you are? Look how rich you are? Look how extravagantly bends your contours? My droppings shall henceforth not fall onto your skin. Soon, you shall be like the sand by the ocean, pale, porous, crushed." Ilier the goat: he was a man faithful to his word, and, never, nevermore did he let a dropping of his fall on Soil. Time waned and Soil grew pale and porous; his grains crushed as the sand by the ocean. Ilier the goat: he wagged his tail, mocking, "Soil, but you are tamed. Soil, but you are humbled. Look how pale you are. Look how coarse you are." Rain came upon Soil, but soil was weak, so her back was eroded. Rain came another day and soil tried to store some water for her friends, the wanderers, but her hands were porous. Rain seeped into the stones beneath Soil. Ilier the goat: he had no hay and had no water, in his pen, in his yard, in his vicinity. "Down the valley," said he, "there is a lea. I'll go and butcher me a bundle of hay. Down the valley there is a stream. I'll go and drag me some water." Ilier the goat: he went with his knife and bucket. The lea had vanished. The stream had disappeared. Ilier the goat: hunger and thirst were the undertakers that saw him off. Punish a pepper in a fire by your side, but only if you are immune to pepper smoke. Peace to your land, Azumba.'

Applaud from the gathering. Zomo Nanna merely nodded; Titiadi, showed him an arrow.

'Address your subjects, fair queen of Taila,' Uono said to Queen Damoya, directing her to the podium.

Damoya did the akimbo of pregnant folk from her throne to the podium. She winked at Zowdor and grinned at the conference members, who grinned back. Carrying his square drum, Zomo Nanna blinked twice at her. Titiadi had an eye on the Azumban and he showed him a bow and arrow.

'I greet you, Azumba,' spoke the queen, winking and smiling at Zowdor. 'Unity transforms into a disease whenever confused with mutuality. Long ago, about the time Raneb ruled Egypt, there lived three men, each with a fist the weight of a rolling rock. They were powerful, and men were fearful of them. They were solid, and men did not trespass where they resided. They lived in the same compound yet they seldom exchanged words. They cared not about love; however, they had great respect for one another. Girdles they all wore: a mini, a medium and a massive. "I shall wrestle this famed trio," said Dodo, demon of the earth. Dodo stole a scorpion's claw while it slept and went with it at sunrise to the residence of the trio. The mini-girdled man was up a tree. The medium-girdled man was sowing some seeds. The massive-girdled man was sitting at his door. Dodo attacked the massive-girdled, whose neighbours saw, yet acted not. Dodo stung him with the scorpion's claw and the massive-girdled fisted Dodo. Dodo thudded onto the ground. The massive-girdled lifted his fist again, but the scorpions poison worked in his body and he passed out. Dodo regained strength after some time and attacked the medium-girdled. The mini-girdled saw and acted not. Dodo stung the medium-girdled with the scorpion's claw and the medium-girdled fisted Dodo. Dodo thudded to the ground. The medium girdled lifted his fist, but the scorpion's poison moved in his body and he fell. Dodo regained strength after a while and did to the mini-girdled as he had done to his neighbours. Dodo threw away the scorpion's claw. "These are strong men," he confessed. "If any two of them at any point fisted me together, I would have thudded to death." Similarity is not the cornerstone of community, in the same way that a market peopled with men bearing blades does not define an army.'

Applaud from the gathering. Zomo Nanna only blinked an eye; Titiadi showed him a bow and arrow.

Tom-toms and square drums came to play. Their music was a tuneful one. The tunes of the tom-toms straightened like stakes and the tunes of the square drums swum through them like weavers. Harmony was in their strain, which tenderly dripped into all ears.

A wizard, good as he may randomly act, cannot for long be captivated by holy drama. Boredom in a wizard cannot be abated as long as the activity of his amusement concurrently amuses his enemy. Titiadi annihilated the tuneful strain with a grumble.

"'Tis been notoriously long,' he grumbled. 'Where is the chosen of Ninaya? Where is the king's concoction? Where is the priestess? I am going right away to the shrine. I shall build Ninaya a small altar, on which he shall show his face and declare his chosen.'

'Hear, people,' quarreled Zomo Nanna, 'the sacrilege of our chief archer. Where Ninaya decrees female purity, he, manly as a metal, swears to go.'

'And why not?' Titiadi grumbled on. 'I came from the womb of women. What prevents me from communing with mother's kind? What has a woman that I have not? What can she do that I cannot?'

'Birth?' challenged Zomo Nanna.

'Birth!' seconded the other conference members.

'Soon!' Titiadi gloomily swore, thrusting a bow and arrow at the conference members.

The stake-like tom-tom tunes and weaver-like square drum tunes returned, teasingly weaving through themselves. A tilt, he, Titiadi, molded his ears into, lest a homogeneous strain drips into them. Bored old wizard, grave was his dislike for time's cautious passage.

What has killed the wizard can kill the priest. Boredom heftier than that which attacked Titiadi attacked the rest of the travelers.

'Nier Uono,' they grumbled, 'now time is truly spent. Something uncanny might have transpired at the shrine.'

'It baffles me as much,' returned Uono.

'Let's send more women there?' suggested Zomo Nanna.

'More women!' seconded the conference members.

The travelers, save Titiadi, nodded.

'I recommend these ones,' Zomo Nanna endorsed the Azumban women carrying beer and eatables.

'Half should go. Half should go again if the first half lingers there unreasonably,' instructed Titiadi.

'Nay,' Zomo Nanna shook his head, 'it is hideously dark and dangerous. Send them all and chances are that a half-dozen may reach the shrine.'

'Send them all!' seconded the conference members.

And all were sent, Zomo Nanna coaching them undertone to the gates of the arena.

Tunefully playing strain, nuisance. No traveler cherished it. Up, the moon was panting, tired of glowing. Time is sourly versatile: impatient whenever there is joy, slothful whenever there is exhaustion. Tired were the travelers of looking forward to the priestess' arrival.

Lo, yonder! Her feet like charging chariots; her arms like speeding swords. She was one of them that were sent to survey the shrine. She dashed into the arena and clapped like a hooligan. 'Go briskly,' she told the gathering. 'Ninaya has led the oracle and its priestess to his tomb. Briskly go!'

Travelers, tom-tom bearers, square drum bearers, all headed north, treading briskly.

Ninaya's tomb, that stately sepulchre neighboured by assorted trees sat with its back shaded by trees; its front was lighted by the moon. Its sides were an amalgamation of bright and dark nothings, which looked like floating pearls to distant onlookers.

Tonight, there were two categories of onlookers: one from the west, the other from the north. The westerners comprised of two kings, a queen, chief custodians, archers, tom-tom bearers and square drum bearers. The northerners were a multitude of women, one carrying a famed oracle and a pot of concoction, and the remainder bearing large oval bags made of raffia. They, the two categories, could hear bumpy clashes between each other's feet and the back of the soil. They could hear the friction caused by the elongation of necks to enable eyes play the spy-game. They could hear the gliding of arms working hard to coerce bodies forward. They could hear the relaxation and contraction of muscles to meet the demands of curious bodies. However, they did not see the feet which clashed with the soil's back, nor the necks which were elongated to enable eyes play spy-games, nor the arms which worked hard to coerce bodies, nor the muscles which relaxed and contracted for curious bodies, because a sugarcane farm protruding into their mutual north-west had obscured their views of each other.

Curiosity guided their steps onto the right-angled edge of the sugarcane farm, from where a solitary step would repair obscurity.

She hopped first, inspired by curiosity, freed from obscurity. A shame it was that there was no competition: winner she would have been, to the honour of her category, winner supreme. She was northerner. She was priestess. She was dancing.

Curiosity's inspiration freed several others from obscurity, all of whom were northerners. Weird. Weird of the westerners that after hasty trekking to meet Azumba's women they now froze their steps, now that the women were come. They were justified in their deed though, taking into account the specifics of the northerners' looks. These were women with face-coats the thickness of a mug's lid, with bodies that were in all regards contourless, with clay-coated feet and hands that were big and muscular, with round rigid breasts, with shabby scarfs smeared with clay, with swaying waists that were inflexible; and these northerners gracelessly swayed them unyielding waists to the front of the tomb. Here, they knelt, save the priestess, who went to the left of the tomb's entrance and kept on dancing.

'Ninaya's symbol is upon them!' proclaimed the Azumbans among the westerners.

'Really?' Uono sobbed, kneeling and peering at the heavens. 'We are thankful, Ninaya. Behold, people, the gift of Ninaya. Healed is our priestess. Her skin glows like glazed vessels. Her muscles are strengthened like swords. Her being is adorned with a triumphal white. Rescue has come, Azumba.'

They, the non-Azumban westerners, stood in bewilderment, peering everywhere – at the priestess, at her followers, at the tomb, at the oracle, at the concoction, at the moon, at their fellow westerners – seeking Ninaya's face or some reasonable sign of him.

Titiadi's eyes sped all about him. His fingers thrust everywhere. 'Uono,' called he, 'do you see Ninaya? Do you see his face? Tell me, Uono?'

Uono sobbed more and peered more.

'Sacrilege,' cried the Azumban westerners, save Uono. 'Deficient faith is a sinful fault in a man. But see, people, our chief archer is he who suffers the deficiency. Doubt tarnishes divinity.'

Non-Azumban westerners, the words of the Azumban westerners triggered nothing in them. They were inquisitive as the chief archer of seeing Ninaya's face, if not, more inquisitive. Their eyes were wide open, as were their ears, seeking signs of divinity.

'What thing about bears more evidence than the garnished skins of those women?' cried a tom-tom bearer.

'What thing about carries more evidence than the strengthened bodies of those women?' cried a square drum bearer.

'What mystery in any mind about possesses more evidence than the power that walks about?' cried Zomo Nanna.

The non-Azumban westerners simply threw a gaze at the Azumban preachers.

Priestess of the Grey Oracle, she squeaked divine nothings. All eyes went to her, but hers went to the non-Azumban westerners, her hands also. She swayed her hands, beckoning them to come, directing them away from the sugarcane farm, leading them by the side of the northerners to the right side of the tomb's entrance. 'Stand there,' she shrilly instructed. The non-Azumban westerners were obedient; Uono joined them.

She beckoned the Azumban westerners to join the northerners. They, the Azumban westerners, went to kneel behind the northerners, their backs facing the northerners.

The westerners, non-Azumban ones, had their eyes on the priestess, who had her eyes on the Azumban westerners, who had their eyes on the place far behind the tomb's front's opposite, by which the northerners had come.

Boredom is bad anytime it has you in prolonged sitting, and worse anytime it has you in prolonged standing. Uono. That face of his had crumpled with boredom. Boredom resulting from prolonged questing for his ancestor's face, from prolonged meandering to find proper space where to examine his priestess of a sister, from prolonged gesturing at his sister's oracle to aid him in his quest; and from the countless boredoms of aged bones.

He started toward, wrong; he meandered toward his sister, meandering his neck five times hastier than the remainder of himself. 'When shall you hand over the concoction?' he put to his sister.

She shook her head and hands, beckoning him to halt, nay, beckoning him to cease meandering.

He meandered ahead. Titiadi hopped after him, inquiring, 'So when shall Ninaya appear?'

The priestess shook the oracle and concoction at Titiadi. 'Desecration!' she madly roared.

Titiadi was discouraged and he tiptoed backwards, to the point where he had been before.

Neither waving nor words could dissuade Uono from meandering further; thus, the priestess resorted to maneuvers.

Through the first row of northerners, she maneuvered. Into the second row of northerners, she maneuvered. Along the third row of northerners, she maneuvered.

Through the first row of northerners, he meandered. Into the second row of northerners, he meandered. Along the third row of northerners, he meandered.

Yet he couldn't reach his maneuvering sister. If he was a meandering stream, she was a maneuvering militia. And she maneuvered to the side of the tomb that she had, before her maneuvers, kept like an inheritance. To the upright westerners went her brother, adding fury to his crumpled countenance.

Tonight, Curiosity was courageous and Time was timid; Curiosity was progressive and Time was backward. Earth shivered and curiosity dared to investigate, by looks, by gestures, by hypothesis. Looks of upright westerners and not of kneelers; gestures of vertical westerners and never of kneelers; hypothesis of perpendicular westerners and ever of their meandering acquaintance.

Lo, there! Afar. Upon the horizon, similar to heaving tides: tides of scarfed heads, tumbling up, lengthening as they closer drew, widening as they closer came; yet with faces thin, and scapulas outsticking, and ribs so flat. On the scapulas rested robes of speckled white. On the ribs lay robes of stained white. Speckles and stains of clayey red. This clayey red was all bout them, on their heads, their faces, their arms, their legs, their scarves. Their smeared skins united with the moon's rays and displayed a cruel shade of glowing brown. Skinny, muscular women were they. Many were they. Women with oval raffia bags were they. Many were the yards that kept them away from their destination.

Aesthetic tom-tom bearers, they nursed the silent wind into a sure rhythm.

Artistic square drum bearers, they nurtured the weak wind into a resolute rhyme.

Sure rhythm and resolute rhyme, this determined the pace of the oncoming women. The slower the rhythmic rhyme, the slower the women. The speedier the rhythmic rhyme, the speedier the women.

She knelt. The priestess knelt. Swaying her waist and chanting:

> 'Veil charges the forth;
> Shroud travels the forte.'

'Shroud travels forth?' spoke the erect westerners among themselves. 'Could be that those ones bring Ninaya? Could be that they bring the better concoction? 'Tis now the hour is ripe. The faces about do tell.'

She straightened. The priestess straightened. Wildly swaying, gyrating through the kneelers, dancing vulgarly, and chanting:

> 'Fall the throne be sworded;
> Cleanse the thing of leeches.'

'Cleanse the throne of leeches?' whispered Titiadi to Uono. 'Ninaya did not sing that. And see how abominably sways your sister.'

'I shall implore her to improve,' Uono promised Titiadi.

'Fall the thing be sworded?' spoke some erect westerners to their neighbours. 'That's harsh to come from her ancestor. Perhaps a foreign spirit sang through her? Or her oracle's been contaminated? Perhaps?'

'To such disapproval,' spoke Uono, 'a brother cannot but sorry. Calm, good people, this now I'll discourse the matter.'

Flowing slyly, no, pouring slyly, nay, meandering, meandering, meandering his neck ten times quicker than the remainder of his body, Uono went to his sister. She did not maneuver; she showed him her coated face and chanted:

> 'Fire the veil of thy fall;
> Smoke the craft of thy foes.'

'Why do you mishandle yourself?' Uono put to her, meandering his neck and waist.

'Tarry, I'll show you,' she responded. 'Now!' she instructed the kneelers.

The female kneelers took bamboo pipes, gourds of water, sticks, crisp herbs and punched wood from their oval bags. They put the herbs in the punches in the wood and rubbed them with sticks. The setup created tiny flames which they used to light the bamboo pipes. Each one of them inhaled some smoke from her own pipe; then, shaking vulgarly they allowed the smoke to leak from their lips. They set their scarves aflame and begun wailing.

'This is an odd night,' said Liyanga, wearing wrinkles of confusion.

'Not to offend Ninaya, but that ritual baffles me,' said one king to the non-Azumban westerners.

They nodded and peered askance at the flaming scarves.

Bawa! Curse the priestess! The oracle thudded, the work of her hand. She smashed the concoction as well.

Uono meandered onto the jiggling oracle, tears in his eyes, fear in his heart, fright on his face, meander in his manner.

The queen looked at the kings; they looked at her; the chief archer looked at the rulers; they looked at him and his archers.

Uono, when he had meandered enough over the oracle, fixed his gaze on his sister and furiously chided, 'What ails you? Are you bewitched?'

'With gladness, I am,' squeaked she, pulling a club from an oval bag.

Bawa! Curse the priestess! The club thudded on Uono's head, the work of his sister's hand.

He wobbled, no; he meandered in pain.

'Let him be!' yelled the tom-tom and square drum bearers to the priestess, who had her club suspended above Uono, determined to hit the meandering one afresh. 'The priestess asked that we spare him.'

On the modicum of earth beside the right side of the tomb's entrance, time terminated. The world converged at a halt. Eyes stuck out as much as their lids could enable them, yet the world was a blur, blurred by uncertainty, uncertainty of non-Azumban minds.

They, the kneeling women, removed their right breasts, which were made of calabash and filled them with water. They washed their faces; the priestess did likewise. Their washed faces were masculine. The clayey coat was a veil: the kneelers from the north and the dancing priestess were all men.

'We must run!' whispered the queen.

'We're late, my queen,' said Titiadi. He kissed her feet. 'But I swear by Kalante that those vile veils shall not take you to the grave.'

'Birth plots our torture; Earth nurtures the evil; Death is attributed with the sin. Our lives are finite, sons of men, yet we mourn the dead who shall see no death,' Zowdor was speaking and eyeing the priestess.

'Distance yourself from death, daring deity,' Titiadi held Zowdor's leg and spoke. 'Live for Taila, for her sovereignty.

The potter's earth has finished its service with me; in pride allow me to spill my blood.'

'Audacious archer,' Yiddi said, touching Titiadi's shoulder, 'if victory comes to this union, your statue shall be mounted where I rest my bones.'

Titiadi's left eye composed a tear. He hugged the triple monarchy, giving them the words: 'This sacrifice is my valediction. Flee, but at such a time when my arrows are superior to their craft.'

A club for Yiddi, a bow and arrow for Zowdor, a machete for Damoya, with these their staunch subject, the commander commanding archers, armed them.

Hilarity. Azumbans – a portion tom-tom bearers, a portion square drum bearers, a portion formerly coated women – laughed. Members of the tom-tom portion dismantled their tom-toms. Members of the square drum portion demolished their square drums. Members of the formerly coated females' portion emptied their oval bags.

Bows and bundles of arrows lay among the debris of the dismantled tom-toms. Machetes rested within the rubble of the demolished square drums. Clubs, catapults and pebbles were the contents that were emptied from the oval bags. The members of the three portions unified their voices in a succinct strain:

'Outnumber our onslaught;
Posthumous pilgrimage.'

He, Titiadi, son of Kalante, chief archer of all Taila, marched to a coaching position, and coached his archers into rows, three rows. The second row shifted three yards away from the first, and the third drifted six yards away from the second.

Finally, the oncoming women reached the square drum and tom-tom bearers. They washed their smeared faces, tearing off their veils of womanhood, and lo, they were made up of Spear Makambes and foreign men. The kneelers arose and shook hands with them.

In the middle of some white-attired folk a path was let; this path faced the rulers. Zomo Nanna's hand was in the priestess-posing man's hand, and his was in Tsambo's. They stood at the rear of the path, their jointed hands flying above their heads. A portable man with a portable trumpet stood before them. Those white-attired folk who let a path walk through their middle clapped and sang a victory song. The threesome strode forth, trailing the portable trumpeter, going for a handshake here, a handshake there, stopping for a hug here, a hug there, striding, striding, till they got into the third quarter of the path.

Shouts Titiadi to the first row of his archers, 'Shoot the oncoming three!'

Archers of his, they put tension between their arrows and the strings of their bows.

Zomo Nanna dived right. Tsambo dived left. The fake priestess dived down. The trumpeter ahead of them dived up. Those of the white-attired folk that were closest to Titiadi's archers dived backwards. The fear of Titiadi's forefinger that presently thrust at them, made them, the white-attired folk who had allowed the path, trot helter-skelter, by which trotting the path was destroyed.

Yiddi nodded sideways, alerting his fellow rulers that flight time had come. They sprinted recklessly away from Titiadi's side, sinuously by the tomb's side and hurriedly into the dark woods neighbouring the tomb.

'Bless the ancestors!' Titiadi yelled after them.

'Yonder, the monarchy! Away, they go! Save us! They're fleeing! They fled!' this alarm came from some white-attired folk.

Tsambo and Zomo Nanna, their eyes returned from exile and got stationed at the shoulders of them that had created them a path. They spied before and behind Titiadi. In the dark woods neighbouring the tomb, they saw the crowns which they had for decades craved, those crowns speeding upon the heads of three blur images whose persons they very well knew.

'Battle bird!' Tsambo cried out.

The trumpeter's head returned from exile. Zomo Nanna saw it first. 'Battle bird,' he said to the trumpeter, 'declare war. WAR!'

Titiadi's archers shot two rounds and fell two batches of the white-attired folk; they were in the course of shooting a third round and felling a third batch of white-attired folk.

Thunderous thundered the trumpeter's trumpet, echoing in the west and inviting a different trumpet sound to thunder in the west and echo in the east. Thereupon, the bawls of dying men choked the audible wind about. Titiadi and his men hearkened: the bawls were from the west, from Wambi. The kingdom had been invaded.

While Titiadi's archers felled their third batch, the white-attired folk ploughed forward; thereby, closing the gap between them and the first row of Titiadi's archers. An arrow was useless now. The assailant's arm was in the heart of the bow. Strength was now the decider. Triumph rested in the domain of the hefty at blows. The first row of Titiadi's archers comprised of women, adolescents and elderly men, who weren't hefty at blows. Azumba and her cohorts kneaded them unconscious with clubs and hefty punches.

Titiadi coached the second row of his archers to the offensive. Archers, they shot. White-attired folk, they charged forth. Some arrows felled some white-attired folk, few of them. The majority of them managed to reach the archers and the battle again came to be decided on strength, so Titiadi lost his second row, which had a composition similar to the first.

Titiadi girded his head with his catapult and threw aside his pebbles. He thrust his two hands at the remnant of his archers. 'Strength to your marrows,' said he to them. 'You are what is left. On this northern front, let's flex our last muscle. Watch the renegades. Let their bad against Taila incite a bad hatred in your hearts. Do your best, remnant of mine.'

The archers discarded their bows and bundled arrows in their palms. 'Naamu!' bellowed they to Titiadi. He clapped away. They raced to the white-attired folk. The archers jabbed and the white-attired folk pounded. The battle was at its bloodiest, and it churned warrior blood, and broke warrior bones, and crushed warrior souls, progressing in this manner till there came a moment when the Azumbans and their cohorts raised their weapons and found all the archers, but their commander, lying lifeless.

The commander commanding archers, few yards dividing him and the white-attired folk, applauded and shed tears for his archers. The white-attired folk put on ceremonial grimaces and swayed their bodies onward. As they came, the commander thrust his finger at them, stating, 'Tonight, I, Titiadi, the son of Kalante, disappear from humanity, having left in the annals of time a lifetime of loyalty to the land of my fathers. Should worth be measured by valour, worthy men shall name me. Should substance be measured by steadfastness, steadfast men shall count me. What shall posterity call you, sons of Ninaya and Limnider? Today, I retire to a place that hasn't a crook. Long live Kalante, long live his Taila.'

Clubs battered his head. Machetes dissected his flesh. Arrows sunk into his eyes. Pebbles pained his bones, and it happened, as will happen to all mortals – good and bad, chaste and immoral, cruel and lenient, affluent and needy, infant and elderly – that the most audacious archer who ever trod anywhere in Taila became inert as the earth.

His murderers, while they were yet about him with triumphal airs, saw the waist, heels, shoulders, head, and neck of an old man meandering, by their legs and to the corpse. This old man, who was in the embrace of an oracle, cried three various tears and proclaimed: 'Here lies the able arm of Taila, lured and robbed. Tonight, the shade that gave us refuge has been chopped down with a hopeless machete.'

'Mutineer! Haggard mutineer!' cursed the fake priestess, pounding the old man with a club.

'Yomyo,' Tsambo mentioned the priestess-posing man's name, 'let him away; his sibling will turn sour.'

Yomyo moved away from the old man.

'Dump him inside the tomb,' Zomo Nanna instructed two men.

Frail, old Uono, his meandering waist was meandered onto a shoulder. His hollow, meandering shoulder was meandered up and maintained in a grip. Into the tomb, the whole of him was ferried, and heavily onto the floor he quickly was meandered.

Outside, especially beside the tomb, icy antipathy bubbled in men. Men looking there, where a triple-monarchy had fled. Against the remembrance of that monarchical flight, they mumbled war songs.

'Comb all Azumba. Find the crowns. Die the rulers. Death the monarchy. Bash the alien lords. Scourge the alien queen. Make their faces crimson. Do you behold particles at all, let them be implacable particles of battle,' thus spoke Tsambo,

Zomo Nanna and Yomyo, as the songs of war grew from mumbles to bellows.

Several of them saw. They who saw nodded around. The sight bolted into their entirety, providing they who had not seen it with knowledge of it. It was a thing of an old fellow and a middle-aged woman brandishing swords. And, curse the duo, they danced, clashed their swords and mentioned names—names of Zowdor, of Yiddi, and of Damoya. They ceased dancing and clashing and mentioning; and only clapped. Clapping five hooliganic claps beside five conspiratorial claps.

'Hail Nsora! Hail Dikomo!' spoke the white-attired folk at the clapping sight.

The sight cleft into two elevations: grateful hands the tools of elevation. The old member of the cleft sight, Nier Nsora his name, was in a higher elevation, and the middle-aged member, Dikomo her name, was in a lower one.

'Comrade,' Yomyo said, swaying before Nsora, 'victor is I. So are you. So is she. So is the whole union. Somewhere, the rulers race, perhaps in some swamps, perhaps on some rocks, perhaps about some canes, but merry more and panic less. Where shall they go? Tonight is ours and we go to take it.'

'In those sugarcanes from whence we observed, we witnessed the fall of Titiadi's Taila,' spoke Dikomo, making monarchical gestures. 'Importance is contained in four crowns. Zomo Nanna shall wear one.' Zomo Nanna nodded aside, as if in trance. 'Tsambo shall wear one.' Tsambo twitched his eyes and sighed. 'Nier Nsora shall wear one.' Nsora nodded specially and grinned. 'What shall be left shall be a woman's. I shall wear it against the straightening of that which Damoya has crooked.' Here she smiled and dogma was spelt on her face. Yomyo gnashed and folded his arms. 'Immediately below the crowns, there shall be a chief archer and chief custodians. That one among us four rulers whose men shall kill the monarchs will decide who becomes chief custodians and chief archer.'

Politics became the war; politics, which is no sport for a man with conscience. The nodding and eye twitching that occurred in the period were condemned to cruel vices, vices that were ruminated upon in quite.

'The gift of tomorrow makes us less ashamed that we are less accomplished,' stated Dikomo, her belly hopping. 'Tonight, we take what was taken from us. Time is a speedy nuisance that feels no nostalgia. The thing cries; let's charge onto fame. At the wave of my hand, people, the flag be hoisted. The trumpet be sounded. The hunt be begun.'

It waved, her rebellious hand. It was hoisted, Nsora's flag. It did not blare, the trumpeter's trumpet, so the hunt was hampered.

Wasn't it Zomo Nanna? Wasn't it the bogus priestess? It was they, for they cornered the trumpeter and his trumpet at a conference, nagging across him, grumbling round him, and frenziedly spinning their heads.

'Do you lack readiness?' Dikomo spoke to the conference. 'Let the crown ahead incite you. Let the archer's mantle urge you on. Let the glory of custodianship be your incentive.'

'No stratagem? No craft?' barked Zomo Nanna, his right knuckles pounding in his left palm. 'In the meshes by man, woman by default is a defective yarn. She calls for the trumpet so she can send men through the dark woods. Native and stranger, she would have sent them both. Giving little thought to the victory that was attained by crafty arms. She errs with Nsora's backing. Confidently, she errs: Nsora's doing.'

Speechless was Dikomo awhile; in which very while Nsora distanced himself from her with the assertion: 'To them whom are hasteful at statements, agility is elusive.

Correction does the cock to the chick; tie the chick's folly to its own nape and there let it be.'

'Back the strategic then. Support the tactical.' rejoined Zomo Nanna.

Nsora agilely said he would. Dikomo moaned dejectedly.

'This is my tactic,' spoke Zomo Nanna, 'that the true natives go through the woods. The men from Yadoma will roam this place. Every other Tailan should go opposite the direction of the natives.'

'Worse than her blunder!' snapped Tsambo, heaving forever. 'We stand before a trio that by itself conquered all Numungu, yet you ask that the task be entrusted to a third of our population. Before the smoke that dazed a swum, a bee is but a plumage. Dogma is another breed of greed.'

Zomo Nanna curled his lips and drooped his cheeks. 'Mutual dogma hasn't the same demeanor as democracy, for in a democracy the fool also can air.' he, with mirth, said. 'Four are the rulers in the figure she inverted. The going shall be decided by mutuality. Nsora, whereas he advocates folly, I say, a strategic split. With what do you identify?'

Nsora glanced at Tsambo's visage—it was mean. And glanced at Zomo Nanna's—it was meaner and more susceptible to grudge. 'With your strategic split,' he voted.

'A dilemma is when the worst is conceived, and not necessarily born,' Tsambo promptly cornered Dikomo, shaking her as he preached. 'What shall you endorse? His blunder? Or my genius?'

Dikomo's head glided about its neck, coming into visual contact with Nsora, communing with him, receiving direction from him. The answer, which had Nsora's endorsement and was given to Tsambo, as loud as it was painful, to the hearing of the lot about, was, 'Bush catchery is in the traits of dogs, yet a dog when alien rather yowls in the bush. I side with the split.'

Her vote admitted the Zomo Warriors into the dark woods, and led Tsambo and his men opposite the direction the Azumbans went. She went with Nsora after the natives. At this time of the deployment, the alien warriors who helped in the battle kept the tomb and its environs.

CHAPTER 8

She lay in his embrace, moaning a maternal pain, tossing her arms and working her legs. With his lips he swallowed her tears and soothed her face; this was her husband.

She held his thumb, so surely a bystander would have thought he was her giver of life. He soothed her hand with fingers from his other hand whose thumb was not held. His eyes guarded about and his eyelids kept blinking; this was her father.

'Hold yourself, Moya,' implored Yiddi her father, 'our flight is far from its destination. The blaring and clanking are done in pursuit of us. Death sees us clearer as we are tighter engulfed.'

'Painful, Pa-Yiddi. My tummy will erupt,' groaned Damoya.

'Naught shall erupt in you, sweet child.'

'Something shall. Tiny, many blades slice me within. I'll drop soon and die.'

'You shan't, Moya, its merely a sensation of maternity.'

She groaned her loudest of the night, tucking her belly and kicking her legs. She fretted in his embrace, which made him as fretful, her husband.

'It's aggravated,' communed her spousal Zowdor with his in-law.

'Let me handle her,' Yiddi communed back, picking and folding her into his own embrace. 'Relax, Zowdor, fret less. We did it once on foreign soil and we'll …'

'Forgive me, Pa-Yiddi?' she went on a wailing spree. 'My willful disposition has left you in grave agony.'

'You are blameless, my child.'

She stretched her hand to Zowdor.

'Hush, sweet Moya,' implored Zowdor, caressing her hand.

'Forgive me, Zowdor?' wailed she.

'Hush,' both men implored.

Damoya rocked her legs off the embrace and they formed a slant on the ground. She spun her bust, swaying her waist and sinking her head downward till the whole of her lay flat on the ground. The men each tried to offer assistance, but she crawled backwards, swerving them in all their efforts.

'Go away,' she implored. 'I'll be the snare of you. Here, I'll end my journey.'

'We won't abandon you,' returned Zowdor, caressing her temple.

'You need help, Moya,' Yiddi entreated.

With docile faces and affectionate gestures, she was beckoned to calm, which beckoning she succumbed to, and while her violence jumped to calm the men heaved, their faces elated. Suddenly, she tucked her tummy and wailed and gnashed.

'It's crumpling my stomach,' she said.

'What is?' queried the men.

'The baby, it's swimming down. I feel slippery inside. It swims. Believe me!'

'We do. We do,' assured the men.

'She may be due?' Yiddi whispered to Zowdor.

'But she's only as pregnant as seven moons?' Zowdor rejoined.

Wails Damoya, 'My soul is slithering out of my skin!'

Yells Yiddi, 'Let's lay her in comfort.'

It was happening on a street on whose flanks lay two warped footpaths. Thus, seeking to lay their daughter and wife on comfortable ground, the father and husband trampled some tall grass at the mouth of the left footpath, weaved the bunch level with the ground and added the attires of their bust for a covering.

Simultaneously, Damoya and them that were speedy about in search of her and her family howled. They who were speedy about were almost as close to her as she was to delivery.

She yet howled and the men took her upon a carriage of their hands to the comfort they had woven on the left footpath, resting her in comfortable majesty. Much moaning, tucking and wobbling brought her to the verge of the grueling duel in all maternity. So it came, as has come to all who dared to born, that as Yiddi waited beneath her maternal throne, a scalp with barely any hair did an appearance do. He cuddled it and followed in the manner of birthaids.

Zowdor was a solace to her maternal soul—he ate her tears, stroked her palms and from his mind, which presently reasoned like a lunatic, spoke into the depths of her heart the things:

> 'Cascade! lone cataract of crimson grace,
> Hush: the tresses of Taluu adorn thy face
> Within two blissful hosts of sultry balm.
> Restful be thy soul while you docile calm;
> Lily: yon tempting bloom and weed of love
> Enamoured as the sweetness of a dove;
> Soft and mild a ditty chimes, nay softer;
> Jocularly, the daisies maneuver;
> Undaunted, we stride, time a toothless foe,
> Among solemn violets devoid of woe;
> Nirvana the kin of affinity,
> Unsullied our pact of eternity.'

The sounds of charging feet closed in on them, and at this time the premature foetus that took on the guilt of bona fide babies was wholly cuddled in Yiddi's palms. A he it was, and it did in the ways of notorious babies.

'This creature is a glutton,' Zowdor nibbled the baby's finger and told.

'Zowdor!' shrieked Damoya, laughing and sobbing, wanting to comment, but not finding the strength to air.

'This creature acts like babies,' Zowdor kissed the baby's cheeks and told.

'Zowdor!' Damoya laughed.

States Yiddi, 'And, and, all baby-like creatures are given gifts of identification, for through such identification society identifies with them.'

'Name him, Zowdor,' shrilly Damoya urged, beaming.

'He won't need a name,' returned Zowdor.

'Why?' asked Yiddi and Damoya.

'Because we shall sacrifice him to the spirits of here.'

Daughter and father, gloomy their faces got.

'A lie that was,' spoke Zowdor, fetching the baby into his palms. 'His eyes have beheld the moon, so I name him Witanda, son of the late lamp. Witanda Nemoso. Men shall admire you, prince of Taila.'

A termination by Yiddi, somewhere along the maternal-after and nature's own evictions unfastened mother from baby, and not long after that, voices came across the street on whose flank Witanda, now an external foetus, was born.

Yiddi leaned backwards and sent his eyes a-spying, spying right, up, left, down; curse the pursuers, two of them trotted along the far horizon upon the street, both of them a-spying here and there.

'There is two of them on the far end,' reported Yiddi to his company.

'Are they headed here?' Zowdor and Damoya asked.

'They aren't in motion now,' Yiddi reported. 'The one faces us with his side, and faces his henchman with his face, his henchman does same. Their fingers are involved with the soil, mapping strategies, doing other things unknown.'

'Do they see this way?' asked Zowdor, cuddling his Witanda.

'To air it with the intensity of a rumour, I'll say they don't.'

'A rumour is as true as a rural myth, and intense as a famed scandal,' pondered Zowdor, aloud. 'If we're to them as invisible as a rumour is believable then we're indeed unseen.'

'Hmm!' returned Yiddi.

'Take Witanda,' Zowdor gave Yiddi the baby.

'Is there a thing I am to do with this little bundle?' Yiddi questioned the relay, kissing Witanda's chest.

'Cross with him to the lean road yonder,' instructed Zowdor. 'I'll lie by the foundation of this growth, spying for your safety. When you are there, you also lower your eyes a-spying, so I can ferry Damoya by your captaining to the other side; where grouped we shall flee.'

Yiddi showed Witanda to Damoya. 'Wish us well,' he told her.

Her throat, so clogged by sorrow, was in a wordless state; therefore, she blessed them with tears and caresses. A hug briefly fastened Yiddi to Zowdor.

As gifted by the recently fallen Titiadi, the weapons were of three makes. Yiddi, the baby in his left grip, gripped a club into his right hand, then heaved, then nodded.

Zowdor the vigilante, seeing the nod of readiness, settled himself by the foundation of the growth. He spied like a poaching wolf, like an idling crab, like a thieving mouse, and like an eloping bitch; then, signaled, 'We cross now, comrade.'

Yiddi waved his club at Zowdor and Damoya. Yiddi hopped into the street. Yiddi moved like a daytime burglar. Yiddi sneaked onward with a guilty countenance. Yiddi gripped Witanda tighter. Yiddi forever heeded Zowdor.

Zowdor. This spied on the kneeling assailants. He observed them in their plot against him and his family. So close was Yiddi to his destination when Zowdor saw one assailant's head stopping still and motioning about. It first motioned that way before starting this way.

'Dodge it!' alerted Zowdor, fidgety and wide-eyed.

'What?' enquired Yiddi, as he directed his gaze to the kneeling assailants.

Clash! His gaze met with an assailant's. This assailant hastily shook his colleague and they together caught a brief final glimpse of Yiddi. Their mouths became wide open as their eyes became wide open. Their feet set into motion and upon that motion their wide-opened mouths cried, 'Tukule!' A cry that was to many a call to duty: many who converged at the far arena where Zowdor's eyes were at sport, a-spying.

Zowdor Nemoso. He, king and spy, father and husband, comrade and in-law, was crushed in his spirit. Pitifully, his father-in-law knelt fretting. More pitifully, his wife lay moaning, tears streaming across her face. Most pitifully, his early son hung in exhausted grips, with a visage that told that the world about was to him a mystery.

In his arms, Zowdor took his Damoya. 'Run!' he told Yiddi. 'Do your flight in that direction, a zigzag flight, an invisible flight, a tactical flight. We shall do ours in this direction. Upon the waters, we shall merge and thus unified we shall properly flee.'

Up. Hasty. Racing. There, abnormally goes Yiddi, speedily in a zigzag, disappearing into the tall grass.

Zowdor tensed his muscles and set about his own flight. He had gone no more than three steps than Damoya wobbled and fell. He angled his hands to scoop her back into his grips.

'I won't go, Zowdor,' she cried, crawling speedily toward the street.

'What are you doing?' Zowdor stopped her.

'Take flight, Zowdor,' wept she, 'I'll distract them while you flee. Go, Zowdor.'

'Believe, Damoya, we shall be safer together,' said Zowdor, caressing her head.

'I want to believe you, Zowdor. But ... look at Pa-Yiddi. We don't know what lies ahead of him. He's already exhausted. With me in your care you shan't be swift. We shall all perish. Go, Zowdor, if you love me. Give ...'

'Shhh!' Zowdor clasped her lips. He ferried her some yards into the grass beside the footpath.

'Where are we going?' she asked him.

He stopped. 'Stay here,' he instructed her. 'I'll go race the villains and lead them afar off.'

'What if ...'

'Hush ... don't ...'

'I love you, Zowdor.'

'I'll forever love you, fair Damoya.'

Zowdor's eyes were watery and he shut them, so that they wept two stout tears. He hurried to Witanda's birthplace, where was a machete and bow and arrows. Possessing the bow and arrows, he launched into the street.

Assailants. They chased their approaching target, the Zowdor Nemoso. They did their fastest race of the night, shouting battle cries, shouting any words that had any tendency of being an emergency signal. The two assailants who had spotted Yiddi first closed in on Zowdor; he felled them with arrows. More assailants were approaching the

Zowdor. He leaped into the bushes right of the street. Leaping and sprinting, he onward went. They went after him. The assailants went, crying, 'Tukule!'

A sinister cry arose from ahead. It was oncoming and distant. 'Osunda! Masanda!' it cried.

Zowdor raced. Zowdor kicked a bevy of grass. Zowdor murdered an inquisitive snail. Zowdor aborted a mango seed. Zowdor did all these while he yet raced. There came a time when there wasn't a bush to race in, when what lay ahead was a plain. Here was he contained in two chases. The chase by which he had come this far; and the chase that had 'Osunda! Masanda!' as battle cry.

Danger dwelled behind and ahead. Peaceful were the sides. Zowdor turned to the side neighbouring his left. Curse the assailants, they craftily secured the space. Zowdor now headed to the side neighbouring his right, and, curse the assailants again, they secured this space as well. The danger ahead had a meaner cry than that behind; thus, Zowdor turned and started away from meaner danger.

'CEASE ATTACKS!' commanded a prancing Zomo Nanna, his two hands waving across each other.

'Conserve the attack!' Tsambo ordered his men.

'CEASE!' roared Zomo Nanna, racing, springing, passing Zowdor, and prancing to Tsambo's men.

'Cease,' Tsambo told his men. He gave Zomo Nanna a hideous stare.

'It's all about the archer's mantle,' stated Zomo Nanna. 'We are surrounded by warmongers, for that reason a coward cannot be lorded over our archers. The bogus priest shall be put in the dimness behind Ninaya's tomb. Whoever shatters his breath shall be chief archer of all Taila.'

'On condition that one of my men shall shoot first?' Tsambo spoke with a voice trailed by quarrelsome echoes.

Zomo Nanna pondered deeply. 'Yes,' he at last accepted.

Twelve men were tasked with transporting Zowdor to the arena of his execution. These men had clubs and contented faces. Zowdor laid down his weapon and showed his palms to this men, telling, 'You are forevermore doomed. The blood of a pregnant woman wails for your head, that of an innocent sailor also, and when I do die, there shall be three wraiths upon your case, all three wailing for your heads.'

Honks Dikomo, whose head was tucked into the hips of two Zomo Warriors, 'Power has already been won by some. Some have slain the pregnant one, and the homeless sailor.'

'My men …' started Tsambo, but was cut off by Zomo Nanna, who dogmatically said, 'Killing the living is what we are about. The dead are dead.'

The twelve carried Zowdor and headed for Ninaya's tomb. Once, his crown fell and a Zomo Warrior picked it up.

'Give me!' roared Tsambo, pulling the crown and fitting it back on Zowdor's head. 'This crown shall not leave this skull until an arrow decides where it should go. Until then, it belongs to none.'

Zomo Nanna shook his eyes.

Zowdor was taken to Ninaya's tomb and bound to one of the thinnest trees behind the tomb.

Zomo Nanna's eyes were an eagle's eyes. His feet were a beaver's tail. His hands were a gorilla's hands. So he moved with an able stick, marking a yard, two yards, three yards, four yards, five yards, ten yards, fifty yards, hundred yards; and leaving a trail of twenty and hundred yards at the end of the marking. 'This is the range, the perfect range,' he told Tsambo.

'My men are very skilled!' Tsambo frowned and responded.

The lot in favour of Zowdor's execution gathered behind Zomo Nanna's range-line. Tsambo stood beside Zomo Nanna, a yard in-between them. Behind Zomo Nanna was

Yomyo and his followers, and Zomo Nanna's Zomo Warriors. Behind Tsambo was the Spear Makambes. Between these two groupings trod Nsora and Dikomo.

'Who shoots first?' Nsora put to the two groups.

'US!' Tsambo quickly stated, pointing at his chest.

'In ten counts, they must shoot,' Zomo Nanna instructed Nsora.

'In ten counts, King Tsambo,' Dikomo said to Tsambo.

Tsambo smiled a dry one. He chose his first archer, equipped him and placed him before the bound target.

Counts Nsora, 'One ... two ... three ... four ... five ... six ...'

Shot!

Darts wide.

'Aw!' cries Tsambo.

'Talentless!' sniggers Zomo Nanna.

'You're next, King Zomo,' Dikomo clapped. 'For ten counts, you shall be in contention of that crown and the archer's mantle.'

Zomo Nanna called his first archer; he showed a bow and arrow to Ninaya's tomb and gave it to this archer.

Counts Nsora, 'One ... two ...'

Shot!

Yards wide.

'Ey!' cries Zomo Nanna, throwing a blow that caught his archer at the nape.

'Craftless!' snickers Tsambo.

Round the second. Spear Makambes dart wide. Tsambo screams, kicking his feet. Zomo Nanna sniggers. Zomo Warriors shoot wide. Zomo Nanna fists two of his men. Tsambo snickers.

Round the third. Tsambo's archer darts terribly wide. 'Tactless!' mocks Zomo Nanna, as Tsambo groans. Zomo

Nanna's archer shoots awfully wide. 'Unreasonable!' teases Tsambo, as Zomo Nanna flies three punches to his men.

Round the fourth. Tsambo coached his archer to the range-line. The arrow was tensed in the bow.

Counts Nsora, 'One ... two ... three ... four ... five ... six ... seven ... eight ...'

Shot!

Narrowly misses.

'Great!' applauded Tsambo. 'You shall shoot in the next round. Aim more prudently and the glory shall be ours to keep.'

'Never!' quarreled Zomo Nanna. 'None shall have a double shot.'

'It is a double measure,' Tsambo returned the grudge. 'I thought the quest was for a competent archer? I was wrong, for if it was, a promising shot would have attracted another shot.'

'Anything apart from shooting the target isn't promising,' sniggered Zomo Nanna.

'Nsora, we're rulers, aren't we?' asked Tsambo.

'We are. We are,' responded Nsora and Dikomo.

'So let's vote,' Tsambo stamped his right foot.

'Yes, vote,' consented the Nuambans.

'Not now,' quarreled Zomo Nanna. 'My men are at the summit of their energies; needless hesitation will kill their morale. Nsora, count for me.'

Zomo Nanna put a man at the range-line. Yomyo went over and whispered into the ear of this man. This man knelt and tensed an arrow in a bow. He shut one eye and Yomyo put his palm some inches above the tip of the arrow, as if to guide the arrow through its whizzy journey.

'Pity!' chuckled Tsambo.

Counts Nsora, 'Lone ... two ... three ... four ... five ... six ... seven ...'

Released. Zooming. There. Crunch, into the head of the diadem, halted.

He yowled; the target yowled and pouted painfully, dangling his head all about, before settling his chin on his chest.

'Mat Modidi!' honked Zomo Nanna, hopping fast, slapping his laps, kissing his teeth a strain, twisting his shoulders.

The Zomo Warriors, Yomyo and his men, these did merriment.

'Nobody dies this soon?' debated Tsambo, gyrating forth, towards the shot target.

'Lay no hand on my catch!' quarreled Zomo Nanna, trailing Tsambo.

That moment, a ghostly gust hit the stillness upon the growth behind the shot target, awakening bats, owls, and sparrows.

'It is no wraith,' Tsambo comforted Zomo Nanna; the both of them calling for backup and putting their backups ahead of them.

Whereupon, a tattered voice squealed, 'Ni.'

And a weathered one echoed, 'Ni-ni-ni-ni-ni.'

The journey to the shot target halted.

Then, the tattered voice squealed, 'Na.'

And the weathered one echoed, 'Na-na-na-na-na.'

The members of the journey strode backwards, aborting the journey altogether.

Yet the tattered voice squealed anew; it squealed, 'Ya.'

And the weathered one echoed, 'Ya-ya-ya-ya-ya.'

Up shot the gust, from behind the target, descending before the retreating members of the journey, in the form of a human skull, and rolling religiously.

Journeymen and their cohorts, off they fled.

'Die!' the tattered voice squealed after them.

'Die-die-die-die!' the weathered voice echoed upon their souls.

Ah, but the venue became desolate and deathly as the ghost towns of Geesa.

It took a while before the tattered voice weaved forth, entangling the echoes of the weathered voice, shaking every leaf along its path, till it was two yards away from the shot target, and here it sobbed like a baby lizard.

'Yiddi?' whispered the shot target, contracting and relaxing its lips. 'Is that you?'

'He lives. He rules,' squealed the tattered voice, crawling to sit behind the tree to which the shot target was bound.

'Hey, Yiddi,' called the shot target, 'untie me. These ropes are climbing plants. Break them. Find a stone.'

'Uono's done all this doings, good king,' squealed the tattered voice.

'I'm grateful, crafty son of Ninaya,' Zowdor thanked Uono. 'Quickly undo the fasteners.'

Uono pounced on, nay, he meandered onto a knot, fisting it, chewing it, pulling it, bending it, wrestling it, so that the knot loosened and disappeared. He meandered onto other similar knots, depriving them of their curly gracefulness.

Zowdor hopped clean of all his roped limitations. He drew the arrow from his crown; it was stuck in its lining and he said to Uono, 'Come with me; Taila is ensnared.'

'My days are fully unfolded,' squeled Uono, meandering his wrists. 'Death whispers in my spirit. My bones shrink. My blood clots. Go, my king. Leave me here, to haunt this place with my final breath. Live long, king of Taila.'

'Farewell, wise Uono,' Zowdor bowed to him.

The duo hugged and parted, the older into the woods, the younger through the woods.

The assailants were in their flight. Ringed segments were created by Zomo Nanna and Yomyo, and their men.

Yomyo's men and most of the Zomo Warriors ringed Nsora, Dikomo, and Tsambo's Spear Makambes. Tsambo was ringed by Zomo Nanna, Yomyo and the remnant of Zomo Nanna's men. Tsambo was armed with a club, which Zomo Nanna smashed away with a bigger club.

'Your present mischief!' Tsambo roared and heaved.

'It is my valediction, Tsambo,' screeched Zomo Nanna, showing Tsambo a curved knife.

'What ... do you mean?' spoke Tsambo, trying to repossess his club, but was pounded on the wrists till his hands were incapable of gripping his club.

'An opportunist is one who prays to his enemy's god,' Zomo Nanna did a cold smile and told Tsambo.

Tsambo, his Spear Makambes, Nsora and Dikomo, death was the end of them all.

CHAPTER 9

'What has your enemy that your friend hasn't? Friendship and enmity, both are brewed in the heart. Do they say the growth is dangerous? You'll safely rest in it if it were not tampered by man. What do you fear? The scandal? Man's work it is. Don't you feel safe behind a gate? From whom do you secure your space? Man is the destruction of himself. The jealous brute who is amazed by jealousy. The envious hypocrite who complains of envy. The unfaithful spouse who battles infidelity. Man's virtues are fantastical and exaggerated, disturbing and notorious.'

The speaker was a kneeler whose hands and legs were wrapped and shackled to a tree. He faced away from this tree. About him, knelt a shackled multitude, some weeping, some dizzy, some hurting, some maimed, most of them bloody.

This speaker was an elderly man and as he peered across the multitude that was shackled about him, he lamented: 'Nature, but show us your might. You're a pathetic coward, looking on, defenseless, while the widow's heart is snapped on the scanty land she acquired by cheerless matrimony. Were you not with the living when the widow's folk, the orphan, slept unfed, or when he cuddled in chilly fields, troubled by callous crickets?'

He spat and bit his lip.

'Why are we coerced by stagnant fetish folk to honour you with tranquil days—Tuesday for your seas and Thursday for your soils? Of what relevance are your elements – water, fire, air, earth – when, the water transports the tyrant; the fire warms him and makes his food; the air gifts him life; and the earth nurtures his grain?'

Smack! His head was scourged with a stick: a stick in the grip of Zomo Nanna.

'Pity, Old Muyamba!' taunted Zomo Nanna, scourging the speaker anew. 'Destiny is like death: you can delay it, but you cannot prevent it. For years you kept me away from my treasure. You plotted against my fame, hampering me with rituals and lies.'

'I kept no treasure, no fame ...' Muyamba defended himself.

'Liar!' Zomo Nanna scourged him afresh. 'You spiked my glory with filth. You mocked my misfortunes. You called the heir of Zomo a coward. You so hated Azumba that you desecrated the shrine of our Grey Oracle.'

'I'm guiltless.'

Smack! 'You hired an alien guise to steal my fame, my destiny, my throne. But bless the Oracle, dust has gone to dust and what lingers is immortal me. Yomyo ...'

The bogus priestess was at the throat of a shackled duo, and he responded to Zomo Nanna's call with a wave of his hand.

'Come, Yomyo. Bring me the remains; the remains of them whom were hired to abort my glory.'

Yomyo bullied forth the shackled duo, slapping one, fisting the other, and propelling them with such a force that left them thudding facedown at Zomo Nanna's feet.

'Old man,' Zomo Nanna laughed, 'I have ridden the flames. My skin is seasoned in the fires of life. The eye of Zomo has guided my steps; it has secured me from the assassins you bought.'

'Assassins I bought!' exclaimed Muyamba.

'My delight will dwindle if my morrow was manifest away from your eyes. Death shall surely come for you, but not before I reduce you to slime. Heed, people of Taila. False is the legend of the trio that conquered Anona. Many were they who conquered Numungu. Our throne was sold to buy that lot. The fake priest and his sailor in-law apparently stole Anona's head and came for the glory. The lot that actually conquered Numungu was with vengeance on the seas last night. These two at my feet were sent to capture the sailor and his daughter. They say they have my royal, that if I would deliver to them the sailor and his daughter, they would return to me my royal. But ... because I am not as naïve as you, I chopped off their tongues and sent warriors to chase off the lot on Nuamba's seas.'

A multitude laughed. This multitude was unshackled and danced about the shackled multitude. Within them lay the carcasses of many Spear Makambes.

'Destroy these ones!' Zomo Nanna passed judgment on the duo at his feet.

Yomyo clapped. Four men marched forth with spears and twisted the weapons through the ribs of the shackled duo.

'Battle birds,' Zomo Nanna cried out.

Two trumpeters run forth.

'Above, a timid sun glows, beaming upon glory me, before it bares its chest and scorches my foes, summon a ceremony, that my head shall be graced in the sight of all who despise me, that he who stole my grace shall himself restore it, that I, the heir of Zomo, shall stand tallest in all Taila.'

'Blare!' whistled the trumpeters' trumpets, upon the south wind, upon the north wind, upon the east wind, upon the west wind.

Victory flags appeared and flew all around the shackled lot. Mirth was in some men and they placed a throne in the front of Muyamba by the side of Zomo Nanna. Songs filled the sky; dancing merrily, Zomo Nanna mounted the throne.

A chest was brought before Muyamba and before it was unlocked, he was unshackled. Inside the chest slept a crown on which was inscribed:

—NINAYA—

'After this, Muyamba from Wambi,' Zomo Nanna shook Muyamba's hand, 'you shall retire. Do this with passion: it is the summation of all your years as kingmaker of Taila. As the battle birds blare, lift that diadem and honour me like you honoured Taila and her royals.'

Zomo Nanna turned to Yomyo and thrust his chin downward. Yomyo clapped at the trumpeters.

'Blare!' wailed the trumpeters' trumpets, upon the arena, into the sky.

Muyamba folded his arms, looking below, defying Zomo Nanna's order with every movement he could manage. When Zomo Nanna had had enough, he flicked his fingers and a dozen archers took stands beside Muyamba, their faces mean as divorce.

Muyamba's countenance drifted from competitive to submissive. He grabbed the crown, and crowned Zomo Nanna, stammering, 'I clown ... you queen ... from all ... Taila.'

Smack! Zomo Nanna scourged him and smiled at the unshackled multitude, whose members were leaping merrily. Then he observed the shackled multitude, whose members were a-doing the melancholy do.

'Remnant of Taila,' he roared at them, 'do none of you cheer for me?'

The shackled multitude, they awfully cheered.

'Come, my courageous,' called Zomo Nanna, clapping. 'Come, crafty Yomyo. I was a stranger, yet you loved me like a brother. Come, Serondo. Come, Yooli. Come, Kranpa.

Come, my sons. My glory is yours also. Come, Bumi and
Sernua. You are my shadow, the eye of my rear. Come, my
warriors.'

In the order they were called, the men lined up before
Zomo Nanna.

'Bow to them,' Zomo Nanna ordered Muyamba, who
obeyed. 'Their stars fly higher in the heavens than yours.
Revere them. Bless them and you shall groan less.'

The six positioned their hands akimbo, eyeing Muyamba.

'Taila,' Zomo Nanna told the shackled lot, 'these are your
governors. My sons shall lead the east. Serondo, you shall
stay with me in Azumba. You are eldest and the mantle
when it is relayed by death will come first to you. Yooli, you
are agile as a hungry harlot; Agunbe shall be your follower.
Kranpa, you smile with prudence. You are slow at words, so
men forever wonder what you think. My enemies will arrive
at Nuamba. Have the vigilance of burglar mice and alert me
ahead of battle.'

Zomo Nanna bowed to his sons; they bowed back.

'Taila,' the Nanna further told, 'Amadi Yomyo shall be my
eyes in Wambi. The thirsty wolf from Yadoma. Look around,
Yomyo ... this is healthy soil. Serve me well and you shall
forever be merry. Bumi, you grew with my son and married
from my compound. You built your own home and
ornamented it with a statue of myself. You are kingmaker of
Taila and governor of Twessi. Sernua, with an arrow you
struck my enemy's head. You made me a victor before my
rival. The archer's mantle has passed to you. Displaying it,
you shall enforce my decrees in Emorna. Taila! A new
system is a new age. Adaptation, though it could be drab, is
safer than rebellion.'

Segments were made in the shackled lot. Wambians
remained in Wambi, while those Tailans from Twessi,
Emorna, Agunbe and Nuamba were returned to their

islands. King was the Nanna of the Zomo clan, and his kingdom was Taila. Reality is blunt.

All Tailans west of Azumba were pained to despair. Theirs was a mortifying servitude. A Life which knew no dignity, knew no rest, knew no reward.

Yaabwe was a son of Maln; a Wambian by birth; married at nineteen; became man at nineteen. His mistress was beautiful and he lusted after her; sweet and he called her Nectara.

That day, he had his Nectara on his back, courting her with verbal vanities. Along the street, he stepped on a ramp of slippery grass and slipped backward.

'Hang on, Nectara!' he panicked.

She gulped. He gyrated and fell forward instead of backward, lest he maims his Nectara. They both laughed.

'You've got a graceful sister,' a voice lusted from a bend on the road.

They both looked. Amadi Yomyo was at the bend with five guards, gazing at Nectara, kissing his lips.

'Avowed!' hinted Yaabwe. 'We ... very married.'

Yomyo slapped his chest. 'I dissolve this union,' he told Yaabwe.

'Not this one,' cried Yaabwe, fidgety. 'I have a sister, beautiful as me, no, as her. Her womb has never conceived. I can take you home and make her your wife.'

'I have chosen,' Yomyo laughed. He showed his face to his guards. 'Get her for me!'

The guards were coming. Yaabwe got up, helped up his Nectara, and said in a low tone, 'Let's flee.'

They, the couple, took flight, running their best, but were caught and returned to Yomyo.

Yomyo held their heads and clashed them. 'You mocked my competence,' he fumed. 'Wambi shall learn from you a principle of obeisance. I shall harm you and march beneath your skulls.'

'Forgive us,' pled Yaabwe. 'We have a son and daughter, very young folk. If you harm us they'll be pained.'

'Behead them,' Yomyo ordered his guards. 'His voice pierces my ear.'

Yaabwe cried as much as Nectara, yet they were segmented, bodies aside, heads aside. Beneath the dark night, Yomyo's men hang the two heads on poles and marched through Wambi, warning, 'The tempest of the east blows over your land; bend and you shall be safe.'

Tyranny suffers a phobia of revolt.

Harvest time came. The tyrants seized all harvest, traded most of it and stored the remnant in their barns. One night, a merchant ship came by. Its captain had before him a coffin and a scale. He tooted a horn and sent two buyers into Taila. They were welcomed into Azumba, where they related the particulars of their trade.

'Hear us!' they announced at Zomo Nanna's court. 'Thus says the merchant: "I, son and brother, lover and avenger, maggot of the sea, pirate of vengeance, poet of grief, I live for you, for the hatred of you. I breathe in your name, in the name of your destruction. I labour for your death, with my gains, with my sweat, with my years. But should you feel remorse and return to me my royals, then I shall give yours to you and undo all my vengeful stratagem." We have nothing to do with this trade: we are envoys, paid servicemen.'

'Wrong,' fumed Zomo Nanna. 'You sold your lives and not a service.'

Zomo Nanna bundled the duo to Wambi and slew them in the sight of Muyamba, quarrelling, 'Your schemes, old man. However, I respect that vengeful pirate: his ambition is as staunch as a mother's love.'

A nonamonth, matured enough to spew a foetus, wore off. On that particular night, time did its ageing below a waning moon. Tugu Tamanga tore into the seas between Wambi and Azumba. Just as is told in the legends of the merchants, her head was buried in a raffia cage. Her eyes were scarlet. Her machete battled the wind above. That night, the goddess queen of Nambo thrust her famed machete at Wambi, bellowing, 'Arise, Wambi! Arise!'

Fear haunted the tyrants. Serondo sent men to secure Azumba's unguarded borders. Yomyo secured Wambi; Kranpa secured Nuamba; Yooli secured Agunbe; Bumi secured Twessi; Sernua secured Emorna. Zomo Nanna. He hid in a lookout, inquiring from his granddaughter – she was bathing her doll below – how his men were faring.

'Granpa,' she told what she knew, 'the people have gone crazy. They say a veiled witch is thieving the seas faraway. Why won't they let her?'

'They shouldn't!'

'They shouldn't?'

'I decree they shouldn't!'

The young girl dashed out. There walked a pedlar in the distance and she yelled after him: 'Get back the seas!'

'Stalemate!' the pedlar returned, pointing west, then went on his way.

The young girl returned to the foot of the lookout. 'A pedlar wishes to trade stalemate,' she reported.

'A pedlar?' asked her grandpa.

'Yes, a pedlar. He didn't show it me, but he hinted west before parting.'

'It's a stalemate!' jubilated her grandpa.

'Do you want it, grandpa?'

'I adore it!'

She raced out. There, faraway, the pedlar walked on. She launched a speedy journey to his invitation.

Yomyo led the western troops from the forested south of Wambi. He led them swiftly and directly, that should he have managed to reach the shoreline at Azumba, Tugu Tamanga and her troops would have been trapped.

The goddess queen of Nambo sent out her coarse, mournful voice a second time. 'Wambi ...' cried she, 'O, Wambi!'

She floated three tiny coffins on the waters. They each carried a flamed candle and a bouquet.

Tugu Tamanga spread her winged robe. 'Beloved ... I go,' she mourned. Her men steered in angles that made the front of her ships become their rear. She sailed forth. She and Yomyo were becoming adjacent. Yomyo did a swift turn with his canoe. 'Retreat!' he ordered the western troops. Yomyo and the western troops withdrew, as swiftly and directly as they had come.

Three white doves were restricted in cages; Tugu Tamanga gave them liberty, and they hovered beneath the night, as amoral as the dead.

Forever, Taila was haunted: the avenging merchant came against the harvest, and the nonamonth brought the goddess queen of Nambo.

CHAPTER 10

These were smelly folk who lived in pungency, who slept with the bats and awoke with the owls; these were gutless pirates who had never, never robbed a ship, though they craved the robbery of one.

'Old buddy,' whispered the younger, very young, 'pray for me, for early youth. When it is I develop an able muscle, I shall purchase a scented field and there we shall retire from the hectic nights.'

'Foul,' whined the older, slapping his hat against the walls of their abode. 'You are a drain on my years. I endure this stinky cave and captain that semi-canoe, hoping you will grow into a bigger boy and assist me to snatch a ship to escape this nightmare, but no, you have the the night evil at heart, garnishing it with romantic retreat. I pray the demons of the ocean prey upon all scented fields, so there shall be none, none to fulfill your curse.'

'But, we're pirates. The world lives there; we live here. The world has norms; we hate society. The world hinges on faith; we have no trust of men. We are the shadows of the night, hidden to light, poachers of he that wanders, be he good or evil.'

'We need the morrow. We need society. Now, we're nothing.'

'No, you are nothing!'

'O, I'm nothing? So what are you?'

'I am the bad bird with the rebel voice of the assembler pirate, who by the day was king of archers, the Titiadi. I am a similar bird with the avenger soul of the famed outlaw who won a stately heart, the Zowdor. The Nemoso!'

'Hush, silence!' cried the older pirate, peeping out of their abode. 'That name will bring a plague here. Don't ever mention it. You willful, mischievous ...'

'Vain cowardice. You are bad company for me,' whined the young pirate, walking away and hiding in the deepest darkness of their abode.

The elder nagged awhile before fetching his fish traps. 'Hey!' he whispered. 'Fellow ... the night's calling ... tonight you'll be coxswain.'

'I'm done serving you, pirate. You are not an honourable man,' replied the younger.

'You don't serve me; we're comrades.'

'O yes, I do. In this cult my voice is fog.'

'What about we do the scales tonight?'

'The scales?'

'Aha.'

'Never. Barter is a sport for honourable men.'

'So you won't play at the scales?'

'Fortunately, I won't.'

'Even if my offer be to stay awake by your side in wait of the coming of the Zowdor Nemoso? Where I'll lead you, you shall behold his metallic teeth and witness his slaying of the tyrant's men. He shall conquer and the pained villagers shall shout his mighty name: Zowdor! Zowdor! Zowdor Nemoso!'

'You promise?'

'I swear it!'

'By your life?'

'You have my word.'

'Whooo! Haaa!' celebrated the younger pirate, hopping to the exit. 'Tonight, the Zowdor shall eliminate the tyranny and the queen shall be brought back from exile. I shall witness him, the legendary outlaw. Let's take the night.'

They sneaked to their semi-canoe, overturned it, and lay, the younger upon the elder, in it, each bearing a paddle and rowing left and right. Two aimless waves passed by; then says the elder: 'Now is the catch.'

The younger, he protested, 'But the bigger kill is yonder?'

'First the catch,' insisted the elder.

'Quickly then, old man, there's bigger business tonight.'

The younger kept watch while the elder hunted for fish. Unflinching was the younger at his duty: fearful was the elder at his. They knew their way about fish hunting, for they caught a herring, two crabs, a bevy of shrimps, and a turtle's baby.

'His moment is come!' the younger beamed.

'Combustibles first,' the elder decreed.

Rowing left and right, they bypassed all the dull, muddy waters of their vicinity, docked on a sparkling sea, from whence the elder submerged himself, swum onto dry land overlooking a cemetery, and aborted some maturing plants, which he called sticks. He re-submerged his body, save his hands which kept the sticks above water, and like a tadpole swum to the semi-canoe.

Whistles the young pirate: 'His moment is here!'

'Only after we've made a festival of this catch,' decreed the old pirate.

They rowed, the younger upon the elder, left and right to their abode, overturned their semi-canoe and sneaked into seclusion.

The elder rested his back, but the younger set to work right away. Near the entrance, there were four square stones, and between these he packed the sticks. He worked a wooden structure to the front of the stones, so that it shrouded them. Now, he worked at causing a flame, with a firm hole, a bundle of crisp leaves, and a durable stick; which flame promptly burst up. He lighted the sticks that lay between the stones. He hung the catch on a metallic thread and held it above the fire. That's a pirate's life: awake in secret, commune in secret, age in secret, die in painful secretive silence. So, in painful secrecy, the sea animals cooked to death, and the pirates had them between their teeth, doing things to them that left them tattered and moist and capable of diving down a throat; and when the pirates saw this capability in them, they ate them.

'His moment looks me in the eye,' the younger said and kissed his knuckles.

'I have a confession,' the elder said; his face was straight as straw.

'Be brief, old man. He that avenges the feeble owns the rest of the night.'

'There isn't ... I mean ... there really isn't any legends of the merchants. I swear it!'

'You ... swear it? Amongst all men, you are the most dishonourable. To you a lie ranks same with the truth. Yiddi ...'

'No names!' cautioned the elder, peeping outside.

'Friend, you were a servant of Diamo, a slave of my dad. Why won't you serve me. You claim to live for me, for the love of Diamo. But you lie. I'm your slave and not your lord. If I was your lord, you would respect me and keep your vows.'

'Son of Diamo, I hold you in high esteem. Upon my lord's last breath, I swore to guard your life, to return you to your Lembe. Around us there's nothing but hatred for Diamo. Diamo's servant shall be buried alive, and his son shall be cooked eternally.'

The young pirate's eyes were wet. 'Is there a Legends of the Merchants?' he demanded.

'There is but it knows no Zowdor, no Damoya, no Titiadi, no Muyamba. These are my brain's own inventions, to entertain you, my lord. Only grow, my boy. All we need is a transport to the adventure you crave, and to the cemetery of my fathers, where I'll sleep like a forming foetus.'

'Very well,' the younger said and lay where he had eaten. He slept obediently, puffing and snoring.

Smiling, the elder crouched over the younger. 'Goodnight, grandson,' bade he. He retired beside the younger, contracting his limbs, and snorting at long intervals.

Those eyes resurrected, same that belonged to the younger. They observed the elder, he was merrily asleep. The younger buried his eyes away from light and rolled away. He rolled back and nudged the elder. The elder sluggishly opened his eyes and observed about: all was well. He went back to his sleep. The younger after a while rolled anew, noisily away. He rolled back and nudged the elder. The elder's eyes opened and looked dizzily about: all was dizzily well. He continued his sleep. After a while, the younger noisily rolled faraway. He rolled back and nudged the elder. The elder motioned his limbs, but his eyes remained shut. The younger stood, strolled away, strolled back and nudged the elder with his foot. The elder motioned his shoulder, but did not open his eyes, and did not stop snoring loudly.

The younger tiptoed to the walls of their abode, by the walls, to the exit, through the exit, to the semi-canoe. He slowly and silently overturned the canoe and got hold of one of the paddles that were tied to it. Steadily, he departed from the place, murmuring, 'False, old wreckage, I go to fame myself.'

His journey traversed the waters and left him and the semi-canoe at the foundation of a projected piece of land, which was Wambi's burial ground. He overturned the canoe and climbed into the cemetery. Here were the reserves of the remains of very dead folk; dead, whether innocent or guilty. An arm bone was stuck in a wreath and lying in a graveyard. The young pirate thought the wreath was colourful, so he wore it around his neck. He held the arm bone in both hands, imagined he was a pirate on a deck of affluent merchants, and flashed the bone as seriously as a famed pirate would.

He broke loose upon the soils ahead of him. He was uncontrollable and crazy, quick and rugged, inquisitive and ambitious; and he dashed into the domain of six dozing guards, who awoke rapidly to this spectacle of ghostly chaos, which was in form skinny as a skeleton, and long as a midget.

They took flight.

'Wait!' shouted the pirate, going after them. 'On whose side are you, the Zowdor, or the tyrant?'

The guards fled faster.

Yon pirate, he pursued; guards, they onward fled; the chase, it until the settlements lingered; and here, where it showed itself to the early-chore maids, their job-maniac husbands, their impish offspring, and the guards that were by tyrants posted among them, there was an anarchy and a race, into which the pirate interwove the words: 'Wait, people! On whose side are you—the Zowdor or the tyrant?'

That way, where reaches a settlement not, went the tyrant's men.

These hid in their abodes: the maids, their husbands, their offspring.

There was at the hip of a primitive barn a window that swung open and showed a lamp that was held. Its holder motioned her head out of the confines of the barn. Her countenance glowed with the brightness of the lamp's light. She was a bald, old woman and when she did open her mouth, it had no teeth. She had wrinkles and two sure eyes. She swung her lamp curiously about, searching hard into the faint darkness around. The pirate had spotted her and was coming to her, speedily and surely. She saw, in his appearance, something like a wilful kid with no sandals.

'Kiti Konaar,' she called to him, 'run this way. Come with your puppet and your garland; come keep me company.

He brought himself before her.

'In my sleep,' she reported to him, 'my ancestors spoke to me. They showed me a stampede. I heard screaming. I heard fear. I heard danger. The tyrants have plotted an evil against Taila.'

'The tyrants?' queried the pirate, looking around.

The old woman searched about anew. 'I see no evidence of their plot, but soon they will strike.'

'Even I support the Zowdor,' the pirate beamed and held high his bone.

'Is that a bone you have here?' the old woman asked, on realizing the puppet was a bone.

'Verily, a fine weapon for a follower of the Zowdor. I brought it from the graveyard.'

'Graveyard! And is that a wreath you've got on your neck?'

'Yep.'

'Spirit of Wazeyme! He has the countenance, the courage, the charisma, the mysterious air of Zowdor, only he stinks like a broken grave. Zowdor!'

'Zowdor?'

'Pull me out; we go to the sage, the friend of the archer.'

'The archer who was chief of all the pirates?'

'Pull me quick!'

The pirate held the old woman by her gown, a mourning gown, and pulled away. She tumbled forth, landing with a somersault that made a bone creak by her scapula.

'Pull me up,' she said to the pirate.

He drew her as if she were some tuber in crispy earth. She placed a hand on his right shoulder, for support. She carried her waist to the right while she motioned forth her right leg, carried it to the left while she motioned forth her left, and that's how she motioned.

The pirate thought her stride was solemn. He carried his own waist right whenever hers went right and left whenever hers went left, his legs doing same as hers. But, queries the bald old woman, 'Is that your gait?'

'Solemnly,' replied the pirate.

Both of their waists were carried right, then left and again and again. At the waist of a bend they turned and went and turned, and swayed and turned. Beside a much vandalized door which secured the exit of an equally vandalized house, the old woman stopped; the pirate did likewise.

The old woman moved her lips. She hesitated. She shut her eyes before reporting, 'Today's case deserves immediate admittance.'

'Nagi,' quarreled a voice from within, 'able-muscled folk have fled from danger, yet you loiter. What is in the making of women that makes gossiping so dear to such? Anyway, I am not awake.'

'Muyamba …' faltered Nagi.

'Muyamba!' ehoed the pirate.

'Whose voice was that?' asked the voice from within.

'On whose side is he?' the pirate asked the old woman.

'On Zowdor's,' she responded.

'What Zowdor?' the voice from within developed dogma.

'An emissary of Zowdor,' reported the old woman.

Time loitered awhile.

BUM! A weight thudded about the ground on the left side of the house.

'Are you fine Muyamba?' asked the old woman. She got no response. She peeped through the door, but a thick cloth tied to the roof near it prevented her from seeing within. The pirate joined her and together they vainly peeped.

An eye emerged by the left corner of the house, spying on the pirate and the old woman. This eye was prudent, so that until it stopped hiding itself, neither the pirate nor the old woman saw it. The man who had the eye showed himself, for his one eye could not give him the good judgment he sought. He was elderly and bearded.

'Muyamba!' the old woman shouted at him.

'Muyamba!' echoed the pirate. 'He that will one day crown the Zowdor and offer him his Damoya. Live long, bearer of the diadems.'

'What is he?' asked Muyamba, moving up to the pirate and giving him a critical look.

'He came from the graveyard,' Nagi reported.

'You came from the graveyard?' Muyamba put to the pirate.

'By the graveyard,' replied the pirate.

'These bone and wreath, they're yours?' queried Muyamba.

'They're for the dead. I borrowed them.'

'Did you see the dead?' Muyamba drew his face closer to the pirate.

'Old man, I am a pirate. I have no want of clairvoyance. Late after you sleep, I lurk upon the waters, in wait for your neighbour, to hit him with a paddle and thieve that which his sweat has bought. I care little about dignity. My dignity is the purity of piracy: abject darkness.'

'What is in Wambi for a pirate?' Muyamba wondered aloud.

'I have come to do my kindred assist, to slay for the outlaw, for the Zowdor!'

Muyamba dragged Nagi aside.

'That is the kindred of my king,' he put rumour in her ear. 'He's come with many to avenge the king's death; with the maggot of the sea, maybe; with the goddess queen, maybe.'

'But he calls the king an outlaw.'

'He might be talking of the king's former life, which you as I know little of.'

'His gait is ghostly,' Nagi reported. 'I suspect he is the phantom of King Zowdor.'

'Even I suspect so: the phantom of King Zowdor. How much they look alike!'

The pirate bent forth, trying to eavesdrop on the conference. Muyamba and Nagi muted.

'When is the hour?' demanded the pirate.

'What hour?' asked Muyamba.

'The hour of the Zowdor the outlaw!'

'Are you come to avenge the king?'

'No, the queen. I'm come to help the Zowdor unite with his Damoya.'

'In spirit?'

'In flesh. I told you, old man; I am a pirate and have no want of clairvoyance.'

'But … you talk of uniting the murdered monarchs?'

'Murdered monarchs?'

'King Zowdor and Queen Damoya.'

'They killed the outlaw?'

'All three monarchs and the chief archer.'

'When you say three monarchs what do you mean? Monarchs? Sounds legendary. Yiddi told me a half story.'

'Yiddi?'

'No names!'

'No …'

'Yes, no names! We're pirates. We bear no dignified identity.'

'That name which you mentioned belongs to the third monarch, the father of Queen Damoya.'

'The name Yiddi?' the pirate cautiously mentioned.

'Mmm!' Muyamba nodded. 'King Yiddi ruled east and King Zowdor ruled west. Queen Damoya was queen of everywhere.'

'And, King Diamo?'

'Diamo was Yiddi's late son. Yiddi mourned him forever.'

'Diamo was no king at all?'

'He was not king,' Nagi reported.

'Yiddi indeed lied,' said the pirate, 'for if Diamo was king of Lembe and king of pirates, what trade would he have with Tailans and their tyrants?'

'Yiddi appeared to you?' the Wambians asked the pirate.

'I live with him.'

'At the graveyard?'

'At Tarada; at the cave that sleeps on the lagoon.'

'Does this Yiddi wear beady eyes most of the time?' asked Muyamba.

'Yes, most of the time,' answered the pirate.

'Does he have a stoop about his shoulders?'

'Yes, about his shoulders.'

'Does he ruffle his beard often?'

'Yes, often he does.'

'Can I come to see this Yiddi?'

'Actually, can we come?' Nagi asked to go as well.

'Never,' swore Muyamba. 'You cannot come, but you can shield our shadows if you want.'

'He met me first,' quarreled Nagi.

'Doesn't matter,' Muyamba counter-quarreled. 'I am the chief custodian of Wambi and kingmaker of all of Taila!'

'Was!' honked Nagi.

'No more. Silence,' decreed the pirate, his eyes winking. 'We pirates do not sail beside a woman. We live secretly and die in silence.'

'At least,' pled Nagi, 'let Wambi see me go with you out of this settlement. I could spy on the guards and tell you where the road is clear.'

'It has the air of piracy,' the pirate smiled, 'mysterious. You shall come, old woman, but as far as the graves.'

'Accepted,' Nagi beamed. 'Get your rod, Muyamba: the going is on.'

'Not now,' decreed the pirate. 'Yiddi has the soul of a rabbit and the cowardice of a deer, if we confront him in daylight he'll flee. He's a follower of the dark, a lover of the dark, a friend of darkness. We shall strike below the night.'

'Done;' consented Nagi, 'below the night.'

'Do you have any food?' the pirate asked the Wambians.

'I have a pregnant crab,' reported the old woman.

'Is she cooked?' the pirate queried.

'Partially.'

'Your first task: cook her wholly.'

The old woman said she would.

'I will give you boiled potatoes and coconut fruits,' promised Muyamba.

Said the pirate, 'This pirate shall consider making friends of such honourable company.'

Muyamba and Nagi grinned.

Continued the pirate, 'Muyamba, you have warred by the side of mighty men. I would call you my brother, should you admit me into your dwelling. Friends, I am a pirate, an ally of moonless nights. Light torments me. It impairs my sight. The virgin sun will emerge in the east and ripen in the west, may my eyes not behold its glory. Hide me this moment.'

Confinement was the pirate's wish, so confined he was, in Muyamba's vandalized house. He ate a potato's flesh before sitting on a Bamboo bed, which he confessed had amazing comfort. Now, his eyes began to flicker. Now, he dozed. Now, he fell backwards. Asleep was the pirate.

'Gone,' Nagi reported adoringly.

'Shut away from society's boredoms,' Muyamba spoke with a smile.

'Muyamba,' reported the she, 'I go to prepare my crab.'

'Good,' commended the Wambian he, 'I also go to fetch the coconut fruits.'

Nagi and Muyamba, they went out through a window. The gaits that moved them away from this point were distinct. Muyamba's waist was rigid and it pounced forth along the street. Nagi dreamt of speed, so she dangled her waist from side to side, causing her head to nod irrationally. Says the she at their parting: 'Won't you get a lad to pluck you the fruits?'

Responds the he: 'Muyamba is able.'

Hence, as the she to her abode went, to do her crab prepare, the he marched pompously to the tallest coconut tree. Muyamba attacked the coconut tree with stones, sticks, sand; he failed; Nagi was watching and she came to him and said, 'Get a lad.'

'Able,' responded Muyamba, walking towards his home.

Yomyo and his guards were there in a distant bush, looking out for the mysterious midget who from a grave came. They saw Nagi looking on as Muyamba went. They monitored Muyamba, along the street, to a side window, into the room the window served. I swear they saw no more of him till he popped out of the same window holding a bow and arrow, and talking into the window.

'His hand work, I told you,' an Azumban cried to Yomyo.

'He truly is a snake,' fumed Yomyo. 'Go search his place; vandalize it. Bring Muyamba in shackles, and do scourge that bald old woman.'

Grumbles his guards, 'What if the midget's wraith is there, somewhere? Shouldn't we spy here by your side?'

'Away from here!' Yomyo chased them. 'Wait, four should return.'

They all returned.

'Four I said.'

None moved a limb.

Yomyo pointed the four he wanted to stay and chased the rest away. They who were chased wore faces like wet wood and strode timidly into the settlements. They waved at Muyamba. He did not notice them. He was on the offensive. He shot a coconut, its neighbour, its sister, its foe; all in all he shot eleven, but they all danced at him, none fretted, none hovered.

'Get a lad,' advised Nagi.

'Able!' bragged Muyamba.

A man of Yomyo lifted a finger. 'Let's tackle his home first?' this man told his colleagues. His colleagues followed him to Muyamba's house.

'Come out, evil midget,' spoke Yomyo's men, in a weak tone. 'We shall burn you and the Wambians.'

The midget did no appearance do.

Their weapons were clubs, so with clubs they drummed on Muyamba's walls, keeping their distance from the window into which Muyamba had spoken. They continually drummed.

'The world is at the bite of vandalism,' a sleepy voice within Muyamba's house spoke. 'Society is risen against the pirate. They know my time. They know I rule the night, so they come as the day breaks, but a pirate is a pirate, whether dark or clear. What if they murdered the Zowdor? Perhaps they did? Death to thee, vandals! Death to thee and thy cohorts!'

He hovers into the window frame. He hovers out of it. He lands.

Yomyo's men see, hear and feel his wrath. His hissing anger infects the wind. Yomyo's men speedily distance themselves. Are they fleeing? O, they are.

The pirate goes after them, but awhile. When he halts, he says, 'I am a pirate; that I am. I am no murderer; I merely hate society. Your death shall be to appease the Zowdor: it shall not be for the sake of killing.'

Yonder, Yomyo departs, leaving his men behind, doing this quickly. His men trail him in his flight.

Victor is the pirate. Gone are the assailants. Muyamba bore witness. Nagi filed a mental report. The pirate sleepily returned to Muyamba's abode.

'He wants a peaceful nap,' Nagi reported to Muyamba.

'I'll tackle that right away,' Muyamba bossily said.

'How?' asked Nagi.

'I'm very efficient, woman. I am Muyamba. I shall keep all Wambi asleep this day and the kindred of my king shall sweetly sleep.'

'How?'

'Watch me.'

Muyamba wanders. He stops by the first house. He knocks. A man sneaks out his head. Says Muyamba to this man: 'Evil roams Wambi. Dwell in your dwelling. Rise to tomorrow's sun. Beware.' The man nods in fright. He draws back his head. He shuts his door. Muyamba eyes Nagi. She lifts her shoulders and rapidly drops them. Muyamba goes to a second house and says there what he had said at the first house, this time to a little girl with wobbly feet. Muyamba does same to many houses. He doesn't stop, even though he is breathing hard. He put nearly every house in Wambi under his spell, his falsehood, his manipulation.

'I've been around awhile,' he did say to Nagi on his return.

She only licked her lips and went to attend to her crab.

Muyamba carried a rock that was able to short coconut tree and hit the hips of this tree. The tree shook. A fruit detached from it and fell. He carried the rock anew and fell another coconut fruit. He fell five fruits in all and dragged them to his dwelling, where he related to Nagi, who came carrying an overcooked she crab, some issues of his manly dignity; stating, 'O, I've been a legend in the circles of tree-climbing folks. When a tree thinks it swings beyond subdue, able men whistle for Muyamba, and once I am come, subdued becomes the tree. I have dared where great sailors dared not.'

'Where?' the pirate awoke and inquired.

'Upon the storm, in the year of Modua. I climbed a swinging sail, good pirate. At the summit of the pole, I warred against storm and wave.'

'Teach me how to climb and war?' begged the pirate.

'Titiadi would have thought you better,' nagged Nagi.

'He would have,' Muyamba conceded, rubbing his palms timidly against each other.

'But the legend says that the Titiadi and Muyamba are the twin a single woman did not born?' the pirate spoke with a puzzled face.

'That is the optimum truth,' Muyamba rejoined.

'Then, what the Titiadi could have done, I, the pirate of Tarada, shall trust Muyamba to accomplish.'

'Off and away!' yelled Muyamba, going through the window. The pirate swallowed the crab's two limbs and followed. Nagi followed. To a coconut tree went this trio.

'Seize above its foundation,' Muyamba coached the pirate.

Pirate from Tarada, he pranced and wrapped himself above the foundation of the coconut tree.

'While arching your back, pull up your legs. Like that. Now elevate your arms, drawing support from your lower body. Good, pirate. Rehearse the first round. Your back arched. Legs up. Arm elevation and there you are. Another round. Back ... legs ... arms ... awesome, pirate.'

'Han! Han! Han! Bijin! Bijin! Bijin!' celebrated the pirate, as he soared.

He higher went and his arm came to interlope with an arm of the tree. Something gave his hand a cold pat. This something tickled his skin and coiled about. Curiosity lured the pirate's head to spy on this something. Snakeful something! Its head was jerked in war, zooming towards pirate skin. The pirate squealed and swerved, and squealed and slid down the tree's stem, and squealed and landed and panted and squealed and smiled.

Says he, 'I, the pirate of Tarada, I did the pirates' do. Friends, I have told you my life, so you need no further telling. I am the outcast, the friend of the night. When it is your neighbour is confronted in daylight, stray your guesses far apart from me: I have no trade with day-men. With a cold heart I go from this encounter, lest the night and the piracy consider me a traitor. Watch out for the early bat; he is the luck of pirates. At his appearance, we shall strike.'

He went to Muyamba's. That pirate went, and ate coconuts and slept away fom all light. He had company, who weren't pirates, and weren't outcasts, and didn't hate the day; therefore, they sat in the midst of the day, looking upon him as he slept, sneaking out this time and the other to spy the vicinity, to make sure no danger lurked about the pirate's nap.

Water is at unity with infinity. Water is sea, infinity is sky. At their horizon a virgin moon yawns and awakens to a virgin night. Lo, oncoming from afar, flapping its wings at the horizon, hovering dizzily, blinking both eyes profusely, a creature with savage teeth and a skin the hue of darkness.

'Eureka!' cried Nagi, whose head had been sticking out all day, causing a partially asleep Muyamba and a perfectly asleep pirate to awaken. 'I spotted the early bat. He's headed for Nuamba.'

The pirate and Muyamba joined her. They looked up about and verily the early bat was upon the sky.

'Curse the day!' bellowed the pirate.

'Curse the day!' echoed Nagi.

'I, the remnant of Diamo; I, the pirate of Tarada; I, the relative of six and twenty pirates; I, who shall avenge the Zowdor; I, who seeks a confession of Yiddi; I call the night to activity.'

Like a captain leading an offensive against raging storms, the pirate hovered through Muyamba's window. Muyamba followed, then Nagi. They hit the streets with various gaits, all lacking harmony and grace, all bereft of speed and perfection, yet capable of attaining a lanky destination, for they reached the cemetery from which the pirate had taken a wreath and an arm bone.

'Do you belong here?' Nagi sought from the pirate.

The pirate's response was in the negative, and after the response he pointed to Tarada, adding the words: 'Below this bereaved night I surge by your side. In your union I entrust my safety. Be to me a sword and I shall be to you a shield. Hate my enemy and I shall adore your friend. Smile at my fortune and I shall share in your misfortune.'

'We shall honour your decree,' reported Nagi.

'Foul,' spoke Muyamba, specially making a face, 'I shall honour his decree. You stay here with these carcasses and divert all future danger.'

'Pirate, your decree is final. Is it not sinful that I who saw the early bat be left out of the struggle?' Nagi said this with a confident akimbo.

'The struggle!' repeated the pirate, his visage entertaining the very sound of it. 'Woman, but I am a pirate, a son of men, a comrade of society's foe. Your kind pray for my doom. His kind offer me a retreat.'

'Hail the pirate ship!' cried Nagi. 'Death to the tyrant, who himself is a man. That morn when Ramod was held, his friend fled and found new company. Disana, that peasant girl, she stayed. She wept at his trial. She wept at his killing. She wept at his grave. She still weeps for him. Hate my kind, but we … have been faithful … to your kind, to the piracy.'

'Come with me!' decreed the pirate.

'Come with us!' Muyamba pretended to like the like the idea.

The pirate launched forth, followed by his company. He halted at the corner of a potruded earth whose base shared a boundary with the sand of the sea, on which sand rested his overturned semi-canoe. He jumped onto the sea sand and beckoned his company to join him, which they did. He marched to the semi-canoe, held it, overturned it, lay in it, and said to his company: 'Come aboard!'

They went to him. 'Where shall we sit?' they asked.

'Night pirates do not sit,' he answered. 'Night pirates lie.'

'Where shall we lie?'

'Upon me.'

They obeyed.

'You're hefty,' grumbled the pirate, shaking himself till the Wambians settled beneath him, and now that he was on top, he ordered, 'Row!'

'Shouldn't we first shove it to sea?' the Wambians asked.

'Row!' that was the pirate's discretion.

The Wambians grabbed paddles from the canoe's sides and rowed boisterously at first, then tediously after, yet the semi-canoe did not move. The pirate examined the situation. 'O pardon me,' he said. 'There's no water. We first have to place the gadget offshore'

The pirate lay in the canoe while the Wambians pushed it to sea. Offshore, they got aboard and started paddling, after the pirate had shaken himself so that they resettled beneath him.

As the paddles counted the seconds, time's maturity brought shrinkage to distance. And when the distance shrank to forty yards of its lifespan, the pirate and his company spotted a restless shadow. This shadow was a-spying and it entered Tarada before the pirate and the Wambians could call to it.

'Just what was that?' company of the pirate, they asked him.

'Sly entity,' answered the pirate. 'He has the tongue of an eastern merchant and the face of a god. Tonight, his falsehood shall be set alight. Row rapidly, friends, this place is cursed by the demons of procrastination, whose disciple we seek.'

Eventually, the Wambians and the pirate reached Tarada. They docked at the front of the smelly cave and the pirate overturned his canoe, commanding, 'We shall first secure the entrance and ask him to surrender. Should he refuse, we shall hunt him down and hold him captive till he confesses all his mischief. With this, I bring Tarada to threat.'

The pirate scurried around and spied above the seas. He scurried to the entrance of Tarada and plunged his head into the cave. 'Join me here. Low risk,' he told the Wambians.

They went with two varieties of gaits and stood by him.

'Exit secured,' said he, peering into the cave. 'Pirate, our business is your head, but why drag it to a noose, if you would be agreeable and give it to us? We've been friends. We've almost been family, only you were dishonourable. We've ridden the night together and we would have been triumphant if you weren't cowardly and disloyal. I am come with the friend of the archer.'

'Muyamba,' Nagi reported the archer's friend's name.

Human feet shuffled on the stony floor within Tarada.

'Succumb,' chanted the pirate. 'Peaceable is the way. Why do you stop, pirate; succumb. You will have no retreat once we're at your heels; surrender.'

'You're outnumbered and doomed, pirate,' Nagi reported. 'Hop out and give up yourself.'

'Quite, woman,' quarreled Muyamba. 'We're yet at negotiations. You are a loophole in our stratagem.'

'I am not!'

'You are! Hence, I, the chief custodian of your kindred, living and late, decree that you sit yonder aloof!'

'That voice!' a shrill, shaky voice spoke from within Tarada.

'You heard it afore?' the pirate asked this voice.

The shrill shaky voice answered not.

'Speak anew,' the pirate told Muyamba.

Muyamba spoke the names of eight breeds of vagabonds.

'Tastes like Muyamba in my ears,' judged the shrill, shaky voice from within.

''Tis Muyamba's vandalized voice,' reported Nagi.

'How many of you have come here to Tarada?' the voice boldly but prudently inquired.

'Smells like the eastern king's voice in my ears,' Nagi reported.

'Indeed,' seconded Muyamba.

'Tell me, Muyamba,' the voice from within spoke, 'how many of you are here?'

'Sounds like him!' celebrated Muyamba. 'There's the pirate, there's Nagi, and there's myself — three of us.'

'This better not be a conspiracy!' warned the young pirate.

'It's not,' reported Nagi.

'Muyamba,' called the voice, 'I see a form, even the frame of a face, but I see not yourself. Align yourself with the light behind you; then perhaps, I shall make you out.'

Muyamba mingled himself with the light behind him, so that its meagre illumination smeared his face. Human feet shuffled toward the exit of the cave.

'He is coming,' reported Nagi.

The feet stopped shuffling and the voice said from where the feet had stopped: 'I have beheld you, beloved of Taila.'

The feet started their stride anew, striding now with bold talkative steps, and as they neared the exit they turned into a shadow, then into an aged fellow with silvery tresses and tattered robes.

Muyamba and Nagi bowed to this aged fellow.

'Longevity to your years, my king,' said Muyamba.

'The tyrants think you're with the dead,' reported Nagi.

'Mutiny!' cried the pirate.

'He is king,' reported Nagi, 'king of the east of Taila. King Zowdor was king of the west, but King Yiddi, he had the eastern issue at his court.'

'He?' the pirate, who was dumbfounded, was pointing at the aged fellow. 'King? Who made him king? He's pirate, pirate, pirate — a bad pirate at that!'

'You mixed it up, pirate,' reported Nagi, skipping desperately. 'You mixed it up anew. You ranked King Zowdor with outlaws and ranked King Yiddi with pirates. Pirate, these waters that transport you all bow to our king, the coconuts and crab that fed you as well. I don't brag the deed, but it would have been merely righteous if you did no defiance of our kings, as a demonstration of your gratitude.'

The pirate was dismayed. He gaped. He slapped his head.

'To whom do you owe your allegiance?' the aged fellow from within asked Nagi.

'To you, my lord. To the monarchy. To Taila,' she reported her answer.

'Then, you've sinned against Taila, against her monarchy.'

'I … have?'

'You called the monarch a pirate.'

'He called you a pirate: I called you the king.'

'His last name is Nemoso. He sat in the belly of a monarch of here. Behold, the prince of all Taila.'

'Hail the prince!' Muyamba and Nagi celebrated.

'Ahh!' the young pirate moaned. 'Did I not forewarn you of his crafty tongue? Yesterday, Diamo was king of Lembe and I was his son. Today, the outlaw is king of Taila and I have become his son. He, pirate, has stopped being pirate and is now the Zowdor's equal.'

'Wait, my prince,' Nagi spoke, a clever glint in her eye, 'I shall this moment unveil to you the court of my mind, which presently is at a durbar.'

'I am pirate. Pirate!' complained the little pirate.

'But you're not,' reported Nagi. 'The points of the verdict are in factual, analytical forms. Our queen was very pregnant when she parted from Wambi. She parted in the flanks of King Yiddi and King Zowdor. Queen Damoya died after childbirth. King Yiddi, the queen's father, fought with death and conquered death like he conquered Anona.'

'Pirate? He conquered Anona Sissi?' the little pirate jubilantly inquired.

'He brutally did,' reported Nagi.

'Not the Zowdor?'

'With King Zowdor.'

'Pirate has been in mighty company?'

'Verily,' reported the she. 'And my verdict further holds that once he was done with death, he took the young prince and reared him in Tarada. Much evidence is in the making of the prince. He has King Zowdor's face, his eyes, his skeleton. This is the son of my king, born of my queen, bred of my king. Thirteen years since the queen went away with her pregnancy, and here you stand, a cohort of the figure. Live long, my prince.'

'I am thirteen. But swear it upon your life that I look like the Zowdor.'

'By my life, you do.'

'Yiddi, I accept this falsehood,' spoke the little pirate. 'I accept you back as my partner, with the condition that you call me the Zowdor, and tell it to every living that you come across that I, Witanda, am the Zowdor.'

'They'll think you a wraith,' reported Nagi.

'Scares them harder; fames me better. And Yiddi, tonight I call the tyranny to threat.'

'Ill stratagem!' yelled Yiddi, his face and head wobbling.

'Huh! Ahh!' groaned the princely pirate, grimacing.

'Just what was that?' Yiddi said and went westward, his eyes looking searchingly ahead.

The prince and the Wambians flanked him, inquiring, 'What did you see?'

'A spy with a flame,' answered he, 'in them bushes onshore.'

'Arm yourselves,' commanded the prince. 'Secure, each one of you, an arc of Tarada. Should you see the sea gull on the wind, give him a message: tell him to summon onto us the fourth cavalry that retrieved the carcass of Kalante.'

'King Zowdor,' spoke Yiddi, 'north and south are both not tampered by spy. Our defense should face east and west. We have to take, the both of us, a subject and man an arc, but I cannot take the female because my bones are weakened with the years. Allow me to take the male to the east, while you take the female west. She shall be safer in your care.'

'Done!' Prince Witanda agreed, taking Nagi's hand. 'Woman, be my eyes and I shall be your strength. Now, I, king of this west avowed to that east, decree that a conquest be pursued.'

He, pirate, prince and king, got armed with a rock. Yiddi took a club. Muyamba drew a stick from the lagoon. Nagi grabbed a broken slab. Tarada's western arc was in the manning of Witanda and Nagi; its eastern arc was in the manning of Yiddi and Muyamba, the latter spying, the former observing his grandson.

'Desert the scare, Muyamba,' Yiddi said, so that Muyamba alone could hear, 'there are no spies I have seen in those bushes.'

'You pulled a joke on the prince?' Muyamba quietly laughed.

'I needed to. Witanda's heart is unflinchingly mischievous. I have to leave Taila, or he'll rally to early death. Help me, Muyamba?'

Muyamba bowed his head diffidently. 'We, the custodianship, have wronged you enormously. It is our craft that has cost you your family, and put you in unpleasant years of exile.'

'No, Muyamba, you were swindled as much as I was.'

'I speak of times before the swindle, my king.'

'Such times?'

Queries Witanda, 'Any progress with the conquest?'

'Cautiously,' returned his allies, and he shifted his attention to his west again.

'We, the custodianship, lied,' resumed Muyamba.

'Concerning what?' asked Yiddi.

'Your return to Lembe.'

'What about it?'

'There were no pirates about.'

'No … pirates?'

'And there wasn't an evil that executes babies. The prince would have been fine.'

'Really?' Yiddi's eyes spoke of anguish and mistrust. His face was a blend of mild hate and agony.

'I'm ashamed, good king,' said Muyamba, fondling his fingers, lowering his eyes. 'I'll help you escape Taila.'

'How?' Yiddi's manner confessed of disbelief.

'By any means; anything you want me to do.'

'What I want, you cannot give, Muyamba. However, I'm grateful for your deep compassion.'

'What do you want, my king?'

'I want a ship and an army?'

'The ships dock between Wambi and Nuamba; I think I could steal one. An army, I could raise one.'

'An army of two-hundred?'

'I can.'

'All of them flawless at archery?'

'I could.'

'When is that moment?'

'It would require some patience.'

'I have waited for thirteen years. I could wait some more, but my grandson.'

'We shall tell him an army shall be raised under his command?'

'Makes him the more crazy.'

'That this army shall sail to Lembe to fetch more warriors, and the union shall return to destroy the tyranny?'

'Great, Yamba. You drew the perfect stratagem. There in Lembe, I would barter my fields to men who know their way about a weapon: if they would fight here, by my side, then they can keep the wealth.'

'Hail the morrow of Taila!' bellowed Muyamba.

'Death to the tyranny!' bellowed Nagi and Witanda, bolting to the eastern arc.

'They fled!' Muyamba married.

'To where?' asked Witanda.

'To their homes,' answered Yiddi.

'There we shall take the conquest,' swore Witanda.

'They have hostages,' warned Muyamba.

'What hostages?' Witanda asked, nearly fuming.

'Your subjects, King Zowdor,' answered Yiddi.

'I am amazed by their genius,' confessed Witanda.

'Even I,' reported Nagi.

'What shall we now do with them?' asked Witanda.

'Outwit them,' spoke Yiddi and Muyamba.

'With what stratagem?' asked Witanda.

'With a stratagem of unexpected battle,' replied Muyamba.

'Tell its particulars?' commanded Witanda.

'You, our kings, shall sail with two-hundred warriors to Lembe, the city of the brave. You shall expand the army and bath every warrior in the chasm at Nuali, which makes men invincible. Your return is the tyrant's doom. Live long, my kings.'

'When is this journey?' Witanda questioned.

'Exactly on the day I'm done mobilizing an army and stealing a ship from the border with Nuamba to the south of Wambi.'

'It takes a dark night and a pirate to steal a ship,' estimated Witanda. 'What does it take to mobilize an army?'

Yiddi took a deep breath.

'Outwitting is the stratagem,' Muyamba reminded Witanda, who nodded intelligently. 'Until such a time when the monarchy has led the army to bath of the potions of invincibility, the return of our monarchs shall be hidden from the tyranny. This is true genius. Let them continue in their arrogant ignorance.'

'Do you think the Zowdor would have consented to this stratagem?' asked Witanda.

'Of course,' swore Yiddi and Muyamba.

'He surely would,' reported Nagi.

'Then, so the stratagem shall be,' decreed the prince.

'I wish to propose a duel of yesteryear,' reported Nagi.

'Speak up,' Witanda permitted her.

Says she, 'Far is Lembe; fatal is the venomous arrow.'

'Mutiny!' cried Muyamba.

'Who does a treason?' investigated Witanda.

'She,' reported Muyamba.

'I am blameless, King Zowdor,' reported Nagi.

Witanda smiled bossily. 'I shall examine your entire proposal, woman,' spoke he, 'and where you err, I shall align you with the justice of my fathers.'

'You are the justice,' Nagi reported and bowed. 'My proposal, which is yards from treason, is that we do what Taila did under Titiadi, who served the monarchy till death.'

'What did Taila do?' the prince demanded, excited.

'Taila mastered the art of archery,' reported the she.

'Archery!' the prince exclaimed, feeling his left palm with his right thumb.

Yiddi's eyes were darting about.

Spoke the she, 'We were an army of women mainly, yet we crushed Numungu in his vengeful raid. The assailant was yet oncoming, when Nier Titiadi signaled the attack. Our arrows feasted on their haughty skins. Sweet was that night of triumph.'

'I decree that the stratagem be, this instant, merged with archery: the archery of the Titiadi!' declared the prince.

'Could complicate it?' argued Yiddi.

'Could mar it?' argued Muyamba.

'Too much fish will not block the sea?' argued Witanda.

Nagi leaped. She clapped. 'Sixteen spies!' reported she. 'There about the bushes!'

'Where?' asked Muyamba.

'There,' reported she.

'I can't see?' spoke Yiddi, searching extensively.

'What do we do?' Nagi asked Witanda.

'I decree that the conquest be resumed,' decreed Witanda.

Witanda and Nagi went west; Yiddi and Muyamba went east.

Nagi stood behind Witanda, pointing her hands ahead of him. 'I lied,' she reported in a whisper.

'Treason,' said Witanda.

'Justifiable,' reported she.

'How is it justified?'

'It is necessary for the morrow of Taila.'

'It cannot be treasonable then.'

'It is about the archery. If you shall give me your command, I shall mobilize the remnant of the archers who fought under Titiadi. With them you can seize Wambi. Your subjects in Twessi, Agunbe, Emorna and Nuamba are more susceptible to rebellion: they rampantly murder the tyrant's men. We only have to send them word that the monarchs are back and have retrieved Wambi.'

'I feel like soap,' confessed the prince.

'Why, my king?' asked Nagi.

'Who shall revere a king who knows nothing about a bow and arrow? What stature magnificent have I, that any man should look upon and shiver? I was a pirate. What honour is there for me? They revered Titiadi, so they fought for him. Why shall they fight for me? Will you do me a favour?'

'Anything, my king?'

'Lead the archers?'

'I am honoured,' she gladly reported.

'I shall concern myself with the troops that shall be posted in the south, persuading them to merge with your archers.'

'At exactly what time should we strike?'

'At the time when the army of the south is stationed at the south coast.'

'How will I know?'

'I shall decree to Muyamba that on the day he comes to inform us that the journey to Lembe is due, he should come in your company. His invitation is your signal: refuse to come see me and go, as he comes, to launch your attack.'

'I am grateful, good king.'

'I am grateful, good subject.'

'Sixteen of them!' Nagi loudly reported.

Muyamba and Yiddi hurried to the western arc.

'Where?' asked Muyamba.

'It was a monkey family,' reported Nagi.

Yiddi and Muyamba frowned.

'Wambians are malnourished. Their sights are impaired. Archery requires able limbs and perfect sight. King Zowdor, I pray you allow the stratagem to go unchanged,' spoke Muyamba.

'My answer is yes,' said Witanda. 'Woman, I mean yes.'

'He means yes?' Yiddi suspiciously asked Muyamba.

'Yes, the stratagem. Nothing changes the plot,' reported Nagi.

'O, the stratagem!' Yiddi heaved and laughed.

'The stratagem!' Muyamba laughed with him.

'Be reminded,' spoke Yiddi, 'that a word of this monarchical return shall not be spoken anywhere in Taila, until a time when the army from here has been unified with the army from Lembe and both have bathed of invincibility. None of you shall visit Tarada before a ship is stolen from Nuamba's coast and an army is stationed in the south. If

there's danger, we shall watch out for ourselves. No one will
know about us if you tell no one about us.'

'I promise to be mute,' reported Nagi.

'You have my word, my silence,' promised Muyamba.

'Fair,' said Witanda. 'She is female, yet she communes
with our kind. She nurtures our cause in her bosom; because
of her good she shall forever tread on our flanks. Muyamba,
I decree that you bring her when you come to inform us of
the readiness of the army and the ship. You are an
honourable man, Muyamba, and I trust I can trust you.'

'Indeed,' Muyamba said unhappily.

'I'm grateful, just king,' Nagi reported, beaming.

A dirge was sang for Zowdor and Damoya, and Titiadi
and his archers. It said Zowdor was an eagle and Zomo
Nanna was a fly and Damoya was a nightingale and Tsambo
was a worm and Titiadi was the king of bees and Yomyo
was a seaweed and Titiadi's archers were a royal swum of
bees and the Zomo Warriors were two lean carrots.

Yiddi the sailor who came to rule a kingdom lay on a
semi-canoe. His back became Muyamba's bed and
Muyamba's back became Nagi's bed. Yiddi's hand held on
to a paddle and with this paddle he rowed. Muyamba held
another paddle and paddled on the flank of the canoe where
Yiddi's paddle was not.

Witanda Pirate, he had a stick in his hand and he darted it
through the emptiness of the dark space above, mumbling,
'Soon ... soon ... soon!'

Yiddi deposited the Wambians at a part of the ocean
which wasn't shore, nor was it deep sea. 'Jump off!' he
shook himself and said. Like orphaned kittens, the
Wambians shuffled to shore.

'Ah, terrible task, but who else can shoulder it?' Muyamba
boasted. 'The future dwells on me. The mere thought of it
makes me tremble. Giant obstacles everywhere. I hate

Yomyo and I hate Zomo Nanna, but I hate more the snoopy guards who religiously guard.'

'We have to outwit the guards,' reported Nagi. 'We have to hide the army away from them.'

'Woman, will not your lips ever tire?' scolded Muyamba.

'I tell you, Nier Muyamba, I've been pondering the thing the whole length of our return and the only perfect veil is Yomyo.'

'Yomyo?'

'If we can buy his friendship, we can use it to purchase the tyranny. We might fail to use him directly against Zomo Nanna, but we might succeed in using him against himself. By toppling him we shall have fractured Zomo Nanna's spine.'

'A bit witty, but reckless.'

'Reckless is when you followed the prince to Tarada. Reckless is when you undertook to mobilize an army and steal a ship. Witty is smiling at Yomyo, so he panics little when he sees you at conference with a mob.'

'Bamaut Nagi, you are a wise woman.'

'My gratitude, loyal chief of Wambi.'

'I accept you into my court. Let's ponder into the future. What shall be our first move?'

'Deama's son was named last week. He is a skinny, innocent creature. I say we take him to Yomyo at daybreak tomorrow and announce that we have named the baby after him. Our goal will be to see what sort of a man Yomyo is. Whether he is gullible or complicated?'

'What if Deama refuses to help us?'

'For this and every other craft of ours, our excuse shall be that Yomyo has sworn to kill all Wambi, if any dishonour him.'

'Incredible, let's go to Deama immediately.'

It was a tiptoe up a protrusion; a sneak along a fence; a race through a field, a settlement , a compound; and Deama's house came into view. Nagi and Muyamba produced themselves before the door of that house, rapping it, shaking it.

'Who's there?' Deama's voice inquired.

'Muyamba,' reported Nagi.

Deama unlocked the door and let the duo in.

'Has the evil ravaged your homes?' he asked them.

Their answer was a nay and two idle smiles, to which he bellowed, 'What recklessness!'

'Recklessness is your mute opposition to Amadi Yomyo,' reported Nagi. 'Recklessness is that bitter glint in your eye when you see a man of Yomyo. Deama, death frowns at you …'

'From where?' Deama jumped.

'Yomyo has sworn by his mother's decay to devour any Wambian who does him no honour, and while he spoke he pointed at your door. Your aunt and I are friends; for this reason, I called Muyamba to help you.'

Deama held Muyamba's hand. 'Help me, Nier Muyamba?' he pled.

'I will, young man,' promised Muyamba. 'However, the only perfect help for you will come from you.'

'From me?'

'Yes. What did you name your son?'

'Boriki.'

'Noisy name!'

'Noisy?'

'Scandalous sound!'

'Scandalous?'

'Dangerous deal!'

'Dan …'

'Keeping the name among your clansmen is the sole remedy.'

'I will do it.'

'And—marching to Yomyo at daybreak and telling him in sober terms that you named your son, whom you'll carry with you, after him.'

'I will do this, very early tomorrow. The charging midget of today: was he Yomyo's doing?'

'Nay, yes, yes. Nagi, why did we not think this?' Muyamba scratched his head.

'Think …' Nagi wondered.

'The demon of today … Yomyo …' hinted Muyamba.

'Ah, awesome,' reported Nagi. 'Deama, you drew our attention to an imminent matter. After the dedication of the baby, the whole procession shall bow to Yomyo and ask him to spare us from the wrath of the demonic midget of today.' Nagi winked neatly at Muyamba, who slyly winked back.

'Deama,' Muyamba spoke, 'this now, Wambi is free of the midget. Go to a score of your clansmen. Tell them exactly as has transpired here and bring them to sleep over; tomorrow, they shall march with us to Yomyo.'

Deama said, 'I am three.' He said to his wife, 'You are four.' He said to tired fellow, who in his house resided, 'Thou art fifth.' He swung an outside door open, dashed out, and shot his way straight to a faraway compound of many. Here, he counted a dozen and five people, whom he convinced to follow him to his home.

'It is set,' told he to Muyamba and Nagi. 'We are a score and two, the baby uncounted.'

'Wait, people,' reported Nagi, 'for the gluttonous voice of the early cock.'

A doze did many, but a doze did not Deama, nor Deama's wife, nor Muyamba, nor Nagi, nor the old man who peered out of the window. Lackadaisically, the early cock crowed.

Deama bundled his baby from sleep. 'To Yomyo's!' he announced and hopped out of his abode. The score and one Wambians in his hall hopped out after him. The procession murmured one half of a dirge and went to Yomyo's residence. The palace gate was opaquely shut.

'King Yomyo, we are come to your feet,' reported Nagi.

Yomyo was there in the palace compound with sleepy eyes, looking out for the ghostly midget who had earlier caused him to flee.

'Is that the midget and his cohorts?' Yomyo asked a man of his.

'I cannot tell?' returned the man.

'You can,' quarreled Yomyo, 'if you go to the lookout and elongate your neck.'

'But the midget, governor?'

'Don't be silly. That midget comes in my name. What shall he call you if he sees your face? Moreover, he's short and seldom looks up. The ground is his domain.'

'Whew!' Yomyo's man exhaled and strode to the ladder that led to the lookout—Nagi's voice was yet yelling. He timidly climbed the ladder and entered the lookout. He spied on the Wambians and quickly returned to Yomyo.

'It's a score Wambians,' he reported, panting.

'Are they with the midget,' asked Yomyo.

'Nay, they're with a baby.'

'Baby?'

'A bony baby.'

'Does he look like the bone of the midget?'

'No.'

'Are they armed?'

'No.'

'Are they muscular?'

'No.'

'Ghomoo, friend of my youth, my oasis in dusty deserts, go behind the gate and introduce yourself as Yomyo. Ask them what they seek here at this hour?'

'I ask to go with two men, governor?' the man called Ghomoo requested.

'You may,' Yomyo replied.

Yomyo's man called two guards and with a face that wasn't Yomyo's went behind the gate, demanding in a mumbling voice: 'What do you want from me?'

'King Yomyo, your demon's wrath,' cried Nagi.

'We beg you; spare our lives,' cried Deama.

'Please call back your dwarf, lest he ravage us with his bone?' pled Muyamba.

'Forgive us, good king,' more than ten Wambian voices begged.

Yomyo had heard it all and he whistled so that Ghomoo made an eye contact with him. He beckoned Ghomoo to come. Ghomoo came.

'Go to the lookout,' Yomyo told Ghomoo. 'Go keep an eye on the Wambians: I'm going behind the gate. Any funny thing, don't hesitate to alert me.'

'At your service, governor,' Ghomoo saluted and marched to the ladder that led to the lookout. He climbed up into the lookout.

Yomyo's chest was bulging arrogantly when he walked to the gate. 'Wambi,' spoke he, meanly, 'the plagues I have planned against you are fatal.'

'Be merciful, good king,' cried Deama. 'You are justified in your wrath, but spare this baby. We named him after you, hoping you shall not harm your own.'

'He is dedicated to your fame, my king,' reported Nagi.

Yomyo laughed formally. 'A baby to glorify me?' he said, yet laughing.

'He is yours,' Muyamba told.

'Haughty voice,' Yomyo laughed on, 'today you've come to my feet, wailing for your life.'

'Clemency, great king,' pled Muyamba.

'Listen, people,' Yomyo spoke sternly, 'this is the anger of a king whose subjects have not paid allegiance. Rebellion makes a murderer of a ruler. You have repented, so I spare your lives. Depart from here, lest the appetite of my midget be whet.'

'He wants us away!' reported Nagi.

'Thank you, good king,' said Deama.

'We're grateful, wise king,' said Muyamba.

All of the Wambians expressed their gratitude, save Deama's son. Deama hopped off and his company followed. Away, they went.

Yomyo laughed and scurried to a place where he could see Ghomoo. 'How far are they?' he asked Ghomoo.

'Fifty and five cowardly steps away,' answered Ghomoo.

Yomyo laughed so much.

CHAPTER II

At the shoulder of a garden which could not see the house that housed Yomyo, Muyamba and Nagi slowed their steps, and onto them came the gift of privacy.

'He is such a gullible moron,' married Muyamba.

'He gives mirth at flattery,' reported Nagi.

'What now?'

'Now, we curse him with his lust. Now, we seduce him into the lustre snare that shall be his end.'

'I've seen him. He'll fall for this, but how does that help us steal a ship?'

'Your influence is in his ways: whose craving you satisfy.'

'What of his cravings shall we satisfy today?'

'Manabi, his wives, his sons, his illness is his curse, his downfall. The old man isn't dead and buried, yet they war for his wealth. Today, we shall take the case up to Yomyo. We shall make him pass judgment on that ailing polygamy.'

'He'll feel like a revered king.'

'The more flattered he is, the less danger we have.'

That day, Manabi's case was taken up to Yomyo, who judged that nothing of the old man shall be shared before his death. In the days that followed, Nagi and Muyamba occupied Yomyo with cases: those of polygamous homes, those of theft, those of assault, and those of many bad that deserved punishment.

Grace and glory are advantages enjoyed by men who have the attention of the mob. This attention Yomyo gained. The praise of the mob, it shall daze thee. O, it dazed Yomyo.

Meanwhile, Muyamba had made a covenant with two-hundred lads. He had told them that Witanda was a kindred of Zowdor, and the bone and wreath which he had, the day he raced through Wambi, were a disguise, that Witanda was sent to deliver a message of revenge, that Witanda said a war was due in few months, that two-hundred warriors were to be sent to Lembe to bath of waters that made men invincible, that this Wambian two-hundred would join another two-hundred who are already invincible, and together the lot would come to destroy the tyranny. Two-hundred Wambian lads were they, who swore to keep the stratagem a secret, and do whatever it took to master the skill of archery.

These two-hundred trained, and hunting was their veil. Every dawn on a third day, Muyamba would lead an eighth of them on a hunting expedition. They would shoot at birds and beasts. Half the game was taken to Yomyo; the other half, they shared with Muyamba.

Nagi assembled all women who had witnessed beyond thirty harvests, but below fifty harvests, and had fought under the command of Titiadi in her biggest chamber.

'The glory of Titiadi shines about you,' she reported to them.

They either beamed or nodded.

'The archers that shall rescue Taila are coming from the south. They hail from Lembe. Their chorus is the screams of their dying foes. The tyranny shall not subdue them,' reported Nagi.

Her audience either pounded their fists or stamped their feet.

'The palace has been allocated to us. When the secret council met, we were singled out as the most competent unit. Our business is to build an arsenal of toxic arrows. Our duty is to shoot down the palace and its dwellers. Our obligation is to withhold the stratagem from every Wambian outside this unit.'

The place became silent and dull.

'Who of you wishes to be let aloof? Show me your face? Do it specially?'

No face was specially shown to Nagi.

'I consider us a union then,' spoke Nagi. 'From today, whenever you are idle, go to the bushes. Make arrows. Intoxicate them. Bring them here for preservation. Don't get caught. Soon, the secret council shall send us word. Soon, we shall overthrow the tyrant. And remember, if this stratagem gets uncovered, Wambi shall be doomed. They chose you because they trust you to keep a secret.'

Nagi reported that the meeting was over, so the assembly dispersed.

Below the mornings, Nagi roamed the meetings of Wambian women, listening for rumours, rumours of the planned attack on the palace. When no rumour was said, she would go her way, speaking, 'Not public yet.'

Below the noons, Nagi's union of archers would converge at her compound with venomous arrows they had produced. Nagi would stack the arrows in her barn and cover them with rags and hay. Within days they got enough arrows and were set for the offensive on the palace. Nagi made them mold two bows each, which bows she stored in her barn toward the attack.

Harvest time. The stone palace sits under a sunny day. It has Amadi Yomyo in its belly. Eight Wambian women are before him, swaying gracefully. To their side is a sculptor, sculpturing a large form, a whale with a shark's head. On the back of this form the letters Z.N. are engraved. From far away, Yomyo's guards and executioners look on.

Muyamba strode in, his hands behind him. He walked to Yomyo and submissively said, 'Great king, I am come to the feet of your throne. I am come with a being propelled by allegiance. Say you're occupied and vanish I will; but, permit me to linger and I will to your feet come and worship you.'

'Muyamba,' Yomyo smiled, 'your life was loaned to death's angels but I have bought it back. I am giver of life. The west pulsates in my palms. I am commander of the east, the morrow and the now of Taila.'

'You deserve to be,' said Muyamba, his voice sympathetic, 'but shall they let you?'

Yomyo stared at Muyamba. Yomyo was wearing a slight frown.

Says Muyamba sympathetically, 'I didn't mean to offend you, my king, but tomorrow's diadem shall not peacefully come to you. His son was kept in Nuamba, where there is much more hiding-hollows than an assailant can search, where a ruler attains a reputation for having an agile eye. Azumba is where the next king shall be nurtured and so a son of his was kept there. You left your land to fight for his. You will die for him and he is aware, yet where did he put you? Wambi, because here Azumba is hated, because here the battle is staged, because here the goddess queen of Nambo who bears a grudge against Azumba shall come to put her plague. Do you remember the first day of your appointment? He said it. He said his son shall rule in Azumba and learn the ways of kings, for when the mantle passes it shall pass to him. Where shall you be, great yomyo?'

Yomyo's eyes reddened. 'Cheats!' he fumed. 'Lice. Ticks. Hypocrites. Parasites.'

Ghomoo came to the scene. 'Are you well, governor?' asked he.

'Ghomoo,' Yomyo was still fuming, 'gaze yonder. That is the fruit of love and allegiance. The whale represents his might; the shark represents his prowess. His enemy, I have called mine. His fight, I have fought and conquered. In his exile, he was an encroachment on my resources, and did I chase him?'

'No,' answered Ghomoo and Muyamba.

'I vacated my piece of Yadoma. I deserted my family. I took my gang with me. We fought for him, for his glory. We died for him, for his glory. I conned the sovereign, then he became king. Yearly, I chase away the goddess queen from Nambo. When the pirate's ship stops at Nuamba, it is I who goes to secure the island. Yet he plots against me, against what I have by bravery and hardwork earned.'

'Shall there be rebellion, governor?' asked Ghomoo.

'Assuredly,' returned Yomyo.

Says Ghomoo, 'I shall, without delay, summon the second and third divisions from the west. I shall summon the fourth, fifth and sixth divisions from the east. I shall decree the confinement of every one of his men who's in our territory and make a seizure of all five islands.'

'You are severely outnumbered,' Muyamba told Ghomoo.

'Very true,' Yomyo agreed with Muyamba.

Says Ghomoo: 'We'll do it next week, at the anniversary of his enthronement.'

'I despise it!' fumed Yomyo, spitting twice. 'My presence will glorify him. He and I, we're done. The next time he sees me, his blood will be oiling my blades.'

'Not promising,' advised Muyamba.

Yomyo and Ghomoo turned attentively to the Wambian, who seemed to know a more cautious plot.

'What day of next week is the anniversary?' asked Muyamba.

'On the sea lady's day, at night. A week before the correct date, lest the vengeful pirate catches him in an alcoholic fit.

O, that greedy king, he has the heart of a wench!' Yomyo spat.

There were a bunch of Zomo Warriors far apart and these, noticing Yomyo was furious, stared attentively at him.

'Out!' he ordered them; they haughtily vacated.

'Attend, my king,' Muyamba told Yomyo. 'Attend the anniversary. Zomo Nanna must not know your bitter heart.'

'I will throw up if I see him again,' Yomyo said.

'Don't, my king,' advised Muyamba. 'Whoever outnumbers his rival shall reign over the morrow of Taila. What you need is the friendship and loyalty of Taila, excepting Azumba. I should have helped you, but death calls to me. My years are used up. Nonetheless, for the sake of Taila I shall do you a favour before I retire. The people will listen to you if I go by your side. They will serve you if a man from my lineage crowns your head. When you return from the anniversary I shall lead you around, to the royals of Taila, and to the sons of the past custodians. Tailans are mute because for the past thirteen years, a war has not haunted them. That is their loyalty to Zomo Nanna. We simply have to make them see that you are the peace, the victory, the conquerer.'

'We shall give you back your position,' promised Ghomoo, 'if you assist us.'

'We shall,' vowed Yomyo.

'I am honoured,' said Muyamba. 'Zowdor was an outlaw from afar, but we made him king. Yiddi and Damoya were Lembeans, but we made them rule Taila. You know why, my king?'

'Why?'

'They were fearless as you. They left their homes and battled on foreign lands.'

Yomyo and Ghomoo beamed.

Later that day, at Muyamba's, Nagi was present as Muyamba.

'Flatterer, your target is dull and talentless,' Nagi said of Yomyo.

'Today, I drew the snare up to his torso,' told Muyamba.

'Tell the details as fully as has happened?'

'Today, I've sown and reared the seed of enmity. I enriched the seed with jealousy, envy, greed and many evils that great rivalries hinge on.'

'Go deeper?'

'I made that gullible moron see that the mantle stands far from him and when it is relayed, it shall be relayed to a son of Zomo. Presently, he and Zomo Nanna share no friendship. The moment is here Nagi: the day of the sea lady.'

'What with her?'

'When the moon dies on her day, Zomo Nanna shall celebrate his dozen and one anniversary. Yomyo is to attend —'

'And then?'

'And then, we steal a ship and send it with two-hundred archers to Lembe. The king will be captain and the prince will be … captain.'

'A ship is not a barrel of beer; you cannot roll and toss it from that far north to that far south. If it motions awhile you're caught.'

'So, what, can I do?'

'Flattery killed their friendship. Same will thieve their ship.'

'Flattery?' Muyamba groomed his beard.

'Spiced with jealousy and envy.'

'Hmmm!'

'Vision the ships that dock at Nuamba.'

'Aha!'

'Vision the symbol on their sails.'

'Aha!'

'It is a vulture.'

'Yep.'

'Which very vulture is represented on the ships and canoes of eastern, western and northern Nuamba.'

'Correctly ...'

'That is the symbol of the Nanna's son. They call him the scavenger, the mortality of men. Our story to Yomyo shall be that here in Taila, the might and wealth of rulers are displayed on the sails, that when your sails are blank, men respect and fear you less, that the merchants, when they pass, record the wealth of kings by the width of their harbours. So he, Yomyo, is badly underrated. We have a ship if he falls for this.'

'Genius is your name, Bamaut Nagi. I know an evil that will ignite fierce envy in him.'

'Tell it to the faintest detail?'

'We have to draw a vulture's head on two white flags and hung them in the north and south. We shall tell Yomyo the vulture has pelted his head and stolen his glory, that only a display of his wealth can win him back his fame.'

'Perfect, Muyamba. That makes this stratagem as dual as the earlier one.'

'Earlier one? Dual?'

'O sorry, triple. Makes three of them.'

'When shall we hung the flags?'

'Tomorrow, at night. We shall get youthful maids to distract the guards while we hung the flags.'

'Sealed.'

Another day was born. Before the night of this day, muyamba and Nagi mobilized two white flags with a vulture's head drawn on them, two gourds of thick starch, six fair maids, six gourds of strong spirit, and six large fishes that were spiced and grilled. The six maids had a gourd of spirit and a large fish each; and Muyamba and Nagi had a flag and a gourd of starch each.

North went Nagi and three maids. South went Muyamba and three maids. Nagi's three maids strode seductively into the camp of the northern guards. One maid broke down in tears. A guard gave her a shoulder to cry on.

'What troubles you, fair one?' this guard asked.

'Today my younger sister got married,' answered she, sobbing harder. 'My father thinks I am burdensome. Who shall marry me?'

'I!' every guard about declared.

She smiled. She and her friends gave the guards their spirits and fishes. The guards ate the fishes and made a festival of the spirits.

Onlooking was Nagi, who was creeping through faraway flora. Behind the flora was the shore, and on the shore were canoes, after which were ships. Nagi splashed the first canoe she met with starch and pasted her flag. Her return was brisk and when she passed the vicinity of the northern guards, she threw a stone behind her which made some leaves squeak. Her maids heard.

'Could that be danger?' they asked the guards.

'You needn't worry,' assured a guard. 'I'll go patrol there.'

'I'm leaving right away,' said one maid, rising and running off.

'We're leaving too,' said the other two, rising and trailing their friend.

'We shall secure you,' promised one guard, moving nine steps after them.

'They'll return,' the guards assured themselves.

Muyamba's maids strode seductively into the vicinity of the southern guards.

'He hates me!' one of them broke down in tears.

'Be comforted by me,' said a guard who went to this maid. 'Who hates you.'

'My uncle,' responded the maid. 'He yelled at me. Then he sent me away.'

'At this hour?'

'He hates me.'

'You're right.'

'Shall I bide here with you?'

'You should.'

'Shall we?' the two other maids asked the other guards.

'For your own good,' answered the guards.

The maids gave their spirits and fishes to the guards. These guards swallowed and chewed the fishes, and sipped all the spirits.

Observing closely was Muyamba, who was maneuvering through distant flora. Old Muyamba went pass a shoreline, stopped by a canoe, spilled some starch on this canoe and pasted his white flag. On his return, when he had bypassed the guards, he threw a stone into some leaves, which briefly squeaked.

'What was that?' the maids asked the guards.

'It isn't something to make you worry,' assured the guards.

'But we're scared,' complained the maids.

'I'll go check it,' said a guard.

'I'm leaving,' said one maid, getting up and running off.

'We're leaving,' said the other two, following her.

'Hey, come back!' a guard called.

'They have nowhere to go,' the guards assured themselves.

The morn that followed. At Yomyo's court. The governor was wandering about in his sleeping gear when Muyamba and Nagi entered the palace.

'We bow to you, kind king,' they bowed and said.

'Greetings, noble subjects,' responded Yomyo.

They went to flank Yomyo and wandered about with him.

'The northern vulture has pelted your head,' reported Nagi.

Yomyo felt his head with his thumbs. 'I can't find it,' he told.

'Your head is your glory,' Muyamba spoke. 'The vulture is your rival.'

'Am I threatened by a rival?' queried Yomyo.

'Great kings mark their territory,' reported Nagi. 'They put their symbols as far as their dominion reaches. Here in Taila, the king puts his symbol on the sails of his ships. This shows his wealth. This shows his might.'

Yomyo nodded upwards. A question yet resided on his face.

'My king,' Muyamba spoke to him, 'your rival is at the neck of your fame.'

'Does this rival have a name?' asked Yomyo, bitter.

'Some call him the scavenger. Some say he is the mortality. Some say he is for ever.' Muyamba told.

'Who's he?' fumed Yomyo.

'He owns Nuamba,' reported Nagi.

'Kranpa!' Yomyo mentioned.

'Yes, that's the rogue,' Nagi furiously reported. 'He put his symbol in your territory. He stuck the vulture's head on your possessions. There were flags in both the north and the south. We burnt and tossed them into the ocean.'

'Ghomoo!' Yomyo called.

'Governor!' Ghomoo responded from an inner chamber.

'Come hastily!' Yomyo ordered.

Ghomoo came.

'We are threatened,' Yomyo told Ghomoo.

'By what?' Ghomoo asked.

'Tell him,' Yomyo said to Nagi and Muyamba.

'Kranpa has disrespected our king,' reported Nagi. 'He has put his vulture symbols in Wambi. We set the flags aflame, but not all. There were two flags – one in the north, one in the south – that we could not burn, for they were tightly stuck to canoes.'

'It happened this morning,' added Muyamba. 'I had gone hunting with the lads when we saw several flags rising in the north and south. At first we thought the flags were pirate flags but once we neared them we saw the symbol of Kranpa. If the vulture symbols engulf Taila, Kranpa would be the most powerful ruler about.'

'Death to him!' yelled Ghomoo. 'Shall we rebel, governor?'

'We shall,' Yomyo said.

'Yet peacefully,' advised Muyamba.

'I say we go to put our own symbols,' reported Nagi.

'What is our symbol?' Muyamba asked.

'We have to think of one,' answered Ghomoo.

'A very rugged rock,' proposed Yomyo.

'What about lion paws?' Nagi put to the men.

'More fearsome,' Yomyo admitted.

'Very fearsome,' Ghomoo clapped.

'We shall put our symbol on the mighty sails of ships and plant it north, west and south,' declared Muyamba.

'East too!' declared Ghomoo.

'It's not safe in the east,' said Muyamba.

'Why?' asked Ghomoo.

'Because Zomo Nanna's hypocritic friendship with our king is to our advantage. We should let it linger until our lord becomes king.'

'When shall we be brave enough to hoist our symbols?' asked Nagi.

'Today! Now!' declared Yomyo.

'Yomyo is fearless!' declared Ghomoo.

Amadi Yomyo: one who once wept for the corpse of a dirty bird; this morn, he called thirty of his men to conference, the all of them Yadomans.

'Each of you, make a flag,' he commanded them, 'and draw in it our emblem, the paw of a lion. The cloth should be white, and the symbol, red.'

'We shall, governor,' his men stated.

Yomyo's men made the flags, a yard long, half a yard wide. They used red clay to draw lion paws in the center of the flags. Ten flags were erected in northern Wambi, and the flag with a vultures head, which leaned on the flank of a canoe, was destroyed. Another ten were sent with a ship captained by Ghomoo to Western Wambi. Yomyo captained a ship and took it with ten flags to southern Wambi. On the sail of the ship that was sent west, a lion paw was gigantically impressed. After removing the flag with a vulture's head from the canoe on which it was, Yomyo smiled on the south coast and ordered that a lion paw be drawn on every sail about, which thing was done, so that he smiled some more. By sunset, all the sails of ships and canoes on the south, west and north of Wambi bore Yomyo's emblem. A grin was Yomyo's last deed before he slept.

Muyamba met with a dozen of his best archers.

'Sharpen your gauge,' he spoke. 'We shall depart on the sea lady's day, on which day Amadi Yomyo shall go to Azumba to celebrate Zomo Nanna's anniversary. You shall go ahead of the other archers. You shall remove the southern guards from their station, a noiseless removal.'

'Hail the Stratagem!' the archers softly celebrated.

'Tell it to the others,' Muyamba told them. 'We shall meet no more. Prepare yourselves. I also prepare myself. I shall alert you with a gong, when our moment is ripe.'

Chanting songs of war, the assembly parted.

'Wambi shall be snobbish anew,' reported Nagi to her archers, who had stuffed themselves in her biggest chamber. 'On the day of the sea lady, Yomyo shall go to meet Zomo Nanna; that's our period. Before the clash, we shall shift all of Wambi to the south coast so that the tyrant's men shall have no hostages. These last few days are Yomyo's funeral: let's honour him with flattery.'

'Death to Yomyo!' Nagi's archers married and parted with her.

The days did their work, maturing laboriously into nights, so that the aged nights died away and new days were born. So, one day, the sea lady's day was born and when Yomyo's departure time was come, there was a crowd about him. Ghomoo stood ahead of Yomyo. Muyamba and Nagi flanked the governor. These four were partially encircled by a lot of Yomyo's men. Women trailed the procession, Wambian women, Nagi's archers.

The women sang a song; so tenderly they sang. They sang Yomyo is a metal; and the coward and his crown are wood. Lightning dived below and a fire was loose upon the land. Victor was the metal. Slime was the wood. This song lingered from the palace to the east coast of Wambi, where Muyamba asked the question: 'Who led the offensive that chased off the pirate of Nuamba?'

And the women responded, 'King Yomyo!'

And Muyamba asked, 'Whose prowess was it that delivered Taila from the metal jaw of Nambo's goddess?'

The women responded, 'King Yomyo!'

'King Yomyo!' Ghomoo loudly echoed. 'Governor, speak, the mob cries your name.'

Yomyo smiled. He faced the women, stating, 'I salute you, loyal subjects. I am the morrow and you are my mob. Now, I part awhile to view our competitor in the eye. Merry in your dwellings, hailing our morrow.'

'Hail King Yomyo!' the women bellowed.

'Muyamba,' Yomyo called, 'oversee my borders. Prevent them from mutiny and rivalry.'

'I shall, mighty Yomyo,' vowed Muyamba.

Yomyo spread his arms over everyone about him. 'My love is my valediction,' said he. 'While I'm gone be safe.'

Ghomoo tooted a horn and Yomyo in the escort of eleven guards went to settle in his ceremonial canoe. The canoe's crew set it in motion. Yomyo's journey was reality.

A song sang the Wambian women. They sang that Yomyo is a cat and the coward is a rat. And Yomyo is at the tail of the rat. That Yomyo's paws shall soon tear the coward's throat; and as they sang, Muyamba struck a noisy gong continuously with his rod.

These guards were southerners, for they guarded Wambi's south coast. A gong sound rapidly echoed into their camp, and about it they said, 'It bids the governor farewell.'

Twelve archers had come hunting, archers of Muyamba. They knelt in a uniform line and the bachelor in their midst softly signaled, 'Lone! Two! Hit!'

They fell, Yomyo's southerners fell.

On the coast east of Wambi, Muyamba called Nagi aside.

'We're set for the going aspect of the stratagem,' said he. 'Come with me to Tarada, to bid the monarchs farewell.'

'My word shall go with you,' reported Nagi. 'Tell the monarchs that as they charge here, I shall charge there, and where we merge victory shall come.'

'But they will be headed south, there?'

'I am aware. It is simply a thing of the diplomacy, assuring rulers of the allegiance of their subjects.'

'But the little monarch really wanted to catch a last glimpse of you.'

'Tell him it's in the interest of the stratagem that I oversee Wambi while you're with them.'

'Very well.'

Muyamba went to the near assembly of Yomyo's men and Nagi's archers. 'I temporarily excuse myself,' he said to them. 'My joints are as exhausted as they are aged. I go to soothe them of the toil of today.'

'Go well,' the assembly said to him.

In the vicinity of the assembly's eyes, Muyamba hurriedly walked, and when he had left their patronage, he did a race, between grass, wood and tombstones, onto a shore that looked across a lagoon, at which place dwelled wrinkled canoes, one of which he got hold of and went upon the waters beyond the shoreline.

Nagi had walked her archers away from Yomyo's men and she reported to them: 'Our first task is to evacuate the people from the settlements. The rumour that we shall spread is that the raid that shall demolish Wambi comes by the north. That the escape rests in the south, on the coast.'

Her archers nodded and went with her to the settlements.

He was faraway with his sailing. Muyamba was. He spotted two attentive shadows, and knowing who they were waved and bowed at them. They also waved and bowed. Paddling and spying about, Muyamba reached them.

'Don't dock,' ordered Yiddi, the longer shadow. 'No message, curse or stratagem shall cause me to longer stay on Tarada. I shall get into my canoe, then advancing on the waters, we shall commune.'

So Yiddi and Witanda, who was the shorter shadow, crawled to their semi-canoe, overturned it and rocked it forth. Side by side, they and Muyamba advanced.

'Where is the woman?' Witanda asked Muyamba.

'She stayed behind,' answered Muyamba, 'but for the good of the stratagem.'

'That loyal old woman,' Witanda grinned.

'And, my kings, she said as you charge … here, she will charge there, and where she meets you victory shall come.'

'Row quickly,' Witanda said to Yiddi.

'Our current pace is perfect,' Yiddi returned.

'Is there something more to be said?' Witanda asked Muyamba.

'But, for a word of caution, nay,' returned Muyamba.

'What word of caution?' asked Yiddi.

Cautioned Muyamba, 'Don't die.'

'Well noted,' said Witanda. 'Anything else to be said?'

'Nay,' returned Muyamba.

'Then see you on the horizon of our merger, where shall be the victory.'

'Farewell, my lords,' bade Muyamba.

'Farewell,' bade Yiddi and Witanda.

South-east went Yiddi and Witanda. East went Muyamba. Muyamba landed where he had set sail. He climbed protruded soil and walked through a graveyard. PU! A trumpet very briefly cried from inside Wambi. Muyamba quickened his steps. The trumpet very briefly cried again. It took a while. It cried again. It cried half of a battle declaration. Muyamba raced away until the settlements. But for four women carrying carcass, the place would have been desolate.

'What has happened here?' Muyamba inquired from them.

They walked to him with the carcass. 'She's dead,' they reported to him.

Muyamba observed the bloody carcass. Bamaut Nagi was dead.

'Tranquil be thy rest, good daughter of Taila,' spoke he to her carcass. 'Women, how did she die?'

'She shot the Yadoman,' reported one woman.

'And shot the Azumban,' reported one other woman.

'Who both were trying to declare war,' reported another.

'So they speared her in the belly,' reported yet another.

Asks Muyamba, perplexed: 'Why did she shoot at them? Why were they trying to declare war?'

'We were …' started a woman, but was interrupted.

'Top secret!' screamed the woman who interrupted her.

'Speak?' quarreled Muyamba, wearing a dizzy surprise on his face. 'Were the men she attacked men of Yomyo?'

'Mmh!' a woman nodded.

'Where are these men?'

'At the palace,' answered the woman.

'And, you apparently were with her?'

'Yes.'

'And all our people?'

'Nay, they went south.'

'To do what?'

'To secure themselves, so they won't be taken hostage.'

PU! A trumpet briefly cried.

'Is the attack still on?' queried Muyamba.

'Yes. We await two-hundred warriors to strengthen our offensive. The tyrants have also sent three men to Azumba, who should be on the seas by now.'

'You let three men go to Azumba.'

'Their escape was crafty.'

'Wambi is doomed. We have to leave Wambi. We have to go faraway, to a safe hideout. There shall be bloodshed if we stay. Every one of us shall be slaughtered.'

'I say we run to Yadoma,' suggested one woman.

'Yomyo comes from Yadoma,' Muyamba reminded her.

'They say Nambo's queen adores us,' said another. 'Why don't we hide in her land?'

'Yes, Nambo!' echoed the other three women.

'NAMBO!' Muyamba consented. 'Let's go hastily to the south and depart with all Wambi to the waist of the ocean, where a goddess rules.'

Nagi's carcass was rested in her abode. Muyamba and the four who carried the carcass sped south, prancing and panting.

With time, their destination became reality, and they saw Yiddi and Witanda at a debate that happened beside Muyamba's two-hundred archers, who stood behind all Wambi.

'We raid tonight,' decreed Witanda. 'Our archers already are at the throat of the tyrant.'

'That shall bring defeat,' cautioned Yiddi.

'We are skilled and motivated,' spoke Witanda.

'We are vulnerable and outnumbered,' cautioned Yiddi.

Muyamba walked to the debate ground.

'Bamaut Nagi is dead, her archers too,' said he.

'They killed her?' Witanda wept.

'And they are gone to alert Azumba. We have to escape now, all Wambi,' Muyamba specially stated.

'To where?' asked Yiddi.

'To Nambo,' replied Muyamba. 'Nambo's queen is our only friend around. That goddess knows our misery.'

'To Nambo!' decreed Yiddi.

'To Nambo!' decreed Witanda.

'To Nambo!' announced Muyamba.

'To Nambo!' celebrated the Wambians.

All eyes patronized the space that led to Azumba. All hearts panted whenever a breeze came from that space.

The ship of the south was currently docked beside an offshore deck. She could have been manned by eighty oarsmen, yet two-hundred and seventy was the population of them that went for her oars. Three captains went aboard her. The one captain, who was chief, was responsible for her routing. The other, who was king, was responsible for her fitness, and for riding her against tide and storm. The final, who was prince, had a flat drum and by ramming it he controlled the pace of the oarsmen. The ship's anchor was drawn and she was set into motion.

Her journey wasn't a lonely pursuit. She was flanked by rows of canoes carrying Wambian people. Tide by tide, she walked the seas, purposeful as a night burglar.

Gwandae was a place of no tides, and here, where the Wambians floated faraway from Taila, they heard the cry of the trumpets of battle, calling their foes to war.

CHAPTER 12

As much of it as we claim to know, it yet outwits us; it is
where we live, what we live. Tugu Tamanga was the name
that became legend, the legend of the shrouded goddess of
Nambo. She emerged upon the tides while Sajruna and
Sasanja where up against each other. Her eyes were crimson.
Her skin was bloodstained. She wore a raffia basket about
her head, and all who beheld her were petrified.

'Disarm!' she thundered.

Sajruna and Sasanja stood peacefully asunder; no
tribesman of any of the two tribes held on to a weapon.

'What transpired afore?' demanded the goddess of the sea.

'They started,' quarreled the chief of Sasanja.

'No, they started,' quarreled the chief of Sajruna.

'Admit it? It was your aimless subjects that crossed into
the waters of Sasanja.'

'The bridge, the divisional rock, the waters about the two,
those are ours, Sajruna's.'

'Pirate, wretched pirate,' cursed the chief of Sasanja.

'Warmonger,' cursed the chief of Sajruna.

'You sons of servitude, shall you now claim Nambo as an
inheritance?'

'Wizard. May the goddess demolish you with lightning!'

Says the goddess of the sea: 'The waters are mine and the
fields therein. Nambo is mine and my peace shall dwell here.
Commander of there, what do they call you?'

Says the chief of Sasanja: 'They call me Abhe; I am chief of
Sasanja.'

'Come,' Tugu called him, which he did before she spoke: 'Glory of Sasanja, you shall be my legs, my foundation, my grip. Walk over to Sajruna.'

Smiling and flexing a linear muscle, Abhe walked to the Sajrunans and stood before their chief, whose head shamefully bowed.

Says the goddess of the sea: 'Commander of those, what do they call you?'

'Calata,' returned the chief of Sajruna, cheerfully. 'I am chief of Sajruna.'

'Walk to me,' said Tamanga, which order Calata obeyed before the goddess spoke: 'Beauty of Sajruna, you shall be my hands, my confidence, my strength. Go to Sasanja.'

Smiling, Calata looked only where his eyes would meet with Abhe's. he walked majestically and stood before Sasanja.

Spoke the mighty goddess: 'Look, you all, upon the sun. Graceful lamp of above, so shall be the glory of this new Nambo. I, Tugu Tamanga, am queen of here. This coast where I have decreed this peace shall carry my fortress: it shall veil the face of Nambo's craft. Abhe, you are chief of Sajruna. Calata, you are chief of Sasanja. I have decreed.'

'Long live the goddess queen!' celebrated the Namboans, save Abhe and Calata, who were busy throwing devilish glances at each other.

Tugu gave them a mean look.

'Hail the queen of Nambo!' yelled Abhe, terrified.

'Hail the queen!' announced Calata, breathing hard.

Thirteen years on, there came a mob and a teenager with a white cloth that swung about a brownish rod. Trumpet sounds sailed behind them, yet they hadn't a trumpet. They sailed swiftly, as though they were some desperate prey, and landed on the coast where Tugu had afore landed.

A fortress sat on the coast. It had two magnificent gates that rigidly rested at the chest of the front wall. On the front roof of this fortress were forty-three spies, two chiefs and the goddess queen of there. The spies spied from behind the pillars of the front roof and were partially visible to the teenager and his mob. The chiefs were stationed four yards away from the pillars. The goddess queen, her nails unkempt, sat on a dusty rock.

'We are come to you with hearts bereft of war!' the teenager noisily announced.

'Ask him why he is come,' Tugu told the chiefs.

Asks Abhe, showing himself to the teenager: 'Why are you come?'

'But, I am a Zowdor,' explained the teenager, 'and those are my subjects.'

'Tell him to repeat his name,' ordered Tugu, her eyes suddenly widening.

'What did you say you are?' Abhe put to the teenager.

'I said, and I am glad you care to know a second time, that I am the Zowdor Nemoso, king of all Taila.'

'Is that a claim of the infant about whom you afore spoke?' Tugu queried from a spy.

The spy nodded.

Tugu Tamanga. That goddess queen, she leaped to her feet and gyrated to a pillar, where the teenager came into view. She was severely angered by the sight of him, so that she quarreled in a demonic tone of voice: 'That is no Zowdor!'

The teenager's body trembled. His swinging cloth and its rod fell and he tumbled backwards. His eyes became shut and his body had no motion.

An elderly man walked two steps and mourned, 'O Witanda!'

The queen looked at the elderly man. Wide-eyed, she gulped as if she had spotted a long lost acquaintance who owed her some treasure. Her eyes became wet. 'Get me a ladder,' she said, in a tone of religious sympathy.

Abhe and Calata fetched her a ladder that lay not faraway.

'Suspend it about the pillar,' she ordered.

It was done, and she got onto the ladder; meanwhile, the elderly man who walked two steps and several others were assembled around the unconscious teenager, trying to revive him.

'It's risky. You can't go down there?' Abhe and Calata said to the queen.

She gave them a mean look and ordered, 'Everyone, depart from this roof. Go summon all the archers and swordsmen at the town square. Tell them to prepare for battle. Go!'

She was obeyed.

She would descend and the people surrounding the teenager would drag him away. She would and they would, so she removed the raffia basket that shrouded her head.

That aspect of the mob that was at least twenty-three years young beamed; all Wambi bowed, after a rumour had loitered around. The goddess queen wore her mask again.

'Long live Queen Damoya!' jubilated the Wambians.

She shed tears, and she smiled, and she went down the ladder, and she went to the teenager. She embraced the elderly man who had walked two steps, yet they spoke not a word to each other. She asked for water, which was brought in a gourd; and with it, and the assistance of several others, revived the unconscious teenager.

Trembling, the teenager pulled away from her and buried his face in the bosom of the elderly man who had walked.

'How ignorant I have been: forgive me Zowdor?' spoke the queen.

'Is she talking to me?' the teenager asked the elderly man.

'She is,' replied the elderly man.

'I've been haughty and dishonest; please spare me?' pled the teenager. 'I am Witanda Nemoso, prince of Taila, son of the Zowdor Nemoso.'

'You indeed are the Zowdor, the remnant of him,' the queen kissed the teenager's nape and said.

'I am?' the teenager turned and beamed.

'Yes, you are,' returned the queen.

Witanda touched the queen's hand. 'They say you came from the sea,' he told her.

'I came from Lembe, from murdering a famous brute, from ruling a kingdom, from marrying the king, from making you his son, from escaping from the teeth of rebellious dying and evil. Then to this oceanic juncture where stood no peace, nor a morrow. The escape was pretence, so I posed as a fearsome goddess of the seas. I am mortal and hungry, and that is a secret I would like you to keep.'

'Yiddi, could be the Damoya!' Witanda announced to the elderly man.

''Tis her,' answered Yiddi, he and Damoya smiling at each other.

Queen Damoya got to her feet. She listened about. 'Those trumpet sounds: who blows them?' asked she.

'Our pursuers,' answered Muyamba from her far side, bowing to her.

'Pursuers from where?' she asked, saluting him.

'Azumba,' said Muyamba.

'Muyamba, today we avenge our dead,' said she.

'Death to the tyranny!' Muyamba bellowed.

'Death to the tyranny!' all Wambi bellowed.

'To the town square!' announced the queen, taking Witanda's hand and speeding off.

Yiddi and the Wambians went after her. She bypassed the magnificent gates of the fortress and travelled the whole length of the wall left of the gates. She did a right turn and travelled the entire length of Nambo's left wall. At the rear of Nambo, she did another right turn and led her son, her father and all Wambi to a narrow gate made of bronze. She clapped. A heavy sound happened behind the gate before it swung open; and it had archers guarding it from inside, the all of them standing in a shooting posture. Nambo's queen led her son, her father, and her Wambian subjects through the gate, through the midst of the archers and to the town square, where dwelled countless archers and two chiefs with war trumpets.

'Nambo,' spoke the queen, 'these are the people of the god of afar, whom we've been trying to rescue for thirteen dim years, and have failed. Today, the great god of afar and his kindred have rescued Wambi, yet the tyrant pursues with heavy hatred. But, death to that tyrant!'

'Death to that tyrant!' all who heard her bellowed.

'Be heavily armed,' spoke the queen. 'We shall go up the front roof of the fortress and cut off the tyrant and his men from there. Abhe and Calata, lead the Namboan offensive. Yiddi, Muyamba, lead the Wambian offensive. Witanda, prince of Wambi, oversee this town square. Make sure all women, infants and elderly folk who are posted here are safe and fed.'

War swore the tyrannical assailant's trumpet, while Wambi, the prey, was creeping up the fortress with her ally to do a defensive build.

This assailant, when he was come onto the shores at Nambo, owned many a man as cruel as he. These men of his, they sniffed at the canoes and the ship that the Wambians had left onshore.

'These are vessels from Taila,' his men reported.

'That alone is why we shall return to Taila carrying the brutalized bodies of many,' spoke Amadi Yomyo, the tyrannical assailant. 'Tear down those gates and shove them out. Be merciless in this dealing.'

Yomyo's men bolted forth. Abhe and Calata ordered their Namboan archers to shoot. Yiddi and Muyamba commanded their Wambian followers to shoot.

Yomyo's men worked at dismantling two gates. Abhe and Calata's men worked at felling the assailant's men. Yiddi and Muyamba's men devoted their arrows to the felling of every man who fought under the command of Amadi Yomyo.

Yomyo's men were totally triumphant. Abhe and Calata's men were almost successful. Yiddi and Muyamba's men were nearly victorious.

Yet Yomyo was the commander who shed a widowed stature of tear, for the gates he dismantled shielded no entrance: behind it was a heavy, insuperable brick wall that would not bawl, no matter how hard it was struck.

'Kill that stubborn wall!' roared Yomyo. 'Strike it harder. Strike it abnormally. Strike it mercilessly. Strike it brutally. You all are useless. I hate you. I hate that wall. I hate that masked sorceress. Hate her, hate her, hate her, hate her Nambo, hate the world, hate every fish that knows the sea, hate every bird that knows to fly. Death to the goddess ...'

SNAP! A venomous arrow darted into Yomyo's throat. Another flew by him. Another flew into his chest. Another flew into his waist. Another flew into his head. One was shot by yiddi; four were shot by others, Namboans maybe, Wambians perhaps, but they shot.

Pitiful were the remnant of the assailant's men, who struck the wall awhile and took flight. Nambo aimed at them. Wambi vengefully targeted them. Nambo shot and

Wambi shot. Bless the queen; victory came to Witanda's
Wambi.

At the town square, where victory found celebration,
Zomo Nanna's Taila was plotted against.

'Azumba's blades are blunt,' the Wambians told the
queen.

'If we strike today, we are a cat and they are a mouse,'
Muyamba told her.

'We shall not rest then,' decreed the queen. 'We shall be
vengefully armed as we set sail to Taila. Upon the night
breeze we shall take on the tyrant.'

'All Taila could help in the fight, my queen,' said
Muyamba.

'How?' the queen asked him.

'I would go ahead of your arrival. I would go to Twessi,
Emorna, Agunbe, and Nuamba, telling every Tailan there
that the monarch has returned and is waging war against
Azumba. That Zomo Nanna has already fallen and all that is
needed is the reclamation of their four islands.'

'That is wise stratagem,' commended the queen. 'You will
go with Abhe and Calata and a hundred archers. Yiddi and I
shall lead the offensive against Azumba. Abhe, choose fifty
of your best archers. Calata, do same. Arm them severely
and go with Muyamba. Remember, you are a lone front,
never split.'

Hundred archers were given toxic bundles of arrows and
very hefty bows. They were put on the seas under the
command of Abhe, Calata and Muyamba. Muyamba
chanted a war ditty and all that were with him hummed a
chorus. Their way, it was toward tyrannical Taila.

He stood. In his lookout he stood. He was more alert than a
community of vigilantes. Once, the wind whistled there, so
there he looked. And whistled here, so here he looked. And

blew that way, so that way he looked. And blew this way, so this way he looked. Till his sight was impaired and his hearing was confused, so that the whistle of the wind was not different from the bray of the monkey, and the world was but a blur, chaotic mist: the world of Zomo Nanna.

Against this chaotic mist, Taila's legendary battle cry arose. Naamu! Naamu! Naamu! It started in Nuamba, infected Agunbe, Emorna and Twessi, before it grew notorious and deathless.

The Nanna of the Zomo clan trembled like eight fowls. 'Sounds like rebellion?' muttered he to his men below.

'Send a spy there,' suggested a Zomo warrior.

'Spy?' Zomo Nanna was audibly pondering.

'Ana the spy,' spoke a Zomo warrior with a sword. 'There he is with his quick eye. Send him, my king.'

'Ana!' called Zomo Nanna.

'Send a swordsman, my king,' protested that Ana. 'A sword can reveal what a thousand spies cannot reveal. Send Hanom. He knows his way about a sword. And lo, this moment he bears a sword.'

'Hanom!' called Zomo Nanna.

'Nay, good king,' Hanom protested. 'I recommended Ana the spy before he recommended me. His eyes are healthy. My sword is blunt. Send him, my king, or send them that possess a spear.'

'Nay, send them that have a club,' protested them that possessed spears.

'Nay, them that possess a bow and arrow,' protested them that had clubs.

The battle bird blared from the rear of Azumba.

'Ah, Yomyo returns,' said them that possessed a bow and arrow, 'and he shall go to crush the rebellion.'

'Yomyo!' Zomo Nanna's face lit and smiled. He gazed into the rear of Azumba. It took a while, and a sail showed its summit. Its chest came into view. That was all Zomo Nanna saw of the vessel. 'Ah Yomyo!' he celebrated. 'The rebels are caught and their cousins shall soon be put to order. Where did Yomyo catch those rebels? Toward Yadoma? Toward Nambo? Where are the sons of Jooti? Bring them forth. Let them sing triumphant, victorious, victorious!'

The north coast, which was Zomo Nanna's rear, was host to his invaders. The queen of Nambo sat on the ship whose sail was visible to the Azumban. On her right, Yiddi sat, blowing a trumpet. On her left, Witanda sat, making majestic faces. Her ship sailed in the middle of many rows of canoes carrying archers with tensed arrows. Once she and every other body got safely onshore, she held her son by the hand and pointed an arrow inland, decreeing, 'WAR!'

Yiddi was commander of them as they charged forth: Namboan and Wambian archers. They combed Azumba, ravaging Azumbans, be they bad or amoral, aged or youthful, haggard or rude, affluent or needy, elegant or disgusting, tired or moody, meek or talkative, agile or gullible, gluttonous or polygamous.

Yiddi led the offensive further, into Zumbi. Here, his eyes met those of the Nanna of Zomo clan of Azumba.

'Break through their lines!' Zomo Nanna commanded. 'Bring down their commander. Charge! Do battle!'

Zomo Nanna's Zomo Warriors launched forth. The first line of Yiddi shot arrows at them. They threw spears at Yiddi's first line.

'Don't merge with them!' Yiddi commanded his archers. 'Fall back as you shoot!'

The Zomo Warriors sought to merge with Yiddi's archers, but the archers hastily retreated while intensifying their offensive.

'They're compact!' spoke Yiddi. 'Encircle them!'

Yiddi's archers sped in circular directions. Seeking to merge with Yiddi's archers, the Zomo Warriors spread out, chasing the archers in all directions. Yiddi's circle was complete. The merger the Zomo Warriors sought became reality, a circular reality that rendered them pitifully outnumbered. Yiddi's victory now rested on the wheels of time, and time's wheels did bring him that victory.

Thus defeated, Zomo Nanna hovered onto the ladder of his lookout and started descending.

'Yonder! The rogue flees!' cried the queen, who was yards away from the front, an impatient Witanda shackled in her grip.

'Seize the palace!' commanded Yiddi.

The archers sped to the north wall of Zomo Nanna's palace and jumped over it into the palace compound. The queen entered the palace in the escort of Yiddi, Witanda and a score and five Wambian archers. Zomo Nanna was not in the palace compound.

'Where did he go?' the queen asked the archers who had jumped over the wall.

'We didn't meet him,' answered they. 'We met six men, but we killed them all, these six at our feet.'

Queen Damoya, she looked at six corpses that lay at the feet of her archers. 'None of them is the rogue,' she said, disturbed. 'Go into every room of this palace and bring to me the rogue.'

She was obeyed. The palace was combed: halls, chambers, kitchens, corridors, yet Zomo Nanna did not become visible. Forty-seven women were rounded up, all palace maids and wives. They were spared.

Frustrated, Yiddi walked to the foundation of the lookout. The structure had four legs, made of wood. At the base of these legs was an oval slab with a handle that was bloodstained. Yiddi held the handle and lifted the slab.

There was a hollow beneath where the slab had been. Yiddi knelt and peeped into the hollow. It was the channel to a westward exit, and a light glittered at that exit.

'He escaped!' Yiddi sadly announced. 'That rogue escaped.'

'He can't be far gone,' said the queen, angered. 'We shall go separate ways, searching for him. Comb the land. Comb it religiously!'

Despairingly, the queen with Yiddi, Witanda and twenty-five archers headed west. The other archers went various directions in search of Zomo Nanna.

When the search became cold as the night, the queen and her company were as far as the west coast of Azumba. They heard the distant mumblings of quarrelsome men and went that direction. When they neared the place where the mumbling was, they saw three sand-bathed men, whose faces faced west. These men were engaged in a fight. The one was buried in the sand up to his knee. The other, a shabby fellow, had his hands tightly hooked to the neck of the buried man, strangling him. The third, a wretched man, lay angrily on the shabby fellow, fisting him.

'Ends here, captive!' vowed the wretched man, throwing a robust fist at the shabby fellow.

'Fist him afresh!' cried the buried man's limited voice.

That shabby fellow was fisted afresh and he squealed, 'In-law, you flaw. In-law, you boost the foe. In-law, I am true. Damoya was queen. Yiddi was king. And I was king. This villain murdered them.'

'I am a royal of Taila,' claimed the buried man's limited voice. 'My hands are pure. Many years ago, this tyrant used foreign charms to ensnare and rule my people. I bought the services of homeless men and overthrew him. The sailor and his daughter, of whom he speaks stately things, were his slaves and he hung them on a scorching noon.'

'Yet he claims a rebel killed them,' spoke the wretched man, throwing a fist. 'Hearken, royal, I shall tell you the craft of this murderer. Long back, I wanted to free my father and sister from Numungu, so I bought warmongers and they helped me conquer the place. It was vain, because an aggressor from this kingdom had already taken them. I came here and poached the seas, listening for rumours, looking out for fact, planning a rescue mission. I captured this man, clothed like a tyrant. He claimed he was king and claimed he was fleeing from rebels. Further into our interactions, I learnt he knew my father and sister. He claimed my father was king of here and my sister was queen, whom he had as wife. He claimed they both were alive and hiding here on this island. He asked me to free him so he could get warriors from that island opposite us. The sound of it was sly so I refused. He then asked me to send my men to call unto him his men. I obliged and sent twenty-three men. This man's men found out his whereabouts and, once they knew where to find him, attacked my men with clubs. Two of my men survived and alerted me on time, so that I escaped this man's evil. For thirteen years, I've tried fruitlessly to trade him for my family. Today, beside Nuamba, eighteen elderly women bowed to him and called him king. They had come to pick paddles to use as weapons against a tyrant. They gave a good account of him, and said, "Queen Damoya and King Yiddi are come and are doing battle in Taila." I freed my captive and asked him to cautiously escort me through the kingdom. He led me through the warring places, so I tried to recapture him, but he fled and got on the seas to this place. Now see what evil he does with you? What wrong did you do him?'

'What wrong could I have done him?' spoke the buried man's limited voice. 'He murders without cause. Unite with me against him, or he'll murder me and turn to you. Fist him off me; then we both shall pounce on him.'

Watery was the queen's eyes as she stared into the faces of her company. 'Zomo Nanna!' she crowed.

'Zomo Nanna!' her company instantaneously crowed back.

The sandy men all turned and gazed at the queen and her company.

'He's fake, Diamo,' Yiddi proclaimed.

The wretched man beamed and weakly fisted the shabby fellow.

'Not Zowdor!' protested the score and five archers. 'Fist Zomo Nanna below!'

'Fist him, Diamo!' crowed the queen.

Wretched Diamo fisted Zomo Nanna. Shabby Zowdor strangled Zomo Nanna's neck. The queen and her company, they joined the struggle, poking Zomo Nanna with many venomous arrows.

Before death ate it and its lord, Zomo Nanna's limited voice announced, 'I'll haunt you! I'll haunt you all! I'll poke you in the jaw!'

'Yiddi,' Witanda merrily aired, 'the legend is fulfilled. The moment of the Zowdor is come, and the tyrannical arm is wraith. We shall give the outlaw his crown and his Damoya, and again mourn the sons of the sailor and the archer.'

''Twas twisted, yet true,' replied Yiddi, in the tone of honourable folk.

Zowdor and Diamo looked at the lad. They both smiled.

'Your son, in-law,' said Diamo, his voice remorseful.

'Mmh!' exclaimed Zowdor, whose eyes suddenly took an interest in Damoya's.

'He's ... like you ... amoral,' Damoya faltered.

Zowdor beamed.

Damoya unveiled her head and went toward Zowdor.

'Taila,' spoke Yiddi, 'the tale of the oceanic goddess is fulfilled: the Zowdor has encountered his Damoya.'

Says Witanda: 'I, once a pirate of Tarada, where the tale was conserved, endorse the claim.'

From Nuamba to Twessi, victory songs soared into the sky, songs that were the dirge at the funeral of Zomo Nanna's Taila. Anew, the kingdom had arisen, as does the legendary bird that from its ashes reincarnates. Every woe hitherto died with the darkness of that night, so when the potter's dew was given, it fell on merry fields.